FIRE

by

Nicki Greenwood

The Elemental Series, Volume 4

FIRE

Cover Art by *Kim Mendoza*

The Wild Rose Press, Inc.
PO Box 708
Adams Basin, NY 14410-0708
Visit us at www.thewildrosepress.com

Publishing History
First Fantasy Rose Edition, 2016
Print ISBN 978-1-5092-0822-7
Digital ISBN 978-1-5092-0823-4

The Elemental Series, Volume 4
Published in the United States of America

This close, Gypsy couldn't help
breathing Ethan's scent—a pleasant blend of sawdust and something smoky that strummed her nerve endings in a constant chord of awareness. And then she was right back there with him on her living room rug, wondering what would have happened if they hadn't been interrupted. Her knees turned to water. "Please," she whispered, unsure what else she meant to say.

"Please…?" he prompted, his husky voice wrapping around her. His body heat drifted against her exposed skin, or maybe she was imagining it.

Desperate, she fumbled for her last shred of willpower. "Pickering needs good men like you."

"Am I?" He canted his head. "A good man?"

Praise for Nicki Greenwood's Elemental Series

EARTH

"Fresh, fast-paced, and riotously colorful…"

~Michelle McAdam, author

~*~

"Emotional…"

~Barbara Witek, author

~*~

"…very enjoyable…"

~Bitten By Books(4 Tombstones)

~*~

WATER

"A touching, humorous story about home being where the heart is. Very refreshing."

~Sizzling Hot Book Reviews

~*~

"Enchanting and charming."

~Romancing The Book

Dedication

For Kevin

Chapter One

"Mommy! *Mommy!*"

The girl's pitiful scream hardly reached Ethan Sutter's ears under the roar of a flame-induced whirlwind. He held up an arm to shield his face and strengthen the protective bubble of power surrounding his body. His skin glowed, and the flames dampened, pushing in and then turning immediately back as though they'd hit an invisible breakwall.

Fire rushed up the wooden skeleton of the old apartment building, devouring the structure but unable to penetrate the protective sphere of his power. Not for lack of trying. It took all his effort to push back the flames snapping hungrily at him with his every step. Wiring snaked along the charred boards, filling the air with a choking electrical smell that he had trouble keeping out of the bubble.

Damned landlords. Didn't matter where he went. It was always the same old story—some greedy bastard saving a buck by not renovating faulty apartment housing to current code. Not until a catastrophe struck, and it was too late. "Kid, where are you?" he shouted.

"Here, I'm here! Help me, help! Please—" The response dissolved into racking coughs, easier to hear.

She was running out of breathable air.

Maybe it wasn't even the housing. Ethan sidestepped a pile of smoldering drywall. Could've been anything this time. Stupid people. Candles, cigarettes, a stove left on. Someone else always paid the price for their negligence…like this girl. When would people learn?

"Help!" The call came more weakly. Even if she'd barricaded herself inside a room, the kid would soon suffocate in this oxygen-robbing heat. If he couldn't get to her fast enough, so would he. His power trapped only so much air inside his protective shield. When that ran out…so would they.

He hurried forward down what was left of the hall, kicking aside more debris with his flameproof boots. He reached a dead end at a closed door. Focusing his power until his hand glowed fiercely white, he grasped the doorknob and turned.

Stuck. "I'm here, kid! Let me in!"

"There's stuff in the way!" she cried. "I can't—" More coughing.

Ethan rammed the door with his shoulder. Pain flashed through his body. Nothing. He slammed against the door again. Weakened by fire and heat, the wood of the jamb splintered, yielding him a measly six or eight inches. "Come on! Hope you're skinny."

The girl's sooty, tearstained face appeared in the crack. When her gaze landed on him, safe behind the protective shield of his power, his skin awash in luminescent waves, her eyes went wide. "Are you an angel?"

"Hardly." He reached for the girl's outstretched arm, then pulled her through the opening.

Once she passed into his sphere, she sucked in a breath from the pocket of fresh air, her eyes wide in a familiar reaction of surprise and relief.

It was short-lived. She gave another terrible, rib-grinding cough. He picked her up, and her arms slid around his neck. Her thin little body slumped against him, and her head thumped onto his chest.

Probably for the best, he considered, ignoring the flash of tightness in his chest brought on by her unshrinking trust. Getting out of here would be a bigger horror show than getting in had been.

The floor gave an ominous crack under his feet. He froze, straining his ears, expecting any minute that the place would give way under his feet. His power was a lot of things, but no proof against a building about to collapse around him. His neck could break as easily as the next guy's.

Fire had its own language. It roared, it growled, it murmured…to average people. Ethan understood the whole range of its vocabulary, and in the inferno now raging around him, he heard a beast about to snap its jaws shut.

He turned for the exit, then ran. A crash sounded behind him, but he didn't stop to look. His heart banged around in his chest with the frenzy of a trapped squirrel. Sparks fell from the obliterated ceiling, sizzling against the wall of his shield. Smoke began to penetrate the bubble. Ethan pressed the girl's face into his shirt and held his breath as he rushed along. Why the hell did he do this? When would *he* learn?

The girl's hair fell over his arm, its blondish ends singed and uneven. A scrap of drywall rained down. He tucked her closer to his body and hunched over, taking the debris against his shoulders. The piece banged off his back, and he grunted in pain. He felt the tear of his shirt as the debris burned a hole, but his skin remained unaffected. So far. *Should start going into these damn things naked,* he thought savagely.

A groan overhead warned him a split second before the ceiling rafters crashed down. He bolted through the hellish rain, stone cold with grim determination. The rest of the hallway fell to pieces around him as he reached the back exit and bullied his way through the broken entry door.

As soon as he made it outside and onto pavement, he snuffed his power. Stumbling with fatigue, he carried the featherweight child around the front of the building.

"Sophie!" screamed a woman. Ethan was immediately surrounded by a man and woman whose panic-stricken faces told him at once that these were the girl's parents.

He released her into the mother's arms only to be waylaid by a team of emergency responders wielding oxygen masks. "Her, get her," he croaked, waving them away toward the girl.

They turned to the child, and Ethan staggered out of the knot of people. Dizzy and shivering with shock, he tottered toward his motorcycle.

"Wait!" cried the mother behind him, her voice thick with emotion. "Thank you! Wait! What's your name?"

Ethan collapsed onto the seat of his bike, started the engine, and then peeled away as if he had a prayer of outrunning the demons in his head.

****

Damn. Out of gas. And in the tiniest, most Podunk little town he'd ever seen.

The engine of Ethan's custom motorcycle coughed

to a halt in front of a kitschy New Age shop with a hand-painted sign in the front window. He squinted past his denim-and-leather-clad reflection in the glass, to an array of clutter he would never buy on his worst day.

That'd be today, actually. He'd saved the girl, but the news back in Montpelier said that an elderly couple and the girl's baby brother hadn't been so lucky.

Every one. He carried every one he lost around with him in his head—each of them one more brick added onto the already-sinking boat that was his life. Checking the news to see if there were casualties was just penance, a splinter he couldn't resist driving into the wound.

He drew in a long breath, full of the sharp scent of autumn leaves. Even kitschy shops had to have a phone. *The Holistic Mystic,* read the shop sign.

Maybe not.

He looked hopefully up and down the street. The other businesses were closed, their signs flipped and windows shuttered, with the rays of the sinking sun glancing off their leaded glass storefront windows.

He turned back to the New Age store with a skeptical frown at the display of candles, geodes, huge apothecary jars, and books on spiritual cleansing.

Of all the shops in all the world where he could have broken down, this was it? Couldn't have been a Laundromat or an insurance agency or something? *Welcome to being me.*

He started toward the door with its *Open* sign, and even reached toward the old-fashioned brass handle.

A slender, long-fingered hand drew aside the lacy curtain in the door's oval window. A face appeared—a woman with striking cheekbones, ivory skin, and such a mass of long, glossy black curls that he thought it couldn't possibly be her real hair. Her dark eyes fixed on him, then went wide. Before he had a chance to knock or protest or even offer a wan smile, she flipped the sign to *Closed*, and he heard the click of the door lock.

Ouch. What did it say about him that not even someone who worked in a kooky New Age store would let him in?

Well, that topped off his rotten day.

Left staring at his own reflection, he decided she might have a point. He looked like a motorcycle gang member in his black jeans, leather jacket, sunglasses, and firefighter boots. His broken-down bike wouldn't have helped her first impression, either. He glared at his normally-beloved machine. *How dare you betray me?* The bike offered no return comment, just sat there looking smugly superior.

Disgruntled, he swiveled back to the shop. "Be glad to get this hunk of metal off your doorstep if I can use your phone," he called.

No answer.

He had a cell phone. Or he would have, if he remembered to charge it. Ethan waited another few minutes, but the curtain didn't so much as twitch.

"People in small towns are supposed to be helpful," he added. He ought to know—he'd grown up in Sagerton, Montana, which had been founded on the principles of Podunk towns. Everyone knew everyone else, or they made up enough stories about the person to satisfy themselves. In the case of Ethan and his foster family, even Sagerton's wildest gossip would never have come close to the truth.

6

He hunched his shoulders under the leather jacket and turned away from the shop. Miss Holistic Mystic probably had a more accurate impression of him in one glance than Sagerton's nosiest had formed in a decade.

Grasping the handlebars, he walked his motorcycle along the street. There had to be a garage here, or maybe that was just wishful thinking. Pickering, Vermont had to be the smallest town he'd been through in over two years.

The town backed up against the shoulder of the Green Mountains, whose trees had just begun to dress out in their autumn colors. Boasting a handful of streets at best, the town proper was a blink-and-you-miss-it stretch of Route 7. He stared up the street as he walked before remembering that even if Pickering did sport a gas station, it, like everything else, was probably closed for the night. He forged on until he found the place— Mason's Convenience Store, a tiny outfit which had flipped its *Closed* sign about ten minutes ago.

Damned small-town hours. Early to bed, early to annoy the passing stranded tourist.

The town planners had, however, spared a slice of land for a commons, which included a gazebo. He'd seen it on his way up the street, and he headed back there with philosophical resignation.

Wouldn't be the first time.

The sun had ducked behind the mountaintops by the time he parked his bike beside the gazebo and stowed his sunglasses and wallet in the hard-sided saddlebags. Summer warmth lingered in the air, but in the shadows, a chill reminded him that the freedom he'd enjoyed all summer was coming to an end. If he planned to continue sleeping outdoors, he'd have to head south for the winter. Even his ability to stay warm had limits.

A few branches littered the grass. Ethan guessed they'd had a recent storm, and not yet cleaned up all the damage. He gathered them, then deposited them in a steel trash barrel standing beside a park bench.

With a sigh, he pulled a cigarette lighter from his pocket. He flicked the lighter wheel, then watched the lick of flame spring to life. It danced, mocking in its liveliness.

Why the hell didn't he just go home to Montana?

Oh, yeah. Cade was there.

Ethan reached for the flame. As he did so, his fingertips began to glow. The lick of fire leaped from the lighter to his hand. Where it touched him, his skin glowed brighter, shielding him from the burn. He sneered and dropped the spit of flame into the trashcan, where it caught in the papers and branches.

The smoky bite of a wood fire wafted upward. Warmth flooded the air as the flames drove away the dark and the evening chill. With an oily resentment, Ethan watched the fire swarm along the branches.

He definitely needed to move south for the winter.

He sprawled his long frame onto the park bench then folded his arms behind his head. The bit of sky he could see over the mountain silhouettes sparkled with unreachable diamonds. He closed his eyes, listening to the pop of dry kindling and the rustle of leaves in the breeze. One by one, crickets began a chorus. Postcard perfect. He wondered how many visits Norman Rockwell had made to this place.

"What do you think you're doing?"

He snapped to a seated position. A police officer

stood over the bench, frowning at Ethan from under the broad brim of his hat. "Keeping warm," Ethan said.

"Outdoor fires are illegal, son."

Son? The guy looked barely older than Ethan. "It's contained."

"Within town limits, without a permit, and in a municipal trash can. I'm gonna have to ask you to put that out."

"You want me to freeze?"

The officer's frown cut a deeper crease across his stern features. "You're gonna have to put that out and move on, unless you want me to charge you with vagrancy."

Ethan decided on a reasonable approach. He spread his hands. "I'm not causing a disturbance, and I'm not panhandling. I'm just a guy trying to stay warm in a town that closes everything after six o'clock. No motels, either."

He knew what the officer saw in him: trouble. *Yeah, mister. In your shoes, I'd tell me to shuffle off, too.*

The officer indicated the fire. "Just do me a favor and be on your way, Mister…"

"Mister Out of Gas," Ethan muttered, shooting another glare at his bike. "Come on, man, as soon as the stores open up in the morning, I'm not your problem anymore."

"That's enough," the officer snapped. He started to reach for his back pocket.

"I'll go, I'll go," said Ethan. Glumly, he levered himself back upright. Long-ass walk to Rutland from here.

Down the sidewalk bordering the park, he spotted

the woman from The Holistic Mystic. She carried an impossibly big woven bag in about a million colors. Hopeful, Ethan beckoned her. "Hey, uh…" He faltered to a stop when he realized he didn't even know her name.

Her gaze fixed on him, tying his tongue. Ethan looked her up and down from her crinkly cotton blouse, to a flowy skirt, to her leather sandals, and then back up to that long, black mane shining in the firelight, just begging him to bury his hands in it. Every word in his head went clean out of it.

Her gaze slid past him, freeing him. "Hollis," she said. "Is something wrong?"

"Do you know this man?" the officer asked.

"She's my phone call," Ethan blurted. "Well, she was gonna let me use it."

The woman turned her stare back on Ethan with perfectly arched brows. He read what she was thinking in her transparent expression: *I was?*

He gave her a pleading look.

Her lashes fluttered as if she were just now coming to the realization that Ethan was bad news. For a second, her bottomless gaze stayed on him, searching. His stomach swooped, and not just from the knowledge that he was going to spend the night in a jail cell.

Needing to break that stare, he arched around to find Hollis ogling her like she was a juicy slab of tenderloin.

Interesting.

Ethan turned back to the woman to find a faint frown on the woman's face. The expression accentuated her full lower lip.

Incredible, wide, kissable lips. Almost too lush for

the rest of her features.

Even more interesting.

She straightened, then came toward him with purpose in her step. "Yes, I know him."

Hollis looked positively pissed off by that little piece of news, but his tone stayed cordial. "Why was he camping out in the park?"

"He was waiting for me to close up shop," she said.

Smooth, Ethan thought with admiration. Almost as good a liar as he was…except he caught the flicker of her lashes. *Got to sell it with your body language, honey, not just your voice.*

With the officer's attention still on the woman, Ethan leaned against the steel trash barrel and thrust a hand behind his back. He flicked his fingers, letting his power surface just enough to dampen the flames inside the can. "As you can see, Officer, she's all closed up now, and I'll be making my phone call and getting out of your life." He shut off the flow of his power. "And look, the fire's almost out. Sorry to bother you. G'night." He strode toward his motorcycle with a wash of gratitude for the woman on the sidewalk. If nothing else, she'd saved him from a humiliating call to Kincade.

The officer sighed and put away the ticket pad he'd pulled from his back pocket. "Just make sure he stays out of trouble, Gypsy."

The woman's gaze returned to Ethan. She tilted her head down the sidewalk toward the north end of town. Ethan grabbed his bike and followed her direction.

"Good night," the officer called.

"Good night, Hollis," she called without looking back. To Ethan's surprise, she slipped a hand into the crook of his elbow. "Just keep going. If he asks, you're my cousin, just in from…"

"Montana," he supplied. Intrigued, he gave her a sidelong appraisal. In the muted glow of the lampposts lined up along the sidewalk, he couldn't tell if she were blushing, but she thrust her chin into the air and marched alongside him with a queenly air.

Okay, he thought. *I'll play.* "It's Ethan, by the way."

"Keep walking," she whispered.

He risked a look over his shoulder. Officer Cranky caught him looking, gave him a frown, then stalked out of the park toward a police cruiser. Once the officer had gotten into his car, Ethan turned back to the woman at his side. "What's with him?"

She squeezed his arm. "Hollis Montgomery. Don't look! He'll just follow us."

He took a closer look at her. "You in trouble with him or something?"

"No." She shook his arm when he tried to turn around again. "Stop looking!"

"Okay, okay." He couldn't help smiling. "Do you evade law enforcement a lot?"

"Just him," she whispered.

They walked all the way to the end of town, then up one of the side streets. Ethan breathed in the fresh, cooling air, spiced with a whiff of pines and someone's wood fire. He'd missed that, bouncing around in big cities. You never got the country out of your blood.

Underneath the scents of autumn, he caught a trace of something like cloves. He suspected that was her. "Gypsy?"

She looked at him, those huge, dark eyes even

darker in the dimming light.

"Your name?" he prompted.

"Gypsophila, after the flower. My great aunt used to own a flower shop. She's the one who named me."

Ethan raised his eyebrows. The name definitely went with the woman: unusual. "Awfully hard to learn to spell that, I bet, when you were a kid."

"Hence the nickname," she said in such a wry tone that he had to smile. She caught it, and then looked quickly away to anything and everything else. He wondered what bothered her most: his attire, or his attention. At last, she glanced behind her.

He did the same. Officer Montgomery had slowed his vehicle at the end of the street. The officer stared in their direction, then hit the gas and drove on. "Takes his job seriously, doesn't he?"

Gypsy let go of Ethan's arm at once. "Yeah. Thanks. I should go." She backed away as if she thought he'd pounce on her.

"Hey, wait. I really do need to make a phone call," he protested. "It's long distance, but I can pay you for the trouble."

Gypsy glanced up the street again. Ethan knew she was about to refuse him. Given the fact that she was anything but the blend-in type, he should have let her…but the words were out before he had a chance to stop them. "I'll pay you extra, even."

****

Good grief, he was gorgeous. Why were the troublemakers always so darned gorgeous? Gypsy stopped just short of wringing her hands in torment. Four boyfriends in five years. Two restraining orders. One arrest. And one who couldn't keep his hands off all the other women in town while he was dating her. You'd think she'd have learned by now. Pickering was running out of options, so Fate must have decided to start importing trouble for her.

Ethan tilted his head. "One phone call. I don't even need to come inside, if your phone's cordless. I swear I don't bite."

Gypsy stared at his mouth, at that full lower lip that gave him a James Dean pout. "Do you even have somewhere to go?"

He nodded toward his bike. "I would, if your gas station were open."

She narrowed her eyes. Nights were still reasonably balmy, especially for a man wearing a leather jacket. She could send him back to the park bench, but as soon as she did, Hollis would likely have him cooling his heels in the town lockup for the night. Not the roof over his head he'd hope for, she guessed, and she'd probably hear it from Hollis in the morning.

On the other hand, she did own a porch swing. "Okay," she said. "One phone call."

He smiled. "Yes, ma'am."

She caught a Western undertone in his drawl, and her stomach gave a completely foolish flip-flop. He smiled at her, all stubble and grin and close-cropped hair the color of old rust. She spun around to hurry down the sidewalk so that he had to jog his bike alongside to keep up. Jitters collected in the bottom of her belly to tingle still farther down.

He stayed silent, and for the last quarter-mile to her house, their only accompaniments were the creak of his leather jacket and the crunch of stray stones under his motorcycle tires as they walked. That grin stayed imprinted on her retinas even when she wasn't looking at him.

She'd be burning lavender incense after a lavender bath tonight for sure. She'd need all the calming effects she could get. Without doubt, she would regret this. "Where's your call going?"

"Nantucket."

"Nantucket?" she echoed.

He must have heard the incredulity in her voice, because he grinned again, setting off a second wave of flip-flops. "My sister, Morgan. She's a chef there. *I* really am from Montana."

"Oh," she said. Jeepers, what sparkling conversation. Maybe he'd tied her tongue in a knot along with her insides. Why hadn't she ever listened to her mother and settled down with the next-door boy in Lubbock?

Oh, right. The next-door boy had never given her the flip-flops, and as much as she loved her mother, she'd listen to Elizabeth Ronan over her own dead body. "That's a nice motorcycle," she said.

"She's my girl," he said with a warmth that, no matter how she fought it, gave Gypsy a rush of envy.

He strode alongside her until she reached her crooked front gate. "This is me," she told him.

With a swooping stomach, she watched him survey the sprawling property in the glow of the yard's floodlight. The gate and its split-rail fence could have used a fresh coat of paint, and the gate itself begged for a new set of hinges. The white farmhouse beyond, though it mingled with beautiful trees just beginning to show off their fall colors, was badly in need of TLC Gypsy's budget couldn't provide. Its fish-scale roof lacked tiles here and there. The siding wanted painting. The sagging porch would have benefited from a few new railing balusters. A few strategically placed pumpkins and hay bales lent seasonal cheer to the old property.

She loved it.

Relieved he couldn't see the worst of it, but stubbornly defensive, she opened the gate. It gave a loud creak, and she tried not to notice when the corner dragged the ground. "Why don't you walk your bike around to the driveway? There's a carriage house. If the owl is there, don't bother her."

"Owl?"

She smiled a little. "I have a resident Saw-whet Owl who likes to perch in the tree nearby and watch for mice. She won't pester you if you don't pester her."

Ethan turned a wary eye on the sky.

Unable to help it, Gypsy laughed. "I don't think she'll eat you. She's no bigger than your hand."

Ethan raised a brow and turned a wry expression on her. Gypsy found herself immediately glad that the dimming light hid most of it. Her flip-flops were bad enough as it was. When he stalked away with his bike, over her graveled drive toward the carriage house, she clenched her hands. "I have a dog," she called. "He can be a little defensive."

His voice floated back to her, full of sarcastic humor. "Great. If the owl doesn't get me, the dog can polish me off."

As soon as she opened her door, Burt hurtled toward her with a deep *Rrrruff!* and began sniffing her with a doggy look of suspicion. She rubbed the big German shepherd's head. "Yep," she said. "I brought home some trouble, baby. With any luck, he won't stay."

The dog waved his tail and gave another muted *Rrrrf,* clearly not buying her hopeful statement any more than she did. Gypsy studied him. Burt topped out around mid-thigh on her—big for a dog by any standard, but especially so for a German shepherd.

If anything was capable of scaring off trouble, it'd be Burt...which was why she'd adopted him, after all. In the wake of Restraining Order Number Two, she marched straight to the pound and found this big, slobbery, cuddly, protective ball of love. Restraining Order Number Two never bothered her again. It was true, what people said: beware of people your dog doesn't like.

Burt usually didn't like the men Gypsy brought home.

She reached for the cordless phone sitting in the charger on the kitchen counter. Ethan from Montana could make all the long distance calls he wanted. He wouldn't last five minutes with Burt. Triumphantly, she carried the phone outside to stand on the porch.

Ethan sauntered back toward her across the front yard. "Owl-free," he reported. "I live to fight another day."

She handed him the phone. "You'll still need to face off with—"

RrrruffruffruffruffRUFF! Burt bolted out of the house through the dog door, then charged toward Ethan like a bullet.

Ethan's jaw dropped. He leaped back so fast, Gypsy expected to see an Ethan-shaped puff of cartoon dust where he'd been standing.

Burt skidded to a stop between them, growling. Ethan made no move forward, so Gypsy walked up beside the dog. Trying desperately not to smile, she handed over the phone.

A full ten seconds passed, underscored by the shepherd's warning snarl. Reaching out as far as his arm length would allow, Ethan took the phone.

The way he kept one wary eye on her dog forced a giggle out of her. "This is Burt." Thinking of Hollis and the park, she conceded that Ethan would need somewhere to sleep. Even though she'd vouched for this perfect stranger, Hollis would be on him in an instant if Gypsy left him to his own devices. "You know," she said, waving to the veranda, "I have a porch swing where you can stay the night. It's been warm, still, and a couple of wool blankets should keep you comfortable enough."

He transferred his guarded look to her. "You sure?"

Those eyes. Even in the floodlight, they speared her, intense like those of the owl that called her property home. "Yeah," she added, feigning indifference with a wave of her hand. "Where else could you go, until everything opens in the morning?"

After a moment of hesitation, he nodded. "I might take you up on that, thanks."

"Great. While you're making your phone call, I'll go get the blankets. Come on, Burt."

With a last, disgruntled *Rrrrf* toward Ethan, the dog trotted behind her back into the house.

As soon as she closed the front door, she heaved a breath she hadn't been able to catch while outside. "What are you *doing*, Gypsophila?"

She'd just invited a man who looked like all the

bad boys she'd ever dated, put together, to stay the night at her home. Even if she were separated from him by a locked door and a very big dog, this had to rank up there as one of her least brilliant ideas ever.

No wonder her mother always called her the scourge of sensible women.

Chapter Two

I saw her in town today. She looked right through me like I don't exist. I've been over to her house to break up fights between her and her jerk boyfriends, for chrissakes. How much more does she want?

****

Ethan ended his call to Morgan, his eldest foster sister, after asking her to wire him some money out of his account. He'd put his finances in her charge since leaving Hope Creek. On the move all the time, he'd decided she was the best choice for a "permanent" mailing address. He'd never leave it to Cade—not because he didn't trust the eldest of his foster siblings to manage his few bills, but because the thought of being in Cade's debt made his stomach turn.

He stood on Gypsy's porch, looking out into the darkened yard. The floodlight must have had a motion sensor. It had turned off several minutes ago. The only remaining light was that from the dim sconce lantern by the front door.

This far out from town, stars studded the sky. He thought he saw a fat little body swoop through the air, and wondered if that might be Gypsy's owl hunting its dinner. Insects chirped, reminding him of nights at Hope Creek. They'd have brought the cows in by now and gone to bed. Irritable, he shook off thoughts of the ranch.

Gypsy brought him the blankets she'd promised, plus a fat pillow embroidered with pumpkins and autumn leaves. He noticed she'd left the giant dog inside, and stifled a rueful smile. No need to reinforce that particular point. She had a loaded canine, and she wasn't afraid to use it.

"Sorry," she said as he tucked the phone under his elbow, then took the pillow off the top of her tilting armful. "It took me a while to find the blankets. I left them in the back of the cedar closet. Moths, you know. They like wool, and hate cedar."

Nervous chatter. Well, he did look like a bundle of trouble. He shrugged and made an effort to sound harmless. "Not an issue."

She showed him to the porch swing, and Ethan tried not to swallow his tongue. He'd be lucky if the thing held him five minutes, let alone all night. More than familiar with the financial difficulties that prevented renovations—having lived through them before—he took the blankets, then laid them out on the swing as if he hadn't noticed it needed fixing. "When does everything open up around here in the mornings?"

"The gas station should be open at six."

"Early to bed, early to rise, and all that?" He lowered himself gingerly onto the swing. It creaked a bit, but by some miracle, it held. He studied her in the feeble glow of the sconce lantern. "Sutter. Ethan Sutter."

She flashed a brief, intriguing smile. "Gypsophila Ronan."

He held out a hand. "Thanks for the rescue back there in the park. I owe you."

He wondered why she'd done it, but then her hand

slipped into his and kicked the thought aside with the sensation of her soft skin, cool against his. He almost jerked his hand back, but by then, she'd closed her fingers around his.

"You don't owe me," she said. "If you spread good karma, you get it back eventually. Have a good night, Mister Sutter."

"Yeah, you, too." They stayed that way, holding hands, for several seconds until Ethan realized neither of them had moved. He dropped her hand on the pretense of getting comfortable on the swing.

"I should warn you," she added with a curious little tremor in her voice, "I let Burt have the run of the house and yard overnight. Living off the main roads the way I do, he's sort of an extra security system."

He snapped his attention back to her. He might dress like a thug, but that kept the nosy people away from him. He'd never hurt a woman in his entire life.

Oh, well. Appearances, and all. He shouldn't have been surprised by her impression.

Definitely not bothered by it.

Gypsy went back into the house, and Ethan stretched out as much as the short, creaky swing would allow. Even then, his long legs hung over the armrest on the opposite end.

Well, that was about as uncomfortable as he could get. He eased onto his side. No luck there, either, because he had to fold himself practically into a ball. When his other side gave him the same problem—in reverse—he tried his back again.

The dog door swung open, and Burt trotted outside, grumbling his canine displeasure at having a stranger on his property.

Dogs, he understood. Once he'd gotten over the sheer size of Gypsy's shepherd, Ethan had admired the animal. He shifted onto his side again. "Hey, Fangs."

The dog pricked its ears and halted with such a human expression of affront at Ethan's indifference that Ethan had to chuckle.

"I bet she feeds you doggy granola, doesn't she?"

Burt gave an uncertain-sounding growl.

Ethan reached into his jacket pocket for a half-finished pack of beef jerky. "Dinner time for me, snack time for you, buddy." He withdrew a large piece, then held it out. "Want it?"

Burt backed away, growling more sharply. His ears flattened.

Lowering his hand, Ethan sat up, careful not to make any sudden motions. Hope Creek had a dog when he was young. Just a mutt, and not half the size of this moose. Ethan guessed if you lived alone, you'd want a dog this big.

He squinted into the darkness beyond the porch. The crickets had organized themselves into a full chorus. The house was set back from the street, and the size of the property meant Gypsy wouldn't have the neighbors breathing down her neck too much. Behind the house, he'd glimpsed a pond, backed by a stretch of forest that climbed up into the Green Mountains. "Your owner doesn't much like people either, does she?" he murmured. That might be the only thing they had in common.

Turning his attention back to Burt, he held out the strip of jerky. When Burt didn't take it, he tossed it onto the floor of the porch.

The dog sniffed it. After only a second's hesitation,

he ate it, then looked expectantly at Ethan.

That easy. Ethan wondered if Gypsy knew her intimidating bodyguard was such a furry pushover. Then again, with teeth that big, on a dog that big, maybe people never got close enough to him to offer a snack.

"One more. It'll be our secret," he said. He tossed down another strip.

After gobbling that down, Burt approached him with a wagging tail. Ethan took a chance that the dog wasn't going to take his hand off and reached out.

Burt sniffed at him, then pushed forward to be petted.

Chuckling, Ethan rubbed the animal's head. Dogs were so much easier than people. "Nice to meet you," he murmured, scratching Burt's chin. He stretched out on the swing again, glad for some company that didn't talk and didn't judge. The quiet soaked into him, and he did his best not to think.

Half an hour later, his back was cramping. He tried flipping again…

…and the swing cracked and dumped him on the porch floor. Pain punched through him from his tailbone upward. Ethan groaned out a curse.

Burt snuffled at his face, then gave him a jerky-scented slurp. "I'm fine, Fangs," he muttered, rolling to a sitting position.

The swing teetered back and forth. Its seat had dropped clean out from under him and now hung at an angle, broken at the armrest joint.

Crap. Nice way of paying back the woman who'd let him use it.

Ethan grabbed the blankets. Resolutely, he laid on

the porch floor beside the dog. "Well, at least I can stretch out now."

Burt did the same, plopping his head on Ethan's chest. Ethan patted the dog's back, then fell asleep.

****

Gypsy woke to the same filtered sunlight and the same tin-tiled ceiling she'd seen for the past five years. The same patchwork bedspread. The same walnut dresser and cheval mirror.

She sat up, then put her feet down on the floor. The same rag rug, too…but Burt wasn't on it.

She called him. No answer.

Then, floating in through her slightly-open window, she heard the sound of hammering.

Curious, she got up, then dressed hastily in a gauzy, frilled skirt and her favorite blouse. She hurried out to the porch.

Burt was gone. Ethan was gone. The swing was gone. The blankets had been folded and lay in a stack on the side table. *What in the world…?*

The hammering started up again. She followed the sound to her carriage house, where she found Ethan in its driveway with a set of sawhorses, some lumber, and her old tool chest.

Burt lay beside the chest. When he saw her, his tail thumped against the graveled driveway, scattering stones and a puff of sawdust. Instead of chasing Ethan off her property, as she'd half-hoped last night, he seemed content to bask in her houseguest's—porch guest's—presence.

That couldn't be a good omen. "What are you doing?" she demanded.

Ethan turned, hammer in hand, then plucked a nail

from his mouth. He pointed it at her porch swing, sitting in the grass beside the driveway. New slats formed its seat. The armrest was on Ethan's makeshift work table, a board laid across the pair of sawhorses. "I broke it last night trying to shoehorn myself into it," he said. "If I didn't fix it, it'd be a pretty miserable way of paying you back for a place to crash last night, so..." He trailed off with a shrug. "You had some wood in the carriage house that didn't look like it was getting used. Lot of dust on it."

Torn between affront that he'd availed himself of her tools, and gratitude that he'd felt it necessary to fix his own mess, she hesitated, digging her sandal into the gravel. Tiny stones worked their way under her toes. Irritable, she tapped her sandal until the stones fell away again. "You don't need to do that."

"I know I don't *need* to, but I should."

He didn't talk like a troublemaker. And if she'd thought him attractive last night under the concealing shadows of dusk, full daylight rendered him positively dazzling. The morning sunlight burnished his hair from last night's rust-red to nearly copper. His hazel eyes were so pale, they almost matched the gold in those of the Saw-whet Owl that lived on her property.

The only other redheaded man she'd ever thought handsome was Prince Harry. Ethan was much more accessible...and much more of a problem. "I have errands to run this morning," she lied.

"Sure. I'll get out of your life as soon as I get this back to the porch. Might want to paint it once the glue dries." He carried the armrest to the swing, and with a little wood glue and hammering, he made it better than it had looked in the five years Gypsy had owned it.

"Give me a hand? Getting it out to the carriage house in pieces wasn't an issue, but getting it back's going to be a two-man job."

Dumbfounded, she watched him gather up the tools. He passed Burt with a friendly murmur, and the dog gave him an adoring look.

Traitor, she fumed. *You're supposed to chase them away for me.* What had happened to her ferocious canine bodyguard?

Spurred into action, she stalked toward the swing and forced out a tone of easy cheer. "Ready when you are."

He hefted his end of the swing, and she lifted the opposite side. Together, they tottered back to the porch with their burden. Even in pieces, the swing must have weighed a ton. She recognized the lumber he'd used as what remained of an old black locust tree she'd had to cut down when she arrived at the farmhouse.

She glanced down at the swing. A better use for the lumber than allowing it to languish in her carriage house for the past five years. Restraining Order Number One had promised to use the wood to fix her fence, and there it sat, ever after.

From the swing, she glanced to Ethan. He'd shed his leather jacket. His gray T-shirt left little of his broad chest and muscular arms to the imagination. Manual labor had brought out the veins in his biceps and forearms. Lifting the hefty swing only made them more prominent. A little shiver ran through her, part apprehension and part something she refused to name.

It took forever to get the swing back to the porch, tethered to it with him on the other end. By the time they'd wrestled it up the few steps and then lowered it to the wide boards of the porch floor, her heart was thundering, and she couldn't blame it on the weight of the swing alone.

She backed away at once, only to come up against Burt, who'd shadowed them back to the house. The dog stared at Ethan with his tail waving and tongue lolling, leaving Gypsy to wonder if her perusal were as obvious. Unoccupied now, she ran out of things to say.

Ethan's gaze lifted to meet hers. After several awkward seconds of her being unable to untie her tongue, he said, "Hope it works out for you."

"It's perfect. Better than it was," she said quickly. "Thanks."

"Welcome." He stepped nearer, enough that the warmth from his recently laboring body drifted across the scant space between them to eddy against the bare skin above the swooping neckline of her blouse. Gypsy froze, staring at the flecks of gold in his eyes that gave them their catlike color. Her heart threatened to pound out of her chest. She'd gone months without such a reaction to a man. Part of Pickering's appeal was its near-lack of bad boys.

Last night's lavender bath had done her no good whatsoever.

His mouth curled into a little smile. She riveted her attention on his lips, trapped by her own fascination. His mouth was made for mischief, for kisses, for long, lazy evenings on the braided rug by her fireplace.

Ethan took another step, an unspoken question in his eyes. When she didn't speak, he said, "I should go get my bike. 'Scuse me?"

"Oh." Dragging herself up out of her fog, she took a step back…

…and tumbled over Burt.

The dog yipped and scooted aside. With a shriek, Gypsy tottered backward down the stairs.

Ethan pounced toward her, but before he could reach her, she slammed onto her back at the base of the steps. Her head struck the ground so hard, she bit her tongue.

The puffy clouds in the sky swam in dizzying circles. Ethan's face appeared overhead. "You all right?"

"Sure," she groaned out, "what's a little concussion?" She rubbed the back of her head. "Thanks, Burt."

The dog's face appeared beside Ethan's. Burt slurped her cheek.

"Get back, you moose," Ethan grumbled, nudging the dog aside and crouching beside Gypsy. He bent close to her face, looking closely into each of her eyes. "Have you had a concussion before?"

"No."

"I have. They get worse each time." He stayed over her, so near his sawdust-and-leather scent filled her nostrils. His hands cupped her face, and the contact startled her into stillness. He stared into her eyes, one after the other, flooding her senses with him. Gypsy made the mistake of breathing deep, and her head began whirling double-time.

He concluded her pupils were fine, then slid an arm around her back. Dizzy already, Gypsy let him lift her back to her feet, which he accomplished as easily as if she weighed nothing. "All right?" he asked.

She blinked, waiting for the multiple Ethans swimming in her vision to resolve back into one face. "I think I'll walk to breakfast."

"As opposed to what? You gonna ride Burt?"

"I was going to take my bicycle." She indicated the light-blue bicycle, with its rack on the back and basket on the front, leaning against the fence beside the gate.

Ethan peered deeper into her face. He couldn't know that most of her inability to see straight was his effect on her, rather than the spill off the porch.

"I don't think I like your eyes, after all."

"You don't need to be rude," she muttered.

He shrugged off her snappishness with a tilt of his head. "I'll walk you to breakfast. I've gotta go into town, anyway."

Her dizziness vanished. "No!"

He jerked back a step as if she'd screamed bloody murder.

Maybe she should have. One evening of him on her porch, she could handle. Even his fixing the swing after breaking it, she could manage. But one more minute in this man's company, with his intoxicating scents whirling around her…that was too much ask of any red-blooded woman. "I'm fine, really. Thank you for fixing the swing. I hope everything works out with your motorcycle."

The look in his eyes hardened, and Gypsy sensed that he'd snatched something of himself away without ever realizing he'd extended it. The emptiness in its place surprised and saddened her. "Yeah, no problem." He stalked away toward the carriage house, presumably to get his jacket and motorcycle and get out of her life, just the way she wanted.

Now who was being rude?

****

Ethan escaped Gypsy's property faster than he'd escaped any big town where he'd ever stayed. He'd never minded when it was time to blow out of Chicago or Phoenix or Atlanta, but those departures were a choice. Leaving Pickering felt just as much like scurrying off with his tail between his legs as leaving Sagerton had been. He walked his bike toward the gas station, seething with disgruntlement. Being an Elemental sucked.

He refused to look up the street to the town's one little diner, where he knew Gypsy had opted to have breakfast before running whatever errands she'd lied about. He was no fool. He knew she wanted him out of her life. A person keeping the world at arm's length had no trouble recognizing another of his kind, after all. If she wanted to be left alone, then she'd chosen the wrong profession. How did such a snoozy little village support a shop full of New Age kookiness? She'd have been more at home in a college town. Here, she stood out like the giant spotlighted geode in her shop window.

Maybe she liked that, after all.

Why the hell would she like that?

Mason's was just opening as he arrived. The gas station attendant sweeping the lot whistled when he saw Ethan's bike. "That sure is a beaut."

"Thanks." Ethan swiped his credit card then went to fill the tank.

"Had her long?"

"A few years," he said.

"Wouldn't mind me one of those."

Staring at the scrolling numbers on the gas pump, Ethan tried not to tap his foot. The quicker he blew this town, the better.

The scrape of a shoe on pavement brought his attention up from the pump. The attendant stood beside his motorcycle. "Y'know you got an oil leak there."

The pump stopped, and Ethan put the nozzle away. Frowning, he bent to peer where the man indicated. Sure enough, a little dribble of oil had collected at a seal. "Damn it."

"Ain't no trouble," the man said. "My brother-in-law owns Clemens Automotive. He'll fix you right up."

Grumbling to himself, Ethan left the gas station for the auto shop. The "ain't no trouble" turned out to be a big one: the seals for Ethan's custom bike with custom parts wouldn't be in for a week, and at a custom price. Ethan glared at his beloved motorcycle, fully aware that he wouldn't ride it anywhere until it was fixed. *You're doing this on purpose, aren't you?*

The bike offered no reply. Superiority on wheels, that machine, even when he griped at it. He should have expected some wear and tear, what with driving it all over the country for two years straight.

Resigned, Ethan left the bike at the shop. He'd have to find a place to stay, no doubt about that. Another attempt at the park bench would only land him in Officer Friendly's not-so-good graces.

He also needed to charge his cell phone so he could call Morgan again. She had transferred some of his money into his regular account, but not much. He didn't have many bills, but he didn't work, either…not regular work. He'd paid cash for his bike out of his share of Hope Creek. He and his siblings still owned a stake in the ranch where they'd all grown up, though Cade and his wife owned most of it and ran it themselves now. Ethan took odd jobs for whatever else he needed, when he needed it.

His stomach rumbled. Food. Good start.

He walked back to the diner. As soon as he opened its door, every pair of eyes in the place turned to him as if he'd announced he was dangerous the moment he walked in.

Every pair but Gypsy's. She sat in a booth across from a woman who was sobbing and dabbing at her face with a handkerchief.

Ethan stopped short, ignoring the patrons' calculating stares. No way would he ask that woman for another night on her porch. He stalked to a barstool at the counter. He'd already sat down before he realized Officer Friendly was sitting two seats away.

Hollis swiveled around then touched a fingertip to the brim of his hat. "Mornin'. Thought you'd be on your way by now."

"Problem with the bike," Ethan said as he hailed the waitress for a coffee.

"That's too bad. You get Clemens to check it out for you?"

"Gotta get parts." Ethan figured a small-town cop ought to be nosy by nature, but he hunched his shoulders and leaned forward onto the counter, hoping his posture would clue Hollis in that he wanted to be left to himself.

"Not a big shop, that," Hollis said.

Ethan gave an inward sigh. When the waitress brought his coffee, he reached toward the sugar and creamer with relief.

"We don't see too many bikes like yours around here," added the officer, "but don't you worry. Roy should have your parts in and get you on your way real soon."

Ethan looked up then. Hollis was staring at him with unnerving, pale-blue eyes.

"Why'nt you go say hi to your cousin, there?" Hollis tilted his head in Gypsy's direction.

Ethan shrugged, not bothering to look. Cousin, was it? No sense enlightening the man if he chose to believe Ethan was related to her. He planned to be long gone before any enlightenment was necessary. "She's busy."

"Ain't now," Hollis added.

Then again, maybe Hollis already knew Ethan bore no relation to her, and was just pushing buttons to see how far he'd get. Irritation danced across Ethan's shoulders. Setting his coffee cup down, he swiveled to look the officer in the eye. When Hollis gave him no more than a mild shrug, Ethan turned all the way around.

Gypsy was talking with a man in the next booth over. She seemed to know him, smiling and nodding to something he was saying. When the man waved a hand to invite her over, though, she lifted the book in her hand, probably illustrating that she was in the middle of something. The man paid his bill, then patted her shoulder and left the diner. She sat alone in the booth, reading her book and sipping at a glass of iced tea.

With a cool look at Hollis, Ethan picked up his coffee and strode toward Gypsy's booth. He slid into the seat opposite her. "Morning, coz."

He'd intended only to stay long enough to ensure that Hollis got an eyeful of him playing family reunion, but the moment Gypsy looked up from her book with a blush coloring her cheekbones, he couldn't move. Fumbling, he blurted, "What's with the weepy woman?"

"I was giving her advice," Gypsy said. "She's going through a tough time right now."

The waitress stopped at their table. "Can I get you anything?"

"Steak and eggs, please," he said without checking the menu. Pretty much every diner everywhere served that, and he found the blush on Gypsy's face a lot more interesting than whatever they put in front of him for breakfast.

The waitress left with his order. Ethan put his elbows on the table and wrapped his hands around the warm coffee cup. Gypsy had gone back to her book. *Dreams and Their Meanings,* it read. He glanced back to Hollis, who gave him a bland smile and a tip of the hat.

Ethan muttered under his breath. That pain in the ass with a badge was just waiting for Ethan to prove he was going to be a problem. *Enjoy the wait, sucker.* "Hey…coz. I've got a favor to ask."

Still blushing behind that book, she raised her gaze to his. Not so shy about being caught fabricating his relationship to her that she'd avoid looking at him, then. He had to admire that. "My bike's going to be in the shop for a week. I need a place to crash on the cheap, and I'm hoping you'll let me have another crack at that porch swing."

"You'll freeze. Overnight temperatures aren't going to stay like they've been."

"I don't get cold." Ethan watched for her reaction. That was as close to an admission of guilt as he ever came, where his power was concerned. He expected her to scoff or raise an eyebrow.

She did neither. The speculation in her eye almost made him reconsider his request to stay at her place for the week, a half-thought-out request he'd only made to rub in her lie about his being her cousin. Why did he even let it bother him?

But as he matched stares with her, the idea of her being his "cousin" floated out of his mind like a falling leaf caught in the wind. In this light, her eyes were the color of black coffee, much darker than his, but striking like her cheekbones, and her skin all the paler because of that bewitching mass of hair. Nature had puzzle-pieced this woman together out of the best of her ancestors, a tailor-made man trap.

If one could get past the *Dreams and Their Meanings*.

Sitting back, Ethan tapped his thumb against his coffee mug. No woman anywhere ever made him do something he didn't want to do. Gypsy Ronan wouldn't be the first.

She closed her book with a snap. Her gaze slid toward Hollis, who was now chatting with the server in pointed disregard of them both. "There's a motel in the next town," she said lightly.

"And you have a house that needs work, and I have a burning desire to not get on Officer Friendly's bad side while I'm here. How about I work off my keep by fixing up that set of stairs you tripped down this morning?"

"I tripped over Burt, not the stairs."

"Well, you're going to trip down those stairs if you let them go much longer. You've got the lumber. Besides…I'm good with my hands." He grinned, letting her make what she would of that.

And she went exactly in the direction he thought she would. The blush flamed across her ivory skin all the way to the roots of her hair. The look on her face, all peachy-pink skin and wide dark eyes, framed by that glorious hair, shot straight to his groin in a jolt of need. Ethan's breath whuffed out before he thought to catch it.

Oh, hell. This was wrong. All wrong. He'd risk a night in jail sleeping on the park bench. Or the gazebo. Or the sidewalk in front of Clemens Automotive. He reached for his wallet to toss a few bills on the table for his coffee and unreceived breakfast.

Gypsy's full lips parted. That wide mouth snagged his attention before her words were even out, and he sat staring at them as her soft voice reached his ears. "Okay. You have a deal."

Chapter Three

The look on Ethan's face was almost as bad as if she'd locked him in a dungeon with a starving dragon. Clearly, it wasn't the response he'd been expecting her to give. Gypsy tried her best not to show that his alarm hurt. She'd extended herself, done something out of her norm. This morning's horoscope had told her to take chances.

So much for that horoscope.

As she was gathering up her things to leave, the waitress brought Ethan's breakfast. His aristocratic nostrils flared. He seemed to change his mind about bolting, thanked her, then tackled his breakfast like he hadn't eaten in a week.

She hesitated. "Don't they feed you in Montana?"

"Sure, but there's also two thousand miles between me and Montana. This is good steak."

"Coming from a Montana man, I guess Pickering should take that as a compliment." She watched him wolf down his food. "You didn't eat dinner, did you?"

"Do you count beef jerky?"

"So that's how you made friends with my dog."

He shrugged. The eggs disappeared into his mouth one after the other, devoured.

Take a chance today, her horoscope had said. *You'll be pleasantly surprised at what comes of it.* She read her horoscope every single morning, and she usually followed it. Ethan was a surprise, all right, but the jury was still out on whether he was a "pleasant" one. More like the last thing she'd expected to roll into quiet little Pickering.

Hollis appeared, looming over the table. "Well, now, I see our visitor's making himself at home."

Flustered, Gypsy stuffed her book into her tote then rose to leave the booth. "Hi, Hollis."

Hollis grinned. From the corner of her eye, Gypsy saw Ethan divide a long look between Hollis and her. "Heading back to the shop now, Gypsy?" Hollis asked.

"In a bit," she admitted. "Excuse me."

"By all means." He moved aside to let her out of the booth.

Gypsy slid out. A few steps toward the door, her conscience pricked her. Hollis might be an overprotective shark where his town was concerned, but she suspected he had it in for Ethan for entirely different reasons. She couldn't leave the poor man to Hollis's torments. He'd done nothing wrong.

Yet, added a little voice inside her. She stifled it. "I'll see you back at the house around noon, Ethan."

His gaze shifted to her, his cat-gold eyes lit with some personal amusement…and a hint of something that touched off an answering bout of flutters in her belly. "Sure thing."

Gypsy hurried out of the diner before she could go back on her horoscope's advice.

Outside, she breathed easier, if only because Ethan wasn't there making her forget how. The morning air carried a crisp little bite of autumn that had her thinking of warm blankets and spice-scented candles. She gazed down the street toward her shop window with a flush of pride. She walked toward it, greeting a few people walking on the sidewalk as she went.

She recognized Rich Pettit, who'd been at breakfast. He stood outside the hardware store loading cans of paint into the back of the rescue truck from the volunteer fire station. "Hi, again. Busy already?"

"Long time, no see," he said, his eyes crinkling at the corners. "Prettying up the station for the fall dance. You going?"

"Not so much," she said. "You?"

He tossed a few rollers into the truck beside the paint cans. "My on-again, off-again lady friend and I are on again, so…" He shrugged and made a noncommittal noise.

She grinned. "Well, that's good. Someone better do your cooking. You've got to be the only firefighter in Vermont who can barely boil water."

"Don't get too excited. The lady friend can't cook, either." He gave a conspiratorial wink as he set the last can of paint in the truck bed. "I might have to sneak over to your house to cheat on her with your apple cobbler and maple glazed pork chops."

"Get back to the station, you," Gypsy teased. She said goodbye to Rich then continued down the sidewalk toward her shop, soaking in the atmosphere of a refreshing Vermont autumn.

Lubbock, Texas might be nice for her parents—accountants, bred from accountants, and as conservative as they came. She loved them even though they drove her mad…loved them so much that she'd tried to please them by going to college for accounting. They had wanted her to follow them into their firm back home…but to Gypsy's relief and their everlasting disappointment, she'd roomed with a woman who had grown up in liberal Pickering.

When the sore thumb from Lubbock arrived in town, she'd expected to stick out here, too, but Pickering welcomed Gypsy with all the warmth her college roommate had professed of it. Her roommate now lived in Lubbock, and Gypsy had moved into the very house in which Paula had grown up. If *that* wasn't a little bit of irony, nothing was.

She entered her shop, then flipped on the overhead and display lights. The warm glow sparkled off the geodes in display cases on the counter. The scent of sage lingered in the air over the faint aroma of old wood. Gypsy inhaled deeply, then sighed, filling herself with the contentment of her shop. If only she could bottle the scent of The Holistic Mystic and all its contents, she'd be happy for life.

She set her tote bag under the counter, then stroked her fingers over the old oak countertop, worn smooth by years of hands crossing its surface. The shop had been an apothecary once. A perfect place to start a store built around healing the spirit. People seemed to need that more and more these days…including herself.

For a little New Age shop in a little New England town, she did well enough to pay the taxes on her property. Her parents' one concession to her move to Vermont was that they'd paid for her house. She suspected they hadn't thought she'd make it here, but her degree in accounting had taught her where to spend and where to save. She might have mostly secondhand possessions, but she managed.

Lots of people came into Pickering from Rutland and the surrounding cities. The recently past Pickering

Fall Festival brought in even more visitors, many of whom stopped at Gypsy's store for gifts. She prided herself on her success in spite of her parents' claims that sooner or later, she would give up and return home.

Too bad she couldn't claim the same success in her relationships. For every romantic failure, she'd simply poured more love into her store. It was enough.

She sighed. It would have to be enough.

And just like that, Ethan walked into her shop. "I was going to ask you— Whoa."

She looked up to find him staring around her store, wide-eyed, with his brows almost up to his rusty-red hairline.

When he didn't speak, she prompted, "Ask me…?"

"Whether you have an outlet outside your house. I have a dead cell phone."

"On the side of the house, and there's one in the carriage house, too, by the side door." She eyed him, watching his clearly-skeptical expression grow more and more incredulous as he surveyed her shop. "Why do you want to stay with me?" As soon as the words left her mouth, she prayed it sounded less skeptical— and less desperate—to him than it did to her. She sounded like she hadn't dated in years. She had…just unsuccessfully.

Ethan wandered across the wide plank floor with the easy, unconscious grace of an alpha predator. He slid between two display tables to pluck a pair of Chinese meditation balls from their ornate little box, then twirled them in his palm. Their faint, soothing chime carried across the shop as they clicked together, and the overhead lights flashed off their cloisonné phoenixes. As Gypsy watched, fascinated in spite of herself, he deftly rolled one up to the tops of his fingers to trickle it along his knuckles, then dropped it back into its box. The other followed.

My, what nimble fingers you have.

An image flashed through her all-too-vivid imagination: Ethan, employing those fingers in ways that drew a shuddering sigh from her lips. She imagined those big hands wrapping around her waist, sliding across her belly, traveling upward under the gauzy hem of her blouse…

How hot would his hands feel against her, a displaced Texan who could never seem to get warm enough in her adopted hometown? Her face heated readily, at least. She tried to look away from his broad shoulders with an entire lack of luck.

Ethan clapped the little box shut then turned around. "So this is what you do?" he asked.

Jerked out of her beautiful daydream, she struggled to focus on the present. His tone plucked at her temper. "Yes," she blurted, spreading her arms. "I do this."

His dark brows lifted, and he went back to strolling the shop as if her reaction hadn't the least effect on him. With his back to her—and those broad shoulders on glorious display, even under his leather jacket—he flipped through a book about tarot. "I appreciate the place to stay."

Gypsy's intuition fluttered. People's postures had a lot to say, even when their mouths didn't. Back turned, eyes averted. Ethan was vulnerable here.

To what? she wondered. It couldn't possibly be her. "It's all right," she assured him as he put the book down to move to an enormous apothecary jar filled with bundles of dried sage. He tapped the glass.

Gypsy took a tentative step toward him. "Are you looking for something?"

His gaze shot to her so quickly, she knew in an instant she'd both hit the nail on the head and bludgeoned his unseen sore spot.

"I should go," he said. "See if I can get started on those porch steps, maybe."

Dismayed, she advanced another few steps. "You really don't have to—"

"Yeah, I do. I pay my way. See you later." He swept out of her shop as fast as he'd come in, leaving her whirling in his wake.

Gypsy stared at the door. The window's lace curtain swung gently as if waving goodbye.

****

She still can't look twice at me. And now there's this new guy in town staying with her. He looks like trouble. I'm gonna have to go right back over to her house and boot him out, I know it. Someone's got to protect her. She's too nice. She needs me, even if she doesn't say it.

****

Ethan hated being without his wheels. He walked back to Gypsy's house, already chafing at being trapped in this town. If frilly bohemian shirts and owls in her garage weren't enough, Gypsy Ronan's shop certainly topped off the list of reasons he should get out of Pickering.

Not the least of which was the shop owner, herself.

And, for some unfathomable, poorly thought out reason, he'd invited himself to a full week on her derelict porch and even offered to fix the thing up.

There had to be a special place in hell for the

stupid.

He turned his hand over to rub a thumb across the deep scar on his right palm. At the tender age of seven, he'd tried cutting the damned glow out of his skin. Old man Rathbone had found him in the garage with tears streaming down his face, and blood streaming from the pocketknife gouge in his hand. He'd had to lie like the devil. A whittling accident, he'd said, without ever thinking to be sure something that looked like a whittling project had been nearby. The old man hadn't questioned it, merely rushed him off to the emergency room for stitches and a tetanus shot.

The Rathbones were gruff and stern, but ultimately kinder than his real parents had ever been to him. Ethan remembered when Social Services had snatched him out of the midst of a domestic screaming match between his birth parents. Holes punched in the walls, the smell of booze in the air. He'd been lucky a neighbor had called in the disturbance, or he might have had holes punched in him next.

As a teenager, he'd gone looking for his parents, only to find his father had been arrested for third degree burglary, and his mother remarried and moved to Canada. He never bothered to find either of them after that.

When he arrived at Gypsy's house, he opened the gate. It scraped the ground with a teeth-jarring screech. He checked the hinges. The top one had come loose from its post.

Things, he could fix. He headed for the carriage house and Gypsy's old toolbox.

A boy was already there—young, maybe into his mid-teens or so, with his electric-blue hair shaved close everywhere but at his forelock, which hung into his eyes.

They stopped as one on seeing each other. The boy held a section of metal pipe so long it dragged the ground. "Uh…hey. Miss Ronan's not here."

"I know," Ethan said dryly. "What are *you* doing?"

The boy flipped his bangs out of his eyes and gave him the haughty look only a teen could achieve. "None of your business."

"Maybe not directly," Ethan conceded, "but I'm staying here for the week, so if you're stealing, it might be my business to tell her so." He started forward again.

"I'm not stealing!"

The affront in the boy's tone brought Ethan to a stop again. "All right," he said, "then why are you here when she's not?"

"I'm building something." Sullen now, the boy dragged the pole toward the side of Gypsy's yard opposite the carriage house.

Ethan jogged forward to lift the end from the ground.

"I don't need your help."

"I know you don't, kid, but to be honest, I'm here to build, too. I promised her a new set of porch steps in exchange for crashing here."

The boy scoffed. "This place needs a new everything."

"Tell me about it." They entered the side yard, where a large, square, white birdhouse with a green roof sat in the grass some way from the house. "You into birds?" Ethan asked.

"*She* is." He waved a hand toward the forest at the back of the property. "She gets a lot of bugs coming from those woods, so she asked me to build her a purple martin house in wood shop."

"Purple martins to go with her Saw-whet Owl. Won't they bother each other?"

"I guess not. They don't eat the same stuff, and the owl doesn't usually hang out on this side of the house. She goes to the woods on the other side of the pond in the daytime."

"What's with the three sections on the pole?"

"It's telescoping, so Gypsy can take it down to clean it when the birds leave for winter. I'm gonna test it once I get it up there." He jerked his chin skyward, presumably toward wherever he intended his handiwork to sit.

Ethan set his end of the pole down as they reached their destination. "How do you know so much about birds?"

"From her."

Ethan nodded. He had never paid much attention to how intricate such a little building was: each "apartment" with a deep porch and an opening of its own, as if the birds were tiny tenants that expected a neat and private entrance.

Even birds had a better home than he ever would.

He watched as the kid attached the house to the pole, then helped him set the pole into a cement-clad base. When they cranked the telescoping pole to its full fifteen feet, the flush of pride on the kid's features was plain.

Ethan smiled. Minus the blue hair, the kid reminded him a little of himself as a teenager. Ethan had given a lot more attitude, though. This boy hadn't yet developed the full coat of prickles. "What now?"

"She says they won't come back until spring, but I wanted to make sure it went up all right," said the boy. He angled a shy look at Ethan. "She says they're better than a bug zapper."

"She says all that, does she?" Ethan muttered, watching the birdhouse silhouetted against the blue sky.

"Yeah."

Ethan closed up the toolbox at the base of the pole. "What's your name?"

"Colin."

Ethan held out his hand. "Ethan. If you have some extra time on your hands, you want to give me a hand getting that porch ready for fixing?"

****

Gypsy arrived home to Ethan sitting on an upturned work bucket in the front yard beside Colin, the boy from town who ran odd jobs for her. Both were covered in sawdust, and a neat stack of boards lay beside her old sawhorses.

She opened her gate, then blinked in startled pleasure when it swung freely, with no scrape and no screech. She looked up to thank the boys.

Ethan looked disturbingly good sitting there in her yard. Of all the things her house needed in the way of improvements, that one seemed to have the biggest impact.

Her mother might be right. Maybe she was hopeless.

Swallowing her apprehension—and choking down a chaser of jitters—she approached them. "Thanks for fixing the gate. I see you've met Colin."

Ethan angled a look at her. "He has a pretty rare gift. He drew that entire birdhouse out of his head, to

48

the exact plans for that bird."

She smiled in spite of herself. "He's got talent," she agreed. She pawed around in her tote for a handful of bills—more than Colin had asked for when she recruited him to build the martin house. "Don't spend it all at once."

Colin's dark eyes went wide as he accepted the money. "Miss Ronan, you don't have to—"

"I absolutely do have to," she interrupted. "You worked on that house all summer."

"Thanks!" Colin gave her one of his infrequent grins, undiluted by the pall of his home life.

Gypsy returned it. Half the reason she'd agreed to letting Colin work odd jobs around her property had been dire need. He needed to—eventually—buy a car. She needed someone to help mow her property. The arrangement had provided an unforeseen benefit to them both: a friend. "Are you two thirsty?"

"Sure," they echoed. Colin tramped ahead of her up to her front door while Ethan trailed behind.

Gypsy's thoughts shifted hard to the man behind her. A whiff of sawdust traveled to her on the breeze, and his heavy bootfalls echoed on the worn wood of the porch. She keyed open the door, acutely aware that she was letting this man into her house.

Colin went to her kitchen fridge without preamble. She had told him from the first day that her fridge was fair game if he came to her house hungry. Some days, she thought with a smile, he all but cleared out her groceries. She never begrudged him that. While she'd never minded living alone, it was nice to provide for someone else.

Two someones, right now. Ethan stalked into the

kitchen behind them, filling up the space just by existing. A little tremor of giddiness flashed through her body.

She strode to the bread box on the counter. "Hungry?"

"Oh, yeah," Colin said, full of enthusiasm. Ethan didn't answer.

She turned around to find him studying her kitchen: vine-and-flower wallpaper; speckled Formica, years out of date; a linoleum floor that might not have seen a new pattern since the home was built. Overall, the tiny space suited a single cook.

His attention shifted to her, and her body temperature shot up several degrees. She averted her gaze to Colin, suddenly very glad to have the boy in the house as a buffer between her and the man currently sending sizzling pulses through her body.

She pulled together two turkey sandwiches, chips, and iced tea, then laid it all on the old, painted wooden kitchen table. "Dig in."

Colin wolfed his portion down with the zeal of a typical teenaged boy. Ethan drew the glass of tea to his lips in a motion that dragged Gypsy's stare away from all else. The rim of the glass touched his sensual mouth, and she only realized she was staring when a drip of mayonnaise landed on her sandal.

She snapped back to herself with an irritated murmur, then snatched a dishrag to wipe up the mess. "Thank you for your work," she said, not looking at them—and especially not Ethan. "Is all that lumber just for my steps?"

"Some of it. I can rip a few boards for the broken spots in your porch if you want. That must've been a really big tree you cut down."

The dog door creaked, and Burt ambled into the kitchen looking for tidbits that might have dropped from the table. With a smile, Gypsy spied Colin slipping him a potato chip.

Ethan rumpled the dog's ears. "What's up, tough guy?"

Burt wagged his tail, then laid his big head on Ethan's knee. *Oh, Burt, you turncoat,* she thought darkly. She turned away to the counter, where she'd stored a basket of tomatoes for her lunches.

An instant later, she sensed Ethan looming up behind her. "More tea?" he asked.

She snatched the glass pitcher then whipped around, all in a fluster.

Ethan stood right in front of her, just missing the swing of the pitcher toward his chest. Tea sloshed upward, then splashed back into the container.

Ethan's brows twitched upward. For a moment, he looked just as startled as she was, as if the two of them had no idea how they'd come to be in each other's space.

And for the life of her, Gypsy couldn't dislike the feeling. His warmth floated across the air to wash up against her skin, and her drafty old house couldn't compete. Agitated by the strength of her reaction, she pushed the pitcher at him.

He grasped the base in one large paw. A fine furrow appeared between his brows, and that sensual mouth turned down at the corners.

A wholly shocking pang of disappointment roiled through her. What did he see when he looked at her that way? "I'd better get...something..." she babbled.

Giving up the tomatoes, the tea, and her kitchen, she hurried upstairs.

****

Ethan didn't expect her to come back down. He and Colin finished their lunch in companionable quiet. Somewhere in the house, a clock tolled one.

After Colin sucked down the rest of his meal, he claimed homework and made himself scarce, leaving Ethan to wonder whether he was once again relegated to the outdoors. He patted Burt. The shepherd wagged his tail and then lay down beside the table.

Ethan pulled a blank postcard from his coat pocket. For no reason, he'd begun mailing them to Morgan and Elsa from wherever he ended up. Elsa told him she'd started a scrapbook of them—why, he couldn't begin to guess.

He flipped the postcard over. *Beautiful Vermont,* it said, with a cookie-cutter picture of a steepled white church swimming in a sea of autumn trees. She'd get a kick out of that: him, in a picture-postcard town in the fall. Maybe he ought to box this up with a jug of maple syrup. With a self-deprecating leer, he took out a pen.
Dear Elsa,

Sending you this postcard so you can see what a joke my life is. Bike broke down. May have to stay here and take up knitting for the winter. Don't worry for me.

Love,
Ethan

He stuffed the pen and postcard back into his pocket. He'd mail it in the morning to Elsa's winter address in California, where she lived with her fiancé and his kid sister. She'd get it and call Ethan, and they'd laugh about it, and he'd envy the hell out of her

52

for having everything she wanted out of life.

More importantly, she wanted everything she had.

The creak of a floorboard alerted him to Gypsy's return to the kitchen. Her arms were full of blankets. "I thought you might be more comfortable in the guest room down here."

Caught sulking, Ethan snarked out a reply before he could stop himself. "I get house privileges?"

As soon as he said it, he regretted it. Crimson flushed across her cheeks. He might be a first-class crank in general, but so far, she hadn't done anything that warranted behaving like one toward her. She'd opened her house to him.

His only problem with her was *him*.

He angled his head and gave her a look of chagrin. "Sorry. Not used to being around...anybody."

"Me, either." With admirable determination, she walked past him through the wide kitchen doorway.

Curious, he followed her back through the sparse living room sporting built-in shelves and old furniture. At the rear of the house's first floor, she opened a paneled doorway to a tiny guest bedroom.

Ethan swallowed a snort. His legs would hang off the bitty twin bed from the knees down. At least there was a wicker bench at the bottom. The only decorations were a dream catcher on the wall over the poster panel headboard, a squatty ceramic lamp on the maple dresser, and an oval runner on the plank floor. Nothing matched. He suspected Gypsy had furnished her house with yard sale finds and castoffs.

Still, not a cramped porch swing. It all went together, in spite of its mismatched first impression. Without liquid assets himself, he doubted he'd do better. God knew he wouldn't ask Cade for extra money, even if he had a place to hang his hat every night. "Thank you."

She set the folded blankets on the bench, avoiding his gaze. "There's a second shower down here, just next door, with towels in the cupboard."

He stared at her for a second, trying to weigh the hesitation in her posture against the fact that she'd just allowed him into her house for a week. "Do you do this a lot? Take in strays?"

"You helped me with the swing and the porch steps. Burt likes you. Colin likes you."

"And you're not worried I'm an ax murderer?"

She met his gaze at last. "I know you're not," she said, with a surety that scared the crap out of him.

Before he could ask what the hell she meant by that, she flitted away. Ethan stood in the middle of a room where his head practically brushed the ceiling, staring at the empty doorway with a sudden conviction that Gypsy wasn't the one who should worry.

Chapter Four

Gypsy hurried upstairs to her room. Burt trotted past her with an aplomb that left her jealous. She went straight to her dresser then lit the fat white candle resting there. Its peaceful glow usually chased away her anxiety, but the man downstairs brought it all rushing right back.

The tarot reading she'd done at the shop after breakfast had determined Ethan had some part to play in her life. The spread had shown her The Lightning-Struck Tower, which bothered her, and then The Hanged Man, even worse. But then she'd laid The Chariot over it.

Ruin. Sacrifice. And then triumph? What did *that* mean?

The combination had been enough to give her doubts. Before the spread, she'd been ready to wave a completely contented goodbye to the man and his motorcycle.

Now? Now, he was making himself comfortable in her spare room.

Maybe—for once—her tarot had been wrong.

Take a chance. Ruin. Sacrifice. Triumph.

Shaking her head, she peered out the front window at the pile of lumber resting in her dooryard. He'd shown himself to be a willing worker, almost as if he expected to provide hard labor in return for a roof over his head. He dressed the part of a loose cannon, but he acted nothing like one.

He didn't like *her*, that much was clear.

The Chariot flashed in her mind's eye. Whatever he was, Ethan Sutter tried hard not to advertise it.

She rarely ended a tarot reading in confusion. She stared out the window toward her carriage house, even though it wasn't visible from her window. Before moving to Vermont, she'd sought advice from a psychic, who'd said Gypsy's spirit guide was the owl. When she moved here and little Aegis the Saw-whet Owl took up residence on her property, Gypsy had been elated. At last, a sign that she'd done the right thing in leaving Texas and everything she ever knew.

Ethan was a whole different kind of sign: *Caution.*

She changed into a pair of jeans and a sweater against the cooling afternoon air, then made her way with Burt back downstairs. Ethan was in the kitchen, finishing up his iced tea. "What do you like for dinner?" she asked brightly.

His gaze followed her around the kitchen. She pretended not to notice, but his laser-hot stare sent pulses of warmth through her body from head to toe. At last, he said, "I don't get it."

"There isn't much to get. You need a place, temporarily, and I have extra room. Boarders aren't that uncommon."

"Have you taken in boarders?"

Blushing, she hunted in her fridge, then emerged with a small roast she'd been planning to cook and slice up for sandwiches. "Beef?"

He shrugged. "I grew up on it. Won't hear me complain."

She set the roast on the counter, then searched her cupboards for the roasting pan, taking more time than necessary.

She sensed, rather than saw, Ethan approaching the sink. As she poked through the base cabinet, the hiss of the tap went on, and then off again. By the time she found the pan, Ethan was drying his hands on a dishtowel. "Put me to work."

Pulling spices from another cupboard, she said, "You don't need to help."

"It's fine," he assured her. "If I'm gonna stay, I'm gonna pull my weight."

She smiled at the cowboy drawl coloring his words. "You cook?"

"I *can*. Montana," he reminded her, unwrapping the roast. "If there's anything we know in Montana, it's cows." He examined the meat. "Nice cut. Local butcher?"

"Yes. He gets it from a farmer who pasture feeds them and doesn't dump chemicals into them. How'd you know?"

He smiled, and the light in his eyes sent a charge of giddiness through her. At the same time, they said, "Grew up on it."

Gypsy laughed, and the mental image of The Lightning-Struck Tower seemed very far away. "You aren't anything like I thought you'd be."

In an instant, his humorous expression vanished under an air so serious, so awash with his own confusion, that she doubted he even knew he projected it. Watching him, she feared to speak, knowing it would puncture some fragile bubble. Instead, she busied herself pulling down ingredients to add to the roast.

Whatever had been in his aura settled back into the business at hand. For the next fifteen minutes, Gypsy soaked in an unfamiliar but completely wonderful sensation of contentment.

Then she identified it. Except for Colin, she hadn't had a houseguest to cook for since her college roommate visited over four months ago. She might have had countless friends and acquaintances in town, but in this big, rambling house, she was all alone.

Ethan's presence filled her home. Oddly, his silence compounded the sensation. In fact, the quieter he remained, the more she focused on his *physical* presence. She'd only just turned on the stove, but the kitchen was as warm as if she'd been baking all morning. She rinsed her hands then picked up the dishtowel to wipe them. The motions didn't distract her from Ethan one bit. When he passed behind her to get the basting broth, a tiny spasm rolled down her spine, as potent as any electric shock.

But most certainly without the pain.

In one day, he'd gone from trouble on two feet to an enigma beyond anything she knew. In spite of past experience, all the signs on which she'd come to depend were pointing her *toward* this man.

Only when she heard the strain of popping stitches did she realize she was wringing the poor dishtowel to pieces. She dropped it at once on the counter with a guilty look toward Ethan. He was busy salting the roast and hadn't noticed. Hot with embarrassment, she cast around for a new task.

The ringing of the doorbell saved her pride. She hurried out of the kitchen to answer it.

Hollis stood on her doorstep with what looked like

a wrapped cake. "Afternoon, Gypsy."

"Hi, Hollis," she replied, careful to keep her tone pleasant but not to inject too much enthusiasm into it. Hollis usually took a friendly response as an invitation to linger. He'd once taken her cheery hello as an excuse to spend three hours at her shop, drifting along among the wares and trying to ask her out in between customers. He never seemed to realize how awkward it was when she politely refused him...again.

He hovered outside her door like a mosquito waiting to get in and irritate her. "My sister made her cinnamon spice cake last night," he said. "She makes so much of it, and when she gives me one, I never eat all of it. I thought I'd bring it over."

By his tone, she suspected he thought she'd invite him in for dinner...but the kitchen was already very full.

Trying not to blush, she held onto the edge of the door, neither closing it in his face nor opening it wider. It was getting harder to combine tact with refusal. She searched for the words.

"While I'm here... Do you have a date for the fire house dance?" Hollis asked.

So that was the reason for the ingratiating smile. Seemed like that was all anyone wanted to talk about today. Small towns did love their big annual events. She stifled a groan and prepared to add Refusal of Date to Refusal of Cake.

Before she could search for the appropriate words, Ethan's deep voice came from behind her. "Afternoon, Officer."

Hollis's sweet-talking behavior vanished like a wisp of incense smoke in the wind. "Mister...?"

"Sutter," Ethan responded.

Hollis's eyes narrowed an infinitesimal fraction. If Gypsy hadn't been watching him, she might not have noticed at all. He turned back to Gypsy as though Ethan were worth no more regard than the worn porch boards under his feet. He held out the cake. "What do you say, Gypsy?"

"To the cake, or the dance?"

"Both." Hollis grinned.

The blush she'd been trying to avoid burst full across her face, sizzling. She pushed open the door. "Yes and thank you to the cake, and…*maybe* to the dance."

Beaming, Hollis handed over the dessert. "Enjoy it. I should get back to the station." His smile faded a little, crystallized somehow into a mockery of warmth. He looked over Gypsy's shoulder as he retreated down the steps. "Well, you and your…?"

"Cousin," she supplied.

"Cousin," Hollis repeated. "Have a real good evening." He thumped down the steps to his cruiser, parked on the gravel driveway outside her gate.

When Hollis left, she closed the door against the crisp air outside. She turned to find Ethan studying her with an expression at least as unsettling as the one Hollis had worn. "You shouldn't have done that," Ethan said.

"Done what?" she asked, pleading with her cheeks to stop burning.

"Made him think he has a chance. He's just going to keep bothering you."

She waved a hand in the air. "I can handle him."

"I'm sure you can. Do you like him?"

She raised a brow. "*Hollis?* Not like *that*."

"Not your type," Ethan guessed. His mouth tilted up at one corner.

Gypsy took a deep breath. This was one of those moment-of-truth points where she could drag out her frustrations, or stop them in their tracks before they multiplied. She decided on swift excision. "My 'type' is bad for me, so maybe I should start shopping for safer material."

He surprised her with a low laugh. His golden eyes crinkled at the corners as he stepped backward, letting her lead the way to the kitchen. "That sounds like a good story."

"Oh, yes," she said acidly, sweeping past him, "unless you're the one who lived it."

"Everyone's kissed a few frogs," he said. His voice mellowed with a sympathetic note that sanded the coarse edges off her irritation.

She pulled out plates and glasses. "Kissing frogs and having them arrested are *not* the same thing."

The amusement on Ethan's face vanished. "What did they do?"

Sighing, she laid the plates on the table. Her cheek throbbed with remembered pain. "Neil was a drinker with a bad temper. The more he drank, the worse his temper." She struggled a moment, then met Ethan's gaze with little more than a veneer of pride in place. "I don't like drinkers."

Ethan held her gaze, his eyes dangerously soft. When he spoke, she detected an oh-so-faint note of bitterness that stoked her curiosity. "Me, either."

Sensing his sore spot, she turned back to her task. Ethan seemed relieved, but her curiosity wasn't. She stole a look at him as he put away the spices she'd left out. Unaware of her observation, he moved around the kitchen with the restless prowl of an animal searching for escape.

One she'd bet he'd been looking for most of his life.

Something at the bottom of her soul tugged hard. Maybe Ethan Sutter was more kindred spirit than she'd realized. She'd had her escape from Texas, from well-meaning but overbearing parents, from a life drowned in decimal points and dollar signs. Who was she to judge him when he might be looking for the same kind of reprieve? The leather jacket and dark clothing and darker expressions might be nothing more than a smokescreen.

Maybe the problem wasn't with him. Maybe it was her.

The words spilled out without her realizing she'd meant to speak. "Dinner will be a couple of hours at least. Can I help with the porch steps?"

But Ethan had already retreated back into his shell. "Sure," was all the answer she got.

He helped her finish setting the table in silence, and then he murmured something about getting the steps ready for work. He left the kitchen. Gypsy stood there holding a platter with the disturbing sense that she'd lost a battle she hadn't even known she'd been willing to fight.

Not with him, but *for* him.

****

Ethan stalked down the creaky porch steps, spoiling for a fight. Gypsy had touched a carelessly exposed nerve. He'd been dumb enough to point it out to her.

Everyone had baggage. Ethan carried around a whole train car.

He gave himself a mental kick. *Quit your sulking.* He stomped toward Gypsy's carriage house, irritable and prickly and wanting least of all to spend an afternoon in her company. Already indebted to her for room and board, he couldn't stand the thought of her poking around in his brain as if she could save him from himself. The last thing he needed was an amateur head shrink, and one that reminded him all too well what it was like to be a society outsider. He hated it. She seemed to revel in it.

Even worse.

Inside the carriage house, he'd found a neglected punching bag hanging on rusty chains from a rafter in the first bay. No doubt, it had been left there by the guy she'd had arrested after he used her as its replacement. Ethan wondered how many times she'd put up with her ex hitting her before she dumped him like the piece of garbage he was.

With a sneer, Ethan shrugged out of his jacket. He dropped it on the rusting shell of a Fifties-era convertible in the next bay. Turning back, he sucker punched the bag. It creaked on its chains, raining down dust, but hung firmly. Encouraged, he pounded the bag some more. The exertion mollified him, and before he knew it, he'd punched his way through Gypsy's baggage and moved on to his own. The bag no longer wore the hazy visage of some woman-beating asshole. Now, the face he projected onto the hapless piece of equipment was an older, grayer version of himself. *Bam. Bam. Bam.* Each hit only polished a lovingly preserved resentment.

"Ethan?" Gypsy's voice echoed into the dim carriage house through the door he'd left open.

He snatched his hands away from the punching bag, still pulsing with frustration.

Her silhouette filled the rectangle of golden afternoon light spilling inside. "Don't you want to work on the porch?"

He steadied the swinging bag with a hand. "Testing it out," he muttered. "Sorry. Should have asked."

She eyed the bag as if it were a slimy bottom feeder in a swamp best avoided. Maybe that was why the carriage house had such a disused air. "It's fine."

No, it wasn't. He could practically see the dots connecting in her head—that he'd be hitting her next. Hell would freeze over before he raised his fists to anyone who didn't fiercely deserve it, let alone a woman.

Brushing his dusty hands off on his jeans, he reined himself back in. He reached for his jacket and swept his gaze over what was left of the car's maroon paint. Tilting his head at the sad hulk, he said, "Who left it?"

"It came with the property."

"That's a damn shame, there," he murmured. "Be real pretty, cruising around town." He glanced at her, intending to check her expression for any residue of wariness, but he was blindsided by the image of her long, black curls fluttering in the wind as she rode around in that fixed-up convertible.

Even more blindsided when he realized the image came complete with him at the wheel. He followed her outside, shaking off the image. Car lust, he told himself. Definitely not the other kind.

Stopping at the pile of lumber, she put a hand on her hip, drawing his attention like a great, big, red arrow to her slender curves. "Put me to work," she said with a brightness that didn't extend to her eyes.

He forced a grin when all he wanted was to get on his bike and zoom out of town, then tossed his jacket over the porch railing. Bending over her ancient toolbox, he extracted a pair of hammers. "Let's get those old boards off."

She took a hammer, then strode toward the sagging boards in question with a capable air that impressed him. He wondered why she hadn't fixed them already.

Burt trotted out to sprawl on the porch and supervise their efforts. Gypsy worked on one side of the steps while he pried loose the other ends of the splitting boards. The longer they worked, in silence, the more he wondered. What had possessed her to trust a man she didn't know to live under her roof, after going through the hell of an abusive boyfriend?

Why me?

He wheeled away from that thought, not wanting to examine it any closer. The last sagging board came away. He tossed it on the pile in the yard, peering at the joists underneath. Not in bad shape, actually. A little repair of the floorboards, and it would be good as new.

The afternoon air had cooled, but he wiped a film of sweat from his brow.

Gypsy noticed. She vaulted over the gaps in the floor to a solid spot. On a small table by the repaired swing, he saw a pitcher and two glasses. She filled one then handed it to him.

He took it with a smile that felt like papier-mâché. The chill of the iced tea slid down his throat and into his belly, but it did nothing to cool the restless heat suffusing his body. He couldn't blame it all on the work. She hadn't said a word about the punching bag all afternoon. He'd have assumed she was over it, if she hadn't been working so hard to act like she wasn't. *Don't get involved,* warned his inner voice.

And there was his basic problem. He barked a laugh.

"What's the joke?"

"One hundred percent on me."

A smile curled her lips, much more welcome than her wariness, if only because her apprehension made *him* uneasy. "Do tell," she prompted.

He shrugged. "I just live in my head a little too much."

"Don't we all? I have entire books on the subject."

"I noticed. Which *Dream* and its *Meaning* were you trying to work out this morning?"

"One for a client. The woman I was sitting with."

"Client," he repeated—not because he cared, so much as because he wanted to keep her talking. Anything was better than silence.

"Sometimes people come to me for help when they're feeling… I don't know. Lost, I guess."

Ethan let out a soft, scoffing breath. He'd been trying to *get* lost for over two years. He wondered if she had any books on how to do that.

Gypsy was watching him, keen-eyed. "You don't believe. It's okay."

I believe more than you think. He flexed his fist around the handle of the hammer, wishing they had more boards to pull up.

"More tea?"

He checked his glass. He'd emptied it in a few swallows. "I got it." He thumped back up the porch, evading the gaps, then paused to scratch Burt behind the ears.

"I'm still amazed at that," Gypsy said. "He hates strangers, and he'd just as soon run most men off the property as look at them."

"Feminist dog," Ethan said, giving Burt a final pat. He smiled into the shepherd's big brown eyes. "It's all right, buddy. I lived with feminists."

"You must mean your sisters."

"Yeah. Both of them are stubborn as oxen. Morgan runs a bed-and-breakfast with her husband, and the other one—Elsa—is getting married next year...in between risking life and limb chasing tornadoes."

Gypsy's eyes went round. "Don't you worry about her?"

"Elsa?" Ethan laid his hammer down and then began picking up the new boards that would replace the sagging ones. "Elsa's going to be the last one standing when the rest of us are a crumpled heap of babbling Armageddon survivors."

"I like her already."

The grin in Gypsy's voice shot sparks down his spine. In spite of his better judgment, Ethan snapped his head around. Gypsy's eyes lit with humor. Incredible on her. Dangerous for him.

Back off quick, he ordered himself. Easy enough to get his head to listen. Other parts, not so much. Gypsy's grin had transformed her from a sober-eyed misfit to a woman of remarkable beauty.

Big mistake in looking. Now, he couldn't tear his eyes away. Before he could rein in that reaction, his mouth went traitor, too. "What's this fire house dance?"

"They do it every fall to raise funds for our fire department. They clear out the fire hall and provide a night of dinner and dancing." Her pale cheeks picked up a little more color, too much to be blamed on the mild autumn sun.

Prickly for no reason, Ethan shouldered a stack of boards. "Hollis? He's just going to keep coming at you."

She gave a gusty sigh. "I know. I hate to hurt his feelings—"

"And he knows that, so he's just going to keep on pushing for a yes. That's its own brand of bullying."

"I never thought of it like that."

"Not much of a dater, are you?"

"I've had dates."

"Clearly of the sort that should be drowned."

She picked up the carton of nails, retrieved Ethan's hammer, and then walked to where he'd laid the first fresh board in its gap. "What makes you such an expert, then?"

Ethan stiffened. His power crackled deep in his bones, a knee-jerk reaction to discomfort. In just a few words, she'd tossed him on the defensive.

He didn't date. He'd *never* dated. A fling or three, just to get the itch out of his system, sure—but *dating*? He'd just as soon feed a woman to a fire-breathing chimera as stick her with a freak like him. He grunted. "I know men, and I know how they think."

Gypsy's eyes narrowed to slits framed by those sinfully thick lashes. Seconds passed, during which he itched to be out from under that shrewd stare. Finally, she knelt to help him ease the board into place. Her attention shifted to the work, but when she spoke, her words were no less discomfiting. "And what do *you* think, Mister Sutter?"

"I think you'd be stupid to encourage that cop. Why don't you just cut him loose with a solid 'no,' once and for all?"

"You think I'm trying to string him along?"

"I think you're too chicken to tell him off." Ethan kicked himself as soon as the retort left his mouth. Why did he let her get to him?

She scoffed, sounding not at all annoyed by his show of temper. The amusement in her voice only goaded him further. "*You* try it some time," she said. "No, wait. You did. That's how I wound up rescuing you from him at the park."

Affecting nonchalance, Ethan shook his head and hammered the board into place. "You're gonna wind up on a date with him."

"No, I'm not."

"Yeah, you are."

"Then you take me."

"Fine." He spat the word out, and then realized what he'd said. Stunned, he forgot his work completely, then slammed his thumb with the hammer.

With a shout of pain, he leaped to his feet and shook his hand in the air. The hammer clattered to the floor.

Gypsy popped up and snatched his hand. "Oh, I'm so sorry! Are you bleeding? Did you break it?"

"I'm fine, I'm fine." He tried to tug his hand out of her grasp, only to find she was holding it too tightly. His pull only drew her closer to him. Unsettled, he met her stare, intending to tell her off just to get her to back away…but there she stood, gazing at him with those mahogany eyes full of worry, and that lush fall of black curls framing her striking features.

Ethan's groin tightened, and his power fizzed dangerously close to the surface. He bit off a primal growl he had no business giving, but couldn't stop sucking in a breath of air laden with an exotic spice he recognized as her perfume.

Bad, bad, all bad. He needed to get the hell out of there before he did something eminently stupid. His power kicked up still higher, warning him to drop everything and run, but his good sense drowned in her intoxicating scent. "Gypsy…"

Those full, wide lips parted on God knew what kind of answer, and Ethan realized he didn't want to hear it. Snared by the lure of her mouth, he bent his head, intending to silence her with a kiss before she said something that would make him regret the heat raging through his body.

He never got the chance.

"Gypsy?" called a voice. A man's voice. Ethan jerked back as if he'd been electrocuted.

Gypsy whirled toward the gate. A beefy man in a windbreaker jacket and baseball cap stood there with a look of unmistakable curiosity on his face. Behind him stood a shiny red pickup with a light bar on the roof and a bed full of lockboxes and water tanks.

Fire truck. Great, Ethan thought. Pickering just kept on hitting him with signs that it was the wrong town in which to break down.

He stole a look at Gypsy. Her cheeks bloomed with color. She blushed more than anyone he'd ever met. Maybe it was her pale skin, or maybe it was his doing.

It might even be the arrival of Fire Marshal Meddlesome that had caused it.

But a sudden, nagging, irritable voice in his head wished it were him.

Chapter Five

"Rich," Gypsy blurted. Her heart thumped as though she'd been caught stealing. She hurried toward the gate—*not* because she was escaping Ethan and that look in his eye, she insisted to herself—and paused in front of Rich. "Get all that paint over to the fire house okay?"

"Yep, but I forgot to tell you. My sister had a little boy last night, and they're both doing great. She said to thank you for the gift basket."

"Oh, she's so welcome. I'm glad everyone's healthy."

She knew Ethan had come up behind her only because Rich's gaze came up and his brows shot skyward, none-too-subtly. She wondered what kind of look Ethan must be wearing to generate that sort of response, but she didn't dare turn to find out.

Burt trotted to the gate with a bark. Rearing up, he set his paws between the posts of the top rail and strained to reach Rich.

Ethan moved into her peripheral vision and shot her an easily-interpreted look: *I thought you said he didn't like men.*

Rich rubbed the dog's head, then extended his hand toward Ethan. Gypsy wondered for an absurd instant whether Ethan would bite the man at her gate instead. "Hi. Rich Pettit. Fire volunteer," he added, nodding toward the vehicle behind him.

The air shivered with a breath of tension. Gypsy stilled, her muscles echoing the frozen moment, but then Ethan reached over the gate. "Ethan Sutter. Hi."

The men shook, Rich with a genial smile, and Ethan returning it with a nod and an assessing gaze. Awareness of how very near she and Ethan stood to one another fizzled down Gypsy's nerve endings. She could practically feel his body heat.

Rich tilted his head back over his shoulder, then eyed Gypsy. "Hollis is putting it about that you're going to the fire hall dance with him."

Was everyone all about the dance today? She couldn't help glancing at Ethan. He returned the look with a raised brow and an upward tilt to one side of his mouth. There was something at once boyish and brooding about that lazy amusement in his eyes. Her cheeks warmed again, all the more noticeable against the slight chill in the afternoon air. "Rich, do you want to come in for some tea?"

"No, don't go to the trouble. I picked up a shift, so I'm headed there now. Just wanted to stop and spread the gratitude."

He grinned, and it looked like he wanted to lean forward and peck her on the cheek as he usually did—they'd known each other as long as she'd lived in town—but he must have caught some intriguing look on Ethan's face, because all he did was back away toward his truck with a parting wave. Gypsy would have given a week's pay to know just what expression had warned poor Rich off. "See you soon," she called by way of apology.

When she turned back around, Ethan's face lacked

any indication whatsoever of his thoughts. The immobilizing glow that had been in his eyes the moment before Rich showed up had disappeared, and she realized with a dismayed shock that she wanted it back. Her lips tingled with the echo of that almost-touch. For just one instant, she'd felt desired again...and it felt wonderful.

Even if she knew that, sooner or later, it would blow up in her face.

A sad, familiar ache swelled in her chest. With a sigh, she retrieved her hammer. "Back to work?"

"Yeah." His voice was gruff, and when Burt nosed at him for attention, he didn't seem to notice.

They worked through the rest of the afternoon. Gypsy allowed the crisp tang of the air and the slanting rays of sunlight to soak into her soul, soothing the ache. Not everyone could be as blessed in life as Rich and his family, a huge, boisterous, well-married lot with a constant gaggle of children at any given cookout or family gathering. He invited her to most of them, and occasionally she went, always coming home with a bone-deep longing. When would that kind of karma come to her?

She paused to get dinner into the oven, but came right back out to continue their work on the porch, most of it wordless. On the upside, they had nearly finished. Ethan worked with single-minded determination, as if this chore meant the survival of the human race. As unobtrusively as possible, she studied the serious frown on his face, as he in turn examined a loose tread and decided it needed to come up and be replaced.

Maybe this kind of work was as cathartic for him as working in her shop was for her. Maybe it helped him with whatever troubled him. And then, stupidly, she began filtering through a half-formed mental list of things that needed to be done around the house.

Only when the yard's floodlight flickered on in the gathering dusk did she realize how long they'd been working. With a murmur of surprise, she put her tools back in the chest. She ventured a look at him. "Dinner should be just about ready."

It was, filling the kitchen with tantalizing scents. Gypsy loved to cook, but with only herself—and an occasionally very spoiled German shepherd—in residence, she rarely had the opportunity to use her skill. The sheer pleasure of sharing a meal with someone else warmed a little space inside her that rarely got much attention.

Ethan disappeared long enough to wash up, then returned to the kitchen while she was still filling the vegetable dish with baked broccoli drizzled in a butter-garlic sauce. Without being asked, he searched through the plate cupboards then finished setting the table.

Pleased, she couldn't resist the smile that tugged at her lips. Not one of her exes had ever considered even coming into the kitchen, unless it was for a beer, until she called out that dinner was ready. Ethan hadn't minded helping with dinner, and clearly didn't share her exes' opinion that cooking was solely a woman's job.

Feminist, indeed.

He noticed her standing there with the vegetable bowl, and his dark-rust brows inched upward. "Problem?"

Embarrassed to be caught staring, she pushed the bowl into his hands. "Not at all."

When he turned his back to set the bowl down on its trivet, she let her gaze slide furtively to the linen drawer. Cloth napkins? Too desperate? Her ears heated.

Yes. Way too desperate. Firmly, she marched to the drawer beside the fridge. Extracting two pot holders and a hot pad, she laid them in the middle of the table. Her shoulder brushed Ethan's.

A static zap flew from her shoulder straight down her spine and into her belly. Gypsy's mouth dropped open on a gasp.

Ethan jerked back as if he thought he'd hurt her. The alarm in his eyes registered far too extreme for a mere static shock.

Was she that repellent after what had almost happened between them outside? Or had he decided it should never have happened at all? Her fluttering heart sank into a disappointed little crevice at the bottom of her stomach. "Excuse me," she murmured, moving aside so he could set the gravy boat on the table.

As they sat down to dinner, Gypsy was suddenly glad for the buffering presence of Burt, who lay on the linoleum between their chairs. She tried to make small talk, thanking Ethan for his work and speculating on what it might take to finish the job. Her attention strayed at every turn to his hands, long-fingered, square-tipped; his forearms, corded with lean muscle, dusted with cinnamon and gold hairs; his short-cropped hair, catching hints of flame in the overhead light. The Hanged Man card flashed through her memory, a man dangling by his foot in helpless frustration—or perhaps resignation at his plight. She tried to envision Ethan, broad-shouldered and big and so vital, reduced to helplessness, and the image wouldn't stick.

"What?"

She blinked. "What, what?"

"You've got a thousand questions on the tip of your tongue," he murmured, setting down his glass. "I can tell. Speak up."

His tone dared her, dared her to ask. *Who are you? What is it about you that makes being in the same room with you feel so electric?* Her skin tingled, underscoring the unspoken question.

His gaze came up, tawny-eyed and watchful, and pinned her in place. "I don't bite."

Until someone got to his soft spot, she guessed. Sensing that was dangerously near, she said, "You can't just linger around until your bike parts come in, and you keep talking about earning your keep. I'd feel much better paying you for your work."

"What sort of work are you looking at?"

"The fence could use some repairs."

Ethan snorted. His eyes crinkled up at the corners in a suddenly-boyish expression that made her heart catch.

She squeezed the handle of her knife as if it were an emergency brake. "What's so funny?"

"Riding fence at Hope Creek was on the top of my Most-Hated Chores list."

Face heating, she blurted, "You don't have to—"

"I don't mind. *Your* fence."

She left off mid-protest, staring. Their gazes collided over the remains of their dinner. That half-felt static charge barreled down her spine and back again, raising goose bumps all over her body until even her loose clothing felt too tight. She opened her mouth. Nothing came out.

One rusty brow arched, an echo of amusement. "You were saying?"

"Fence?" she echoed weakly. The word ended on a question, and she fumed at herself for her cowardice. What in the world was the matter with her? She was a fiercely independent woman who'd started a successful business miles from her childhood home and everything she knew. She'd carved a place for herself in the world. People accepted her here…mostly. She'd defied everything her parents expected of her and built a life here in Pickering.

A very lonely one.

As she met Ethan's stare again, her stomach swooped. The look in his eyes promised anything but *lonely*.

****

Heat poured through Ethan's veins, a tidal surge of one hundred percent lust. Gypsy's pulse flickered in the hollow of her throat. It took everything he had not to stare like a hungry wolf at the way her fair skin flooded with rosier hues. Under that soft-knit sweater, her chest rose and fell with rapid, shallow breaths. He made the mistake of looking—just a glance, because damn it, he couldn't help it. The wash-thin fabric hugged small breasts that begged for a man's hands.

He ripped his stare away to what remained of his food, but the image of stroking his hands down that beautiful ivory skin had engraved itself into his memory. Not trusting himself to look at her again, he said, "Besides the fence?"

She hesitated, seeming just as lost as he, as if they'd arrived on the stage of a bad-dream play knowing only half their lines. "Paint. Roof tiles.

Cosmetics, really. I'll pay you." Her voice shook a little.

Grateful for the distraction, he glanced around at the crown molding and sturdy oak doorframes. "Good bones," he agreed.

God, her cheekbones. That hair. No way was that her real hair. He stared hard at the aged wallpaper and imagined plunging his hands into that luxurious, dark, curling silk. After a day in her company, he'd been stupid to think himself immunized against the shape of her body, the swing of her hair, the spice-kissed scent of her skin that he'd catch on the air as she passed by.

Hell, no. More like a loading dose of sex appeal.

The animal urges roared faster through his body, crashing against each other with equal force. *Yes, kiss her. No, run for it. Yes, take her. No, book out of here.* He ground his teeth and surged out of his seat. "I need a shower."

She was only beginning to form a response before he'd stormed out of the kitchen and lost the rest of her words under the scream of voices in his head.

Away from her, the air thinned and cooled like the respite after escaping a burning house. He hauled in as much of it as his lungs would take and flexed his fists, wanting another go at that punching bag in the carriage house.

Instead, he opted for a shower so cold, it should have turned his lips blue. But his power, his damnable power, protected him from such bone-chilling distractions. He didn't even have to call on it. He burned from the inside, a furnace that began in the pit of his belly as if he could catch fire himself, rather than harnessing an existing flame.

Or was that because of her?

He swore and slapped a hand to the tiled shower wall, then hung his head and let the shower spray pour down on his scalp. The icy water sluiced down his body and splashed into soapy swirls at his feet. He watched the suds circle the drain. Like his life. Like the life of anyone dumb enough to be near him.

No better after washing up, he shut himself in the tiny shoebox room she'd designated for him. He'd found a yellowed car repair manual for the convertible in the carriage house, and leafed through it now, hoping it would settle his mind before bed.

The tick of dog claws on hardwood alerted him to Burt's presence outside the door. For an instant, he imagined Gypsy standing out there beside the dog, wondering what to say to him, wondering if she'd somehow pissed him off. He tensed with the reflex to get up and assure her that it was all on him—then, just as quickly, sat back against the old headboard. His body still vibrated with frustrated need. If he opened that door, he doubted he could stop himself from acting on the demand.

After a while, Burt went away, but his tensions didn't. He spent the rest of a very sleepless night poring through the car manual, searching for answers that weren't there.

In the morning, he found the house empty of all but Burt and the scent of coffee. A half-filled carafe remained on the coffeepot burner, keeping warm. Beside it lay a note:

At the shop. Stop by if you can.—Gypsy

No reference to last night. He'd half thought she'd see him politely out of her house before locking the door against him forevermore. Even half hoped it. But apparently, he wasn't to be let off the hook so easily.

He fixed himself an English muffin, gave Burt most of it, then saw himself out with a tumbler of coffee. The rest of the porch boards lay in a neat stack, under a tarp where they'd been left the night before.

Well, then. He'd been an ass, no question, and the best way to apologize might just be to make himself useful around here. *All right, Sutter. Consider this your temp job.*

Those, he knew. Odd jobs had become his life since going on the road. Bike parts didn't grow on trees, and he needed something to do while he waited for them to come in, or he'd be right back to thinking about…

He reared back from that thought immediately and clapped his hands over the top board on the stack. Burt had followed him outside, and now the dog lay in a companionable sprawl beside the toolbox. With a tacit pat on the dog's head, Ethan started the day's tasks.

He worked best when he worked alone, allowing the job to soak up his attention and keep him from thinking too much about other things. At home, his sisters and Cade had often praised his single-minded, workaholic nature. Ethan doubted they understood why he really did it. It wasn't altruistic—not since old Jim Rathbone had died and left Ethan without the only man he'd ever looked up to. The simple truth was, the work filled holes.

Unfortunately, work ended. By midday, he'd nailed the last new board in place and removed a few splintered balusters in readiness for new ones.

If she'd had a lathe in that carriage house, he'd

have taken some of the lumber and cut new balusters. Sinking onto the newly-hung porch swing, he eyed his handiwork.

Not bad. A little more effort, and the porch would be good as new.

Burt joined him, laying his big, furry head on Ethan's knee. Ethan sat back in the swing, scratching behind the dog's ears. "How much do you think a five-gallon bucket of porch paint goes for in this one-horse town?"

Burt slurped at his hand in reply.

Yawning widely, Ethan stretched the kinks out of his shoulders and peered across the yard. Crows jabbered, raw-throated, from somewhere far away. When the work ended, he usually hated it and searched for the next big undertaking. He sucked in the cool air. No chatter in his head. No self-recrimination. No frustration. Just him, the dog, and a peaceful day.

Almost too easy.

Burt sighed through his nose and pushed his head under Ethan's hand again. Giving the shepherd a crooked smile, Ethan studied the fence across the yard. Not much to do there but shore up or replace a few posts and get it ready for paint. Quick work for a guy who had fence work in his blood. "Come on, mutt. Let's get that done and then head to town."

After attending to the damaged posts, he grabbed Burt's leash from the hook beside the door and they headed into town.

The first couple of blocks in, he began to notice he was receiving some strange looks. An old-timer sweeping the sidewalk in front of the barber shop took one look at him and dodged back into his doorway as if he expected Ethan to bite him, never mind the dog. A pair of children pulling a wagon full of fall flowers stopped dead in the middle of the walk, big-eyed, forcing Ethan and Burt to swerve around them. One young woman clapped eyes on him and detoured into the nearest building—a dentist's office—like she'd rather visit the oral surgeon than have to pass him on the street.

Ethan paused, intending to check his reflection in a shop window—Was he that scary?—only to find himself at The Holistic Mystic. A little sign in the corner of the display window read *Shirt and Shoes Required—No Pets Please*. Ethan doubted people would be going around without shirt and shoes in this chilly weather...and Burt wasn't a pet. He was family.

He pushed open the door, bracing himself against the expected wave of New Age oddity.

A few customers browsed Gypsy's merchandise. Another waited at the counter while Gypsy rang up her purchases and put them in a little green paper bag with the store logo on the front. "Have a great day," Gypsy said as the customer bid her goodbye. Then she saw Ethan, and her eyes went wide. "What happened to *you*?"

"What do you mean, what happened to me?"

"You've got blood all over you. Did you get in a fight with barbed wire?"

He took a closer look at himself. He'd worked himself into a sweat in no more than a T-shirt against the cool air. Bloody scratches and splinter scrapes criss-crossed his arms. His skin bore the odd scar or two, old and pale against his tan, from debris that had fallen on him in fires. He sneered at his own stupidity. He should have put his coat back on.

"Here," Gypsy said, her voice gone dangerously gentle. "Kayla, can you keep an eye on the counter?"

"Sure," responded an elfin blonde wearing an apron in the same green as the shop's bags.

Gypsy slipped out from behind the counter, her eyes all concern. Ethan froze at that look, as unable to move as if every neuron in his body had misfired at once in total confusion. "Burt, down," Gypsy said. "Stay."

The dog obeyed, settling to the floor in front of the counter with a contented sigh.

The touch of her hand on Ethan's back jarred him to his senses. He jerked forward, going where she herded him only to avoid the feel of her long fingers against his spine through his thin shirt.

She showed him through a doorway into the back of her shop, a cluttered storeroom that forced him to walk too close to her. Down a wooden stairway they went, into the belly of the building. Gypsy flicked on a switch. One naked light bulb lit a cellar lined with shelves and an old Hoosier kitchen cabinet. In the middle of the floor stood a single, long wooden table, pockmarked with scorch marks, scratches, and stains.

Ethan's skin shivered, every hair rising to attention. He'd have retreated back upstairs, but Gypsy came down the steps just behind him.

The table was strewn with little bowls, candles, and jars of unrecognizable plants that released their pungency into the air. Thick leather books had been stacked at one end beside a half-burnt twist of what looked like some sort of braided leaves. If the upstairs of her shop had announced her as unusual, the cellar screamed it. "What is this?" he demanded.

"Partly, my workshop," she said, "but also a medicine cabinet." She passed him on the bottom step, stirring the herb-laden air with her own scent, and went to the cabinet. She took down three bottles, a bowl, and a folded cloth. "Come and sit," she invited.

Ethan would rather have stuck his head into the mouth of a rabid lion.

"Those will get infected if they're not cleaned. You're covered in dirt and sawdust."

He stalked the few steps forward then dropped onto an ancient stool. "Do the townies know you're into witchcraft?"

She slanted a look at him. "Wicca isn't pointy hats and broomsticks. It's a faith, like any other." She filled the bowl with water from a tub sink in the corner then set it on the table. Ethan watched her add a few drops of God knew what to the water then dip the cloth into it. A new scent filled the space, a grassy and fresh counterpoint to the still cellar air. "The people of Pickering are more tolerant than…some others," she added, making him wonder what sort of ridicule she'd endured in the past for her oddities.

She laid the cloth against his scrapes. He'd expected it to sting, but the cool sensation soothed the cuts as she cleaned them. Unable to think of anything else to say, he swept his gaze around the room, the shelves, and the table. He grabbed the nearest book, a tiny, linen-bound tome smelling of age and something almost minty. He flipped open the stained cover to stare at the yellowed title page. "Do any of these *Spells of Healing and Power* actually work?"

She smiled, her attention on her task. "Faith isn't

that simple—do a thing, and get an automatic result. It requires a little participation. If you believe the ritual of a spell can bring healing and inner peace, then yes, it works."

He couldn't help the soft scoff that escaped him. Hoping to find inner peace sure as hell wasn't going to bring it. He'd been trying for a couple of years. If driving across the country hadn't turned it up, he doubted a few candles and some incense would do the trick. Flip, flip. The pages crinkled. *For Balance in Your Work,* he read. The spell called for ingredients whose names he couldn't pronounce.

"Thanks for walking Burt," she said, derailing him from learning how to arrange his workspace for the best results.

He shrugged. "We needed a break from repairs. The porch is done, but you could use some new balusters and paint."

She smiled again. "We? You sound like he's helping you."

"He is." Ethan flashed a grin. "How many guys can say their assistants don't talk back?"

When their gazes met, a spark of heat shot through him. Dangerous, that look on her face. Playful. Teasing. Almost enough to make a man forget what he was. What *she* was.

He tore his attention back to the book, then began flipping restlessly through the pages again.

To Correct Imbalance in Oneself. It looked like just another hokey, empty charade aimed at convincing the gullible they could control their own fate…until he started reading.

Imbalance, it said. *Remove,* it said. *Dispel*

unwanted energies causing feelings of stress and disproportion, it said.

His power was sure as hell unwanted, and no question about it being stressful.

He scanned the page, wondering whether she had all these ingredients. A surreptitious glance at the cellar's shelves confirmed all the jars neatly labeled. If he needed ingredients for a spell, Gypsy's shop was sure to have them. It might be just a bunch of crackpot incense and candles, but he'd believe in flying pigs as long as they could dispel his damned ability.

Suddenly cheerful, he waved off the rest of her ministrations. "I'm good now, thanks. Burt and I will take a walk to the hardware store and get that paint."

Her brows lifted, but she smiled. "I'll get you the money. Let me run upstairs for my bag."

She preceded him up the steps. He followed the swing of her hips with an admiring glance and didn't even kick himself for it. When she was almost at the top, he slipped the little spell book into his back pocket.

****

Why does he get her? I'm just as good. Better, even. I've been here, looking out for her, keeping her out of trouble, for five years. Then this hotshot comes to town, and I'm back to being practically invisible. He's no good for her. I can see it. Why can't she?

Chapter Six

"What are you doing for Thanksgiving?" asked Kayla.

Gypsy smiled at her petite blond shop assistant over her cup of green tea. "My parents invited me home, but I have to stick around town. You?"

"Probably just dinner at my parents' house. Don't tell me you're going to spend the holiday alone. You're coming with me. Besides, I need the moral support. Ever since I went on college break, Mom and Dad have been after me to spend quality time with them."

Gypsy laughed. "We'll see."

Kayla went on as if Gypsy had given her a definite yes. "Ooh, bring your pumpkin cobbler. I love that stuff! And segueing neatly onto the subject of love," she added, her blue eyes lighting up, "how about you bring that tall drink of 'Yes, please' with you?"

"Ethan?" Gypsy blurted. She felt the blush even before she thought to stem it.

Kayla snickered. "So? Are you sensing chemistry? An aura? Compatible star signs?"

"Ethan will probably be gone before Thanksgiving."

Kayla looked around the not-busy coffee house. "I'd like to submit for the record, Your Honor, the defendant's refusal to answer the question."

"Ugh! You're such a scorch."

"Come. Please come. I'll stop bugging you if you come." Kayla affected a pout.

"Oh, all right."

"You have to bring your mystery man."

Gypsy groaned. "Kay…"

"No excuses. I need as many topics of conversation as I can get to diffuse the yearly battle over the wishbone. It's getting pretty ugly, you know." Kayla dimpled.

Gypsy tried hard to scowl, but Kayla was one of those buoyant people who always seemed to get her way with a bare minimum of effort. She conceded defeat with a smile. "All right. Pumpkin cobbler, it is."

Brightening, Kayla reached for her coffee. "I owe you one."

Shaking her head, Gypsy lifted her teacup. "FYI, I'm stockpiling your owes."

"For what?" Kayla's eyes twinkled as she reached for a shortbread biscuit.

"I'll let you know when I think of something suitably difficult."

Kayla's cell phone emitted a muted chime. She picked it up, and while she spoke into it, Gypsy finished off her tea.

Ethan was probably at home right now, painting. He'd been awfully strange when visiting her at the shop, first standoffish, and then so cheerful it piqued her sense of something not quite right. When she pressed him—carefully—he shrugged it off with a comment about house repairs clearing his head.

Whatever went on in his head, she doubted porch and fence paint could clear it. He gave off an aura of frustration that boiled around him like bruise-colored storm clouds.

The fire house siren wailed faintly outside. Gypsy frowned. Not the right time of day for evening break.

Kayla put down her cell. "You know my sister works at the fire station?"

"Yeah."

"They just got an alarm call from the old Buswell place."

Gypsy gave a moan of dismay. "Is anyone hurt?"

Kayla shook her head. "Don't know yet. That must be what that's about." She tipped her head toward the windows.

Sudden dread pricked at Gypsy's nerves, almost a premonition. She struggled to stifle it. "I'd better get home," she said as calmly as possible. "Call me later and let me know what you find out."

"I will."

Gypsy left the coffee house with a nagging sense of worry. Many of her friends and neighbors volunteered at the fire department. In such a small town, they depended on each other in emergencies. She loved that about Pickering, but she worried each time the volunteers went on a call. At any time, an accident could befall one of the townspeople she'd come to care about.

When she arrived home, the porch had been laid with a board to prevent people from walking on the newly-painted surface until it cured. Burt was locked inside. She let him out the back door on his leash, wondering where Ethan had gone.

The breeze had cooled, but not enough to warrant the shivers now cascading through her. The scent of something burning drifted on the air. Her hands itched for the motions of a protection spell. She thought of the little altar in her bedroom. She thought about Rich, with his brand-new nephew. In her mind, she drew a circle of protection around her friend.

The Buswell place. She tugged Burt's leash, urging him around the house toward the fence gate. "So mote it be," she whispered.

****

Ethan heard the sirens of the fire trucks faintly over the thundering flames, but he doubted the rescue team would be able to enter the engulfed house by now. He was already inside it and wondering how the hell he'd get out.

With one arm around an elderly man and another around a young boy, he struggled to extend the bubble of his power around all four of them. The smoke and flames pushed in against his flagging shield.

The old man and the boy had both regarded him with blatant shock when he arrived in the midst of the out-of-control blaze—but given the choice between going with Ethan and perishing in a house fire, they'd made the expected decision.

At least he was still preferable to a horrible death. Question was, how did he plan to get out of Pickering before they blabbed his supernatural deed to the town?

The back door by which Ethan had gotten into the house was awash in flame. No retreat that way. Squinting into the smoke and gauging their escape by the tingling of his power, he shepherded his charges toward the front hall. They made it there, but a fallen beam blocked the door. From beyond the blackened rubble, Ethan heard a rhythmic slamming.

A fire axe, he guessed. One of the rescue team was

fighting to get inside.

The man and boy had their wetted shirts over their noses. Both looked to him for their next move. *Help,* their eyes pleaded.

Working on it, he told them silently. He focused his attention on the tingling under his skin. How much time did he have? How much juice? Could he force it high enough to thrust the bubble around all three of them while helping to lift that beam blocking the door?

Screw it. He punched his power to its limit.

The temperature dropped. He bent to the fallen beam and jerked on it as hard as possible. A spear of pain shot through his side where a piece of burning rubble fell against him. The heat of the beam against his hands struggled to penetrate his power. He forced it back—*temperature down, temperature down*—until the burn faded to an annoyance. The beam tumbled aside.

Slam, slam, slam. The blade of the firefighter's axe bit through the fire-weakened door, and a face appeared. "Go, go!" Ethan shouted to the man and boy.

They tumbled out through the hole the firefighter had made. Ethan followed, letting the last of his power flow outward behind him as he escaped. Exhausted, he tumbled into the arms of the firefighter and his brethren.

Blankets. Whirling emergency lights. People wielding oxygen masks. Everything went blurry. Amid the spinning of his head, Ethan thought he heard the barking of a dog.

The firefighter's radio crackled. "Trapped at the second floor window. Need help."

Ethan's power fizzed. He broke free of the firefighter's grasp and scrambled back inside, ignoring the shouts urging him to stop.

The stairs were still intact, but going fast. Ethan rushed upward through the haze, using what remained of his power to keep the smoke and fire at bay.

On the second floor, he found the trapped firefighter at a broken bedroom window behind a wall of flame. The fireman jerked in obvious alarm when Ethan burst through the fiery wall. He had an axe in one hand and a bundle in the other arm. Ethan beckoned to the man, but just as he made to hurry the fireman through the blaze, the ceiling collapsed, pinning them against the window.

Ethan cursed himself and struggled to expand his power. With their lives at stake, anonymity was a moot point. Maybe the fireman wouldn't notice the glow of his skin under the smoke and firelight. The bubble stretched, resisted, then stretched an infinitesimal bit more. Ethan stood closest to the window's broken pane. "Hey!" he called, his voice hoarse with smoke. The snarling blaze engulfed his shout. Precious seconds ticked by as the wall of fire stalked them, ever closer.

With relief, he saw a group of firemen angling a ladder truck toward the window. The fireman beckoned for him to exit first. Ethan glanced toward the wriggling mass of cloth in the man's arms.

A baby.

His power shrank inward, and he cursed. Out of time.

He shoved the fireman toward the ladder as another of his brethren was ascending to the top. The firefighter handed the baby through the broken window. He and Ethan leaped for the ladder as the flame burst through the rest of the window, raining glass and wooden splinters. He scrambled down the ladder, clinging with shaking limbs, then fell the last few feet into a heap that sent lances of pain shooting up from his ankle.

Weak with exhaustion, he let the men usher him toward a waiting ambulance. Technicians milled around him, poking here, swabbing there, offering him oxygen. Images swirled together in one unrecognizable mass, and he couldn't bring himself to care. *This is it,* he vowed. *I'm done with all of it. I'll leave if I have to walk.*

Then he saw Gypsy's worried face. "Let me through!" she cried. "Please, let me through!"

The terror in her voice jarred awake something warm and painfully sweet, and his mental argument washed away like fallen leaves in a river. Ethan swayed where he sat on the bumper of the ambulance, too tired to fight off the sensation, and instead examined it with detached curiosity. "I'm fine," he croaked, his words muffled by the oxygen mask. Gypsy reached him and, ignoring him, slid her hands over his face, his hair, his shoulders. Burt whined and nosed at his charred jeans.

Ethan let his lips curl upward in a faint smile. He'd been right. Barking dog.

"You've got balls of steel, is what," said a voice.

He looked up to find the firefighter he'd rescued approaching him. The man removed his helmet and face shield.

Rich Pettit.

Rich scanned him, still smiling, but when he stopped at Ethan's fireproof boots the smile faded. "You've done this before."

Ethan held the man's gaze. No point denying it now. He nodded.

Gypsy looked back and forth between them, but Ethan fixed his attention on Rich's shrewd stare. Seconds crawled past. His skin itched under his burnt shirt. He'd put it back on, against the EMTs' advice, after they insisted on doctoring him.

"Volunteer?" Rich asked.

With a sigh, Ethan lowered the oxygen mask from his face. "Something like that."

"Pettit, the EMTs want to see you!" called a voice.

Rich acknowledged the call with a wave. He turned back to Ethan and slid his firefighter gloves off. He extended his hand. "I should haul into you for doing something that crazy, but off the record, I'm damn glad you did. Thank you."

Ethan stifled a guilty frown and shook Rich's hand. "It's nothing."

Rich went to answer the EMTs' summons. The moment he left, Gypsy rounded on Ethan with wide eyes and touched his shoulder as if to be certain he was actually in one piece. "It's not nothing! You saved his life!"

"Look, don't make a big deal out of it."

"Why not?" Instead of getting angry, she regarded him with something like curiosity. "His parents will make a big deal. His sister will make a big deal. It *is* a big deal."

"Not to a guy who was dumb enough to walk into a burning building, it isn't."

"Ethan, you just saved three people tonight. Why does that bother you?"

He hunched his shoulders, then gritted his teeth at the sting of his burn. It would scar. *Add it to the bunch.* To Gypsy, he said nothing.

Burt wasn't so easily ignored. He whined and shoved his nose under Ethan's hand. Ethan rubbed the dog's head automatically. So much easier to deal with than people. Much easier than her, with those searchlight eyes.

Gypsy looked back and forth between them. He avoided her gaze, but her dismay was as loud as the roar of the still-burning house fire. He stared across the dooryard at the swarm of firefighters and the outline of flames against the darkening sky. Several steps away, the old man and boy huddled in blankets on top of a stretcher, watching their home burn. Grimacing, Ethan handed the oxygen mask to the nearest EMT. "I'm fine," he said again.

The young tech took the mask, but Ethan rose, then walked away before the kid could add anything further. His ankle protested but supported him. Just sore, probably.

Gypsy caught up with him once he reached the road. "You should go back," she called.

"Yep."

"What do you have against the good thing you just did?"

He swiveled around. "Why do you care?"

"Why do you *not*?" She gestured toward the silhouette of the blazing house. "The Buswells are going to have a Thanksgiving and a Christmas—with each other, even if they don't have their house—because of what you did. I don't understand."

He stalked away again. "They say humility is good for the soul."

"This isn't humility, it's hiding." She jogged up alongside him, still with that curiosity that pricked at his nerves more than anger would have done.

"What do you want to hear?" he demanded. "I don't need your judgment."

"No. You need a friend."

"I don't need pity, either."

"Who said 'pity?' I think what you did was amazing, and no one back there would disagree with me. You have a gift."

He stopped dead, glaring at her, unsure whether to be worried or insulted or a little of both.

She searched his face with those black-coffee eyes, apparently confused by what she saw because those wide, lush lips pursed in a faint frown. "Selflessness, Ethan. You risked your life for people you don't even know. Do you realize what a rare thing that is?"

His anger with her shifted into a rush of self-loathing. Of all the things he'd ever been called or called himself, *selfless* hadn't been one of them. He hunched his shoulders again under the charred, chafing shirt. The EMTs had offered him a rescue blanket, which he'd refused. Pain was almost as good a distraction as manual labor. Maybe better. "Let's just get out of here."

Gypsy studied him. After a moment, her lips curved upward in a little smile. Before he knew what she was doing, she slid her hand into his and started walking again as if it were the most natural thing in the world. Ethan was too startled to resist.

By the time they reached her gate, his side had begun to sting again. That would smart for a few days, he decided with a grimace. He welcomed it.

She swung the gate open, then unclipped Burt from his leash. The shepherd darted across the lawn after a plump little body, which burst upward in a feathery flutter. Aegis, who must have landed on the ground to catch her evening meal. The little owl evaded the dog easily, swooping into the tree by Gypsy's carriage house. "Nice try, buddy," Ethan called, "but I doubt you'll get her."

Gypsy chuckled. "He never gives up. It's practically a game between them." Humor colored her soft voice, but she looked sidelong at Ethan, and he knew Burt's antics were the last thing on her mind. The way she studied him, he expected her to add to their earlier argument over his barging into a burning house, but instead she said, "Why don't you hop into the shower, and I'll get us something to eat?"

The evasion was more than welcome, but he followed her up the steps searching for something to say that might wrap up this mess of an evening. He doubted he'd heard the last of it, from Gypsy or Rich or any of the zillion town residents who'd gathered at the spectacle.

When he finished his shower, he found Gypsy arranging a tray of coffee cups and a carafe on the coffee table in front of the living room fireplace. She had lit a fire to chase away the evening chill in the old house, and Ethan hesitated before entering the room. His exhausted power was a mere hum deep in his bones, but enough to force him to make a wide circuit to the couch.

Gypsy had turned from the coffee table. She fiddled with the old stereo on one of the sagging built-ins flanking the fireplace. Eerie synthesizer sounds erupted from the stereo speakers. "What on earth is that?" he demanded.

"New Age," she said, as if it should have been plainly understood.

He stifled a grimace and joined her at the shelf, still giving the fireplace as wide a berth as possible. A selection of CDs lined the shelf above the stereo—most of them unrecognizable to him. He avoided these and reached for the buttons. "May I?"

She gave him a narrow-eyed look, but waved him on.

Ethan switched the machine to the radio and found a channel playing rock music. "That's better."

"You have no sense of culture," she said, but her playful tone plucked at his awareness of her.

"All right," he said, flipping to a pop station. "More your speed?"

"Not even on the same racetrack," she said, crossing her arms. A dimple flickered at the corner of her mouth.

"Fine, you try. New Age is out, though."

"Is it?"

"Yep."

"Screeching guitars is out, too." She tuned the station to classical music.

"Nope. I'll be asleep in five seconds." He reached for the buttons.

Grinning, she elbowed him aside while clearly trying to avoid his injuries. "Don't you dare. It's still my turn. You got two stations."

Something jumped in his belly. Unable to resist, he shouldered into her, ignoring the sting of his scrapes and burns. "You're gonna have me catatonic with that stuff. Step aside, lady."

"I will not."

Laughing, he jostled her. "You will so. Get."

"No!" Still giggling, she reached a new station. A smoky voice spilled out into the room, evoking the Thirties in melodic song.

More than that, it resurrected the ghost of the Rathbone farm in its heyday, while Ethan was still young and careless. He heard his own laughter echo forward over twenty-something years, and saw himself learning to dance with his feet on top of Ma Rathbone's as they circled the old kitchen.

He'd staggered Gypsy back a step. She came forward again, reaching for the tuner.

"No, stop," he said.

She paused with her hand in mid-reach. "Billie Holiday?"

The curiosity in her voice wiggled under his defenses. He slammed a damper over his memories. "Sure. It works."

She drew her hand back, studying him with those too-seeing eyes. "So, you like jazz." With a sudden smile, she held up her arms. "We have to practice, if you're going to take me to the fire house dance."

With a faint, outward breath of equal parts amusement and resignation, he stepped toward her. He slid one hand into her left and laid the other on her waist, wondering dimly when he'd last danced with a woman. He'd never even attended prom—just hung around outside with some of the guys. For an instant, he stiffened, not wanting to be in her personal space…but then he looked up.

Her eyes were wide and soft. Her smile lingered at the corners of her lips. Where he hesitated, she moved with an easy confidence that he envied bitterly. They swayed in slow circles around the living room. The popping of the wood fire accented the song. Ethan drowned it out and focused on her eyes. *Stop thinking!*

It was easy with her, he realized. Gypsy lived in the moment. Unless she was prying in her quietly nosy way, he could forget about everything but now. Relaxing into the slow tempo of the music, he circled the room with her. Gradually, the silence in his head allowed other sensations to filter forth: the softness of her hand, the gentle curve of her hip accentuating a slim waist, the swish of her long hair falling against his fingers.

He liked it. Too much.

The realization hit him like a blast of superheated air, and left him with the same lack of oxygen. He hadn't let himself get this near a woman in several years, and now his body woke to the sensation with an eagerness born of long denial. He tightened his grip on her, pure reflex.

Her eyes widened a little, but she swung into the next circle around the room with him. Ethan tried like hell not to let it show as he wallowed in the thoroughly pleasurable feeling of holding a woman in his arms. He barely even noticed when they slowed and finally stopped in the middle of the room. Every sense in his body urging him still closer to her focused on her lips.

Now, it had to be now, or he'd never do it. He lowered his mouth to hers.

Their lips met as if the kiss had always been meant to happen. In an instant, Ethan knew he'd made a damning mistake. She fit into his embrace like they'd been molded together once, and the pieces then lamentably lost for decades. The curves of her body.

The shapes of her long, slender fingers. He spread his hand across her back, and every inch of her was an echo of something beautiful that made him forget himself.

All too soon, the song ended, and they were left standing there with the murmur of the deejay chattering nonsense in his ears. He stepped back from Gypsy's arms, but couldn't rip his stare from her face.

Artwork. Like a priceless antique, and just as out of reach for a guy like him. Disgusted, he pulled farther away…

…but Gypsy snared him back with a staying hand on his arm. "Where are you going?"

Her voice stroked along his nerves, reawakening his power. Dismayed, he froze in place, but damned if he was going to let his reaction to her chase him out of the room.

"I don't bite," she murmured, "I promise."

The unidentifiable spice scent of her perfume whirled in the air under his nose. She may not bite, but everything about her chewed his good sense to ribbons. Another song began on the radio, this one a seductive, husky-voiced melody singing of starlit nights and wistful memories of a faraway lover.

With a little smile, she drew close again, easy in her movements in a way he'd never be. One hand settled on his chest, and his senses, taut as piano wire, centered on that barely-there weight as if she'd cemented him where he stood. "I haven't danced in so long. This is nice."

"This from the woman who knows all about the yearly fire house dance?"

"Just because I know about it doesn't mean I dance. It might have escaped your notice, but there aren't a lot of men knocking down my door here in Pickering."

"Officer Friendly knocks pretty hard."

"Oh, you noticed?" Her light sarcasm fluttered the edges of his power.

Ethan leaned closer, regretting he'd brought the man up. His body tensed with awareness of a different sort. "Let's forget him."

"Teach me that one."

Swooping in, his male pride fully at the fore, Ethan claimed her lips with the intent to make her forget her own name.

But he realized too late the snare was on him, not her. Her mouth opened for him in a show of hunger that shook him by his roots. She was so tiny in his arms, a slender slip that would flutter away like an evaporated dream if he let go of her.

Of that, his body had no intentions. He gave a warning hum, low in his throat. Instead of retreating, she pressed forward against him. Adrenaline purled through him, and he tightened his grasp. She molded to him with a sigh that stirred his exhausted power even more.

Shut up, shut up, he told it. For once, he wanted something unmarred by that freakish power, untainted by its presence in his body. He stuffed it back down into the darkest reaches of his thoughts and filled them instead with her. He threaded his fingers into her long, sable-black curls, tugging gently until she tipped her head back to expose the graceful, slender arch of her throat. Greedily, he pressed his mouth to her tender skin, so delicate he felt the frantic throb of her pulse under his lips. Some faraway part of him considered asking her if she was sure about this, but he refused to let the question escape him. Any chance he gave her to reconsider this was a chance she might take…and after kissing her, he doubted he could stand not having more.

Her long fingers tangled in his shirt, tugged at his collar, sought skin under the thin fabric. "More," she whispered.

He couldn't tell if she was saying "more" to the kisses or to the need to feel more of him, skin to skin, but his body heartily shouted yes to both. He jerked back to strip his shirt off, then flung it down and returned to kissing her like a man driven by demons. Which he was. *Shut up,* he ordered his power again. Only at her touch on his bare torso did it concede a grumbling retreat. Fiercely, he drowned it in the sensation of her.

He tugged her down to the braided rug on the hardwood floor. She lay back underneath him, her hair aglow in the flickering firelight like a living thing made to bewitch him. He filtered the glossy curls through his fingers, hardly able to believe that such a breathtaking mane could belong to a flesh-and-blood woman, and not some goddess cursed to walk the earth.

He stripped her shirt away, ravenous, needing to see that the rest of her was as real as her hair.

And oh, God, it was. He worshipped every unwrapped inch of her skin with kisses. She dug her fingers into his back and gave a cry when he reached her breasts, small and perfect, curving over the top of her scrap-of-silk bra. "Get this damn thing off," he growled, pulling at the front clasp. "I need to see you."

She laid her long-fingered hands over his, guiding them, while her polished-onyx eyes locked on his. No shrinking violet, Gypsy. She knew what she wanted, and went for it with a will that set his groin pulsing eagerly. The bra fell away. He spread his hands over her curves with a bitten-off oath that might have been a prayer. She arched into his hands. Ethan soaked in the feel of her, starving for it. He skimmed his thumbs across the taut, dusky nipples crowning each sweet breast and relished every sigh his touch pulled from her.

Lowering himself to the rug, he returned to her mouth, paying those gorgeous lips their full due with no intent to rush things.

Gypsy was of another mindset entirely. Her hands flew to his pants, seeking, pulling at the fly. His cock tightened and throbbed in mutinous agreement with her eagerness. Staring down at the angel lying beneath him, Ethan hesitated, feeling like the worst sort of pretender. Who was he to reach for anything that resembled a normal life?

And then, in a blinding instant, he thought about the little spell book he'd stashed in his room, and he realized that it might just be possible to have everything. All he needed to trade for it was a power he'd never even wanted.

Her gaze came up to his, heavy-lidded and luminous in the firelight. A little frown tugged at her gorgeous mouth. "Ethan?"

He snapped his attention back to her face, letting his gaze rove over her features with a hunger that went bone-deep. Pressing his body fully against hers, he stroked along her skin until his hand found the waistband of her jeans. He grinned at the question in her eyes. "Hell, yes."

Chapter Seven

Ethan peeled away her jeans and underwear with the reverence of a man handling a priceless porcelain vase. Gypsy wanted to smile—almost did—but then his searching fingers reached the curls between her legs. His thumb circled the bud between her already slick folds, lighting a white-hot spark that exploded into liquid fire. Gypsy gave a bitten-off shout of surprise at the intensity of sensation coursing through her body. With one touch, he awakened a yearning she'd buried for what seemed centuries.

Ethan held her gaze the whole while, with a wicked little tilt at the corner of his lips that brought out the flirting hint of a dimple in one cheek. He stroked her expertly, keeping her at the peak of a climax that went on for an eternity until all she knew was the look in his firelit amber eyes.

Gasping for breath, she reached for him only to have him arch back. "Ah-ah," he chastised her. "Not done yet." He lowered himself back down to press against her in an exquisite crush. The bare skin of his chest and belly sizzled against hers, chasing away any lingering chill in her drafty old house.

With his fingers still working their magnificent magic, he brought his mouth to the tip of her breast, stroking the nipple with his tongue until she thought she'd lose her mind with pleasure. Hot shivers rippled outward to the very ends of her toes. Just when she thought she couldn't take any more, Ethan ground himself against her center, easing that pleasurable agony of emptiness with his own body. The rough denim of his jeans dragged over her sensitized flesh until she was shivering again. Near wild with wanting him, she grappled at his pants.

All she received for her trouble was a chuckle. He didn't even lift his mouth from her breast, merely pinned her questing hand with his and went on spinning her into trembling ecstasy.

Oh, goddess, what had she done? This man would forever ruin her for anyone else. He touched her with an awareness of her body more intimate than any she'd ever known. Each contact of his hands or his lips—or the torturous, wonderful heat of him between her legs—sent bursts of euphoria along her nerves, like a virtuoso symphony of bliss.

She'd been so wrong. He had more than one gift.

He arched his hips against her, and in a rush of madness and exhilaration, she found herself sweeping over the edge of her climax. He suckled her hard, and distantly, she heard herself scream his name.

Rar-Rar-Raar-RUFFRUFF! A crash sounded, and running feet and jingling dog tags preceded the arrival of a very outraged German shepherd into the living room.

Ethan's head flew up. Wrapping his body around hers, he rolled with her toward the fireplace, then held up a staying arm. "Whoa, whoa, *whoa*, dog!"

Burt skidded to a halt before them, growling. Gypsy couldn't help it—she erupted in giggles.

Ethan fixed her with a glare. "Glad you find this

funny. If I had my pants off, I could be missing valuable parts right now."

"I'm fine, Burt," Gypsy wheezed. She stretched an arm out from under Ethan to wave the dog away. "Go upstairs."

"Yeah, go upstairs," Ethan grumbled, but Gypsy caught the telltale glint of humor in his eye. "You're not invited."

Burt shoved his nose at both of them as if to assure himself that they were all right. He snuffed and trotted out of the room, the very picture of canine disgruntlement.

Turning back to her, Ethan raised a brow. "You weren't kidding about your furry alarm system."

She squirmed out from underneath him. "I'd better make sure he didn't break something in the kitchen."

From his spot on the floor, Ethan hooked a hand around her ankle. "Deserting me?"

She looked back. The wicked light in his eyes halted her forward motion. Under that devilish gleam, she sensed a cloudiness, a darkness hovering at the edges of his humor as if he thought she might really be ducking out on him. She teetered between checking for irreparable damage to her kitchen, and ignoring it in favor of the much more compelling distraction on her living room rug. "Ten seconds."

"Five seconds," he called. His husky voice sent new shivers of delight dancing across her bare skin. She felt his gaze on her as she went, and the tremors converged into tingles of sensation in places he'd so recently lavished with his attention.

Burt had merely knocked over a couple of chairs and a stack of clean dishtowels on his rush to the living room. One of the chair legs had cracked. With a sigh, she righted them both, then pushed the damaged one back against the wall. Good thing she was boarding a man who was so talented with his hands.

Standing there, stark naked in the middle of her kitchen, she allowed herself a very girlish and very un-Gypsy-like grin of excitement. A little voice warned her of The Lightning-Struck Tower in her—or Ethan's—future.

This was all going to end very badly.

Her giddiness faded. Frowning, she scooped up the dishtowels only to wring them fretfully in her hands. No spell could solve a bad love life. Early in her devotions to Wicca, she'd tried, with disastrous results. She still wasn't convinced that those foolish attempts hadn't ruined any future chances she might have. Her track record spoke for itself, after all.

"Horribly lacking in naked women in here," Ethan called, his voice awash with teasing.

Gypsy struggled to turn her mind from the damning mental image of The Tower card. In her living room was a flesh-and-blood man who'd just sent her into outer space with his touch. And as wonderful as that had been, she knew it could only wind up a train wreck.

Mournfully, she let the last of her euphoria slip away. She laid the stack of dishtowels on the table then returned to the living room at a somber trudge. She hesitated in the doorway, aching with wistfulness. Ethan sat facing the fireplace, cross-legged, still shirtless. She stared at his powerful shoulders, broad and sculpted with muscle, faintly scarred. They tapered to a lean waist, emphasized all the more in the silhouette of fire glow. Possibly the most gorgeous back in all of mankind's history.

He seemed to sense that she'd returned to the room, because he arched around. His smile faded a little. "What? Did he knock over the fridge?"

Mute, she shook her head. Her feet wouldn't move.

His smile disappeared entirely. That cloudiness slammed down over his features, shutting her out. He got to his feet. His gorgeous body, so lithe and catlike moments before, arched and stiffened like that of a defensive bear.

"Ethan…"

"No. Never mind. I get it."

"No, you don't."

"I do. Don't waste your time explaining."

"It's not a waste."

Ethan was shaking his head even as she spoke, denying her protest. "Maybe Burt saved us both from a big mistake." He swept up his shirt, not looking at her, then stalked to the coffee table to lift one of the still-steaming mugs from its tray. "Thanks for the drink."

He left the room, heading down the hall toward his bedroom. With her eyes stinging, Gypsy watched him go.

See? she told herself. *Worst love life ever.*

****

As much as he wanted to slam it, Ethan took care to close the door softly. He was pissed, and she knew he was pissed, but he didn't have to advertise it.

It wasn't at her.

What the hell had he been thinking? Well, no, wrong question. He'd been thinking of her hair running through his fingers, her hot-silk skin under his hands, and the way his name sounded on her lips when she came. He'd been thinking that he wanted to do that to her for the rest of the night, and the night after that, and a million nights after, no matter how sore and tired he was from the bullshit at that farmhouse.

Leaning back against the door, he dropped his shirt on the wicker bench at the foot of the bed. He should never have let it get that far. Shouldn't even have started anything. He had no right and no business, not with his life a mess that would only infect hers. *Dumbass.*

Well, since he wouldn't be sleeping tonight, he could do something productive. He reached into the dresser drawer for the spell book he'd lifted from her shop.

On his way into the house earlier, he'd snagged a slip of notepaper and a pencil from a little tray she kept by the fridge. He swept them from the dresser top, still skeptical that anything in a book was going to fix his life.

Or lack of one.

With a sigh, he dropped onto his bed and flipped through the book. He found the page he was looking for, but when he began to read the list of ingredients, the words swam together. He thought it was fatigue until the third or fourth time his thoughts wandered back to Gypsy's face—more specifically, her face each time he brought her to a shuddering climax.

He dropped the book on the worn bedspread to rub at his eyes, half hoping to scrub the images of her away. His body still resonated with eager responses to her crying his name. Ethan dropped his head back against the paneled headboard, welcoming the jarring thump if only because it gave him something else on which to focus.

All right, Sutter. You're gonna fix whatever else needs fixing here, and when your bike parts come in, you're getting the hell out.

Telling himself that sure as hell didn't make it any easier to sleep that night.

****

The next morning, Gypsy acted as though their evening by her fireplace had never happened. Unfortunately for Ethan, it only took one look at her for his body to go on overload again. She fussed with the coffee maker. In her gauzy, long-sleeved shirt and swishy skirt, she was an easily unwrapped temptation. He gritted his teeth around a grunt that meant "Good morning." The fewer words he said, the less likely he'd be to lure her back to that rug and their unfinished business. Part of him was still furious…but most of him was all for making her take a sick day so he could go on exploring the gorgeous body she hid under all those drape-y clothes. Even now, he tapped his fingers restlessly against his thigh where he leaned against the counter.

"I won't be home until late this evening. Rich asked me earlier this week if I'd stop at the fire house after work and talk over the dance decorations with the chief." She hesitated, still fooling with the coffee carafe. "Do you want to come down?"

Ethan slid a furtive look at her. *Now you want me?* His blood simmered, but then an image of himself teetering at the top of a ladder with a fist full of streamers popped into his head. He couldn't help cracking a smile at the ridiculous notion. "What use would I be with dance decorations?"

He must have injected enough humor into his answer to put her off her guard, because she smiled...which turned out even worse for him. His power, fully rested after a night of inactivity, if not sleep, fizzled under the surface of his skin at the mischief that smile brought to mind.

Grinding his teeth, Ethan left his casual spot at the counter. He didn't dare move toward her. Instead, he stalked to the broken chair. "This part of the damage from yesterday?" He left his reference to their interrupted evening deliberately vague.

She didn't miss a trick. "Ethan, last night after Burt... It wasn't about you."

He surveyed the broken rung and cracked chair leg. Oak. Probably not hard to replace if he got his hands on a large enough dowel and a lathe. Some glue, some clamps, maybe a strap to keep it together while it dried...

"It was me," she said, much closer.

He twisted around to find her right there in his personal space. The scent of her hit him before he was ready, and he had to bite down on the instantly vivid reminder of her naked underneath him.

All right, so they were going to have this out after all. Letting on much more indifference than he felt, he shrugged. "What do you want me to say, Gypsy?"

"Something. Anything."

A fine shudder went through him as he remembered her gasp when he touched his lips to her body. He stifled it viciously. "You want an out for breaking it off last night? Fine. It's all good."

"No." The ferocity in her voice and the spark in

her eyes brought him to a surprised halt. She sighed, and the fight went back out of her as fast as it had appeared. She met his gaze, steady and unnerving. "I'm sorry. I'm a little gun-shy."

Was she asking him for a second chance? He stiffened as though she'd hit him with an electric shock. Some distant part of him gnashed its teeth at the way a word or motion from her jerked him back and forth, like a dog shaking a rope toy.

With a monstrous effort, he stepped back. "I'll see you after work." Before she could say anything further, he stalked outside.

The air, cool and crisp with the tang of dying leaves and light frost, swept away the lingering scent of her and cleared his head. He headed for the carriage house and its punching bag. He had to wait for the dew to burn off before he'd be able to use the porch paint. The intervening hours would be a good time to beat the thought of her out of his head by wearing out his body.

Maybe then he'd stop seeing her naked every time he looked at her.

****

Work was no help at all. The store bustled more than usual with "leaf peepers" from all over the country flocking into Vermont for its breathtaking display of fall color. Gypsy greeted each customer with a cheerful smile and absolutely no ability to concentrate. Thank the goddess for her assistant, Kayla, who worked during the busiest shifts and college breaks.

"Miss? Could I get some help with a book?" one man asked.

He sounded put out, and Gypsy realized he'd had to ask more than once before she heard him. "I'm so sorry," she said, adjusting the sage-green apron she wore when grinding herbs. "What can I help you find?"

"My fiancée wants a book about chakras, and I can't find the author."

She hurried out from behind the compounding bench where she'd been pulverizing dried lavender for her hand-stitched scented sachets. The normally calming perfume filling the air had zero effect. Good thing she hadn't intended it for her own use.

After helping the customer find his book, she noticed stock was low in a few titles. "Be right back, Kay."

"Sure thing," her assistant called from behind the register.

Gypsy waded into the cramped storeroom. Nope, no more chakra books there.

She turned on the cellar light then descended the stairs. Ethan's sawdust scent seemed to linger in the still air underneath the more common smells of dried herbs.

Or her overactive imagination was simply putting forward the things it wanted her to think about instead of work. Here in the quiet basement of her shop, that was all too easy.

With a sigh, she approached the boxes stacked on a pallet in the back corner. As she reached the table, she paused.

Where was that little book? She'd been using it for a client who came to the shop regularly. Bending, she checked under the table. No, the floor was clean and swept, as usual. A quick search of the cellar confirmed it missing.

Ethan.

Standing there in the middle of her shop basement with her hands on her hips, she frowned. Why would Ethan want a battered little spell book worth nothing to anyone who didn't believe in Wicca?

She carried the box of chakra books back upstairs. "Kayla, you didn't move anything downstairs, did you?"

"Oh, yeah," the girl called. "There was a box of patchouli in the Hoosier cabinet. Had to restock the essential oils. We were getting low."

That settled it. Gypsy didn't begrudge Ethan the book, but he might have asked, and she'd have given it freely. Why the secrecy? Did it have something to do with those tarot cards?

The rest of the day teemed with customers, but in spite of the busyness, it never seemed to end. When Gypsy found herself checking the clock for the dozenth time and the end of her day was still an hour off, she gave in. "Kay, I'm going to head out. Close up shop for me?"

"Sure. Hot date?" The girl's blue eyes sparkled with mischief behind her chic pair of glasses.

"Your brother's still way too young for me," Gypsy teased back, handing the young woman the keys.

"I know, but I keep hoping for you to get a great guy."

Gypsy grabbed her bag before Kayla could bring up the subject of Ethan and the impending Thanksgiving feast. "Thanks." She hurried from the shop.

Outside, she took a deep breath. Pickering in the autumn. Her favorite time of year, when the summer heat dissipated and she started to think sweaters and baking.

The long, leisurely walk to the fire house finally had some effect on her swimming head, and she forgot about Ethan for the first time that day. The sun gave just enough warmth to make her lightweight cardigan proof against a chill. She waved to a few familiar neighbors as she turned the corner toward the fire house.

When she arrived, Rich and two of the volunteers were washing one of the rescue trucks. Seeing her, Rich grinned. "Come to help?"

"Came to sketch," she responded, lifting her bag. "I had a few ideas about decorations for Jim. I'll just set up while I wait for Ethan."

"He's already here."

She stopped in mid-stride. "Oh?"

Rich must have read something unbearably amusing in her expression, because he left off winding a hose to pass her a wink. She could tell he was stifling a chuckle, but to his credit, he didn't comment on her shock. "He's inside, talking to Jim."

"Why?"

"Go in and ask him yourself."

Gypsy had never been able to contain her curiosity. This morning, he'd acted like she would have to drag him to the fire house. Squaring her shoulders, she marched inside.

Fire Chief Jim McIntyre was visible through the glass windows of the upstairs office. He was on his feet, pacing back and forth. From the look on his face and the way he gestured to someone sitting in the chair before the desk, he was frustrated.

Gypsy couldn't blame him. Ethan frustrated her,

too…just a bit differently.

When she knocked at the office door, Jim opened it. "Oh, good. Will you talk sense to him?"

No preamble. Gypsy raised her eyebrows and looked toward the chair. Ethan sat there, as innocent as a lamb. "What did you do?" she demanded.

He scowled. "What did *I* do? I didn't do anything. I'm *not* doing anything."

"That's the problem," Jim said. "This man's got more balls than five of my best guys. I need a volunteer like him in this town."

"I didn't say anything about volunteering," Ethan sulked. "I'm in town for maybe a week. She's got me doing repairs at her house, and I'm not even a resident. When am I supposed to come save the world?"

Gypsy passed a look back and forth between them. After a moment, she turned to Jim. "Can we have a minute?"

The chief shrugged. "Sure. *Mi* office *es su* office." He ducked out, calling to his men as he shut the door.

She clasped her hands in front of her then fiddled with one of her rings. Before coming up to the office, she'd had an idea of what to say to Ethan. Now that he was here in front of her, distracting her by existing, the English language seemed to have lost all meaning. "Um…"

"No. I've said 'no' to him three times, and it's 'no' to you, too."

She stilled her fidgeting. The response spilled out of her. "Is it?"

His gaze shot up to meet hers. The sudden intensity there set her blood racing, and the chain reaction started all over again: wanting him, then fearing what might come of it, then drawing back into herself.

Ethan swooped up out of the chair. He stalked closer, not predatory in his motions, but wary. "What did I do to you that bothers you so much?"

She let her bag slide off her shoulder to hold it in front of her, a poor shield against the heat in his eyes. "I…I wanted… It was…"

He loomed so close she couldn't think. Lowering her gaze from that dangerous look in his eyes only brought his broad chest into sharper focus. Looking away from that gave her a view of sculpted biceps. His arms were faintly scarred here and there, like the rest of his body when she'd seen him without his shirt. A glorious body, made to make a woman forget herself. *Oh, goddess…* "You should volunteer," she blurted. "It's not regular pay, but you do get a stipend per call. You could use the extra money for your bike parts, and doing chores around my house isn't going to put enough in your pocket to—"

He stepped still closer, stopping her talking, close enough to breathe her air but not touch her. "I don't give one good goddamn about volunteering."

She looked up then, bursting with affront for him. How could he devalue what he'd done for the Buswells so easily? "You saved lives last night."

"Yeah, that's great."

This close, Gypsy couldn't help breathing Ethan's scent—a pleasant blend of sawdust and something smoky that strummed her nerve endings in a constant chord of awareness. And then she was right back there with him on her living room rug, wondering what would have happened if they hadn't been interrupted. Her knees turned to water. "Please," she whispered, unsure what else she meant to say.

"Please…?" he prompted, his husky voice wrapping around her. His body heat drifted against her exposed skin, or maybe she was imagining it.

Desperate, she fumbled for her last shred of willpower. "Pickering needs good men like you."

"Am I?" He canted his head. "A good man?"

She swallowed. "*I* think so."

He ducked his head toward her. Her heartbeat drummed against her ribs, frantic in anticipation of his kiss, but he paused mere inches from her lips. "That makes one."

And then he was gone.

Gypsy touched her fingers to her lips, unsettled and sure of only one thing: she'd be kicking herself forever for missing that chance.

Chapter Eight

Ethan muttered his way down the steps from the chief's office. Jim was in one of the bays with Rich. "So," the chief called, "did she talk you into it?"

Ethan ground his teeth. He didn't need the money from fire calls. It wasn't about that. If volunteering would have brought his bike parts in faster, that might be something. But volunteering at a place that would force him to use his power, when all he wanted was to forget it? The idea fried him.

The look on her face, though—like she thought he could save the world, if only he'd agree to it... It chafed him how much he liked that. He'd never given a crap about anyone's approval. He listened to others' opinions, and then did what he damn well pleased.

But Gypsy had worked her way under his skin, and he couldn't tell if it was a balm or a splinter.

He descended to the garage floor. Rich walked toward him, all anticipation. He probably thought the Pickering VFD was the be-all and end-all, and why would anyone dream of declining the offer to join it? Ethan opened his mouth to turn him down flat.

Rich frowned as he reached Ethan. "Look, man," he said, subdued, "you took a huge risk last night. Took injuries. But you did the town a huge favor. Oliver Buswell is one of the town fathers. Been around for ages. Everyone loves him. And you saved my ass, so if

I didn't say it last night…thank you. Seriously."

Ethan resisted the urge to arch his shoulders under the discomfiting scrutiny of Rich's stare. "It's all good."

Rich nodded. "You already have some pretty badass fire boots. I have no idea how you got in and out of there without full gear, so you must have nerves of steel, too. What do you say?"

In his mind's eye, Ethan was back in the upstairs office, so close to Gypsy that it would have taken only a miniscule motion to kiss her. She believed in him, for whatever insane reason and without really knowing him. Why?

He refocused on Rich. He opened his mouth to refuse, but his mind stayed on Gypsy, and what emerged shocked him. "Give me some time to think about it."

With a huge grin, Rich clapped him on the shoulder as if he'd accepted. Ethan stifled a wince— must be burns there. "You do that, my friend." He rejoined his fellow firefighters in the bay.

Gypsy came down the stairs while Ethan was still cursing his own stupidity. "Did you come to help out with decorations after all?" she asked.

"Something like that," he muttered.

"Listen," she said, suddenly not looking him in the eye, "I want to apologize again—"

Irritated, he waved off the rest of her apology. "Forget it."

Her cheeks picked up a little color. Ethan made a fast mental count of the days remaining until the mechanic would have his bike parts in. Definitely too long. "How long will this take?"

She angled her head, studying him with those X-ray eyes as if she could read every wrong thought he'd ever had. "Why did you come?"

He scoffed. "You asked me."

"No. Why did you come to talk to the chief?"

He looked away from her to the men washing the truck outside, to the few guys catcalling to each other from the second floor balcony, to the younger men stowing gear. The burns he'd sustained stung faintly. He avoided her gaze, but her nearness was no less distracting. She saw something in him that didn't exist—some kind of hero that put other people before his own problems. That wasn't him...but a small, surprising part of him wished it were.

Maybe that was why he hadn't said no.

He shrugged off the lingering sting of the burns. "Let's just do this and get home."

Throughout the talk about streamers and tablecloths, Ethan was able to shut down the chatter in his head. Volunteer fire departments didn't have much money. Stipends were provided out of grants from the state and whatnot, and there were few full-time, paid positions, if any. Chief McIntyre was paid, but he considered the position a privilege.

Some privilege, risking your neck every time some idiot left the oven on. But Jim directed Gypsy's efforts with a cheer that suggested he thought being Fire Chief in Podunk, U.S.A. was the greatest job a man could have. Ethan watched him laugh with Gypsy as they talked over placement of the balloons and the deejay's equipment, and the resulting sting wasn't from his burns.

Envy.

What was it like having little more to worry about than how to organize a small-town dance? Clocking in at your job every day and going home every night without running from who you were?

He eyed Gypsy's bag where she'd left it on a folding chair. Easy enough to sneak her shop keys and go look for the stuff he needed for that spell.

If it wasn't just a lot of bullshit.

He could have asked her for the ingredients. Whenever anyone asked her about her hocus-pocus interests, she was only too eager to share what she knew. Asking her would involve answering questions about *why* he wanted them, though, and he'd sooner face a firing squad.

"Sutter, since you're here to help, do you think you could get a couple of stepladders out of the loft?" McIntyre called. Louder, he added, "Jenks! Show Sutter where the ladders are, would you?"

Ethan expected another burly fireman to answer the summons, but Colin emerged from the locker area. "Hey," he said, flipping his blue hair out of his eyes. "Are you volunteering here?"

"I'd put it at indentured servitude," Ethan said, sliding a wry look at Gypsy.

"Sweet. Me, too." The kid started off on a speed commentary that Ethan only half heard as he led the way to the fire house loft.

Ethan followed him up the stairs, nodding to a couple of men and women as he passed. He recognized some of them from town. "Lot of people here. Is there a law about volunteering?"

"Pickering's tight. Everybody's up in everybody else's business. I can't wait to get out of here once I get a car."

Ethan took a closer look at the kid. Probably resembled Ethan more than he'd first thought, complete with crappy home life. No wonder Gypsy had suckered up and taken him on like a project. Shrugging, Ethan said, "It's not so bad."

Colin scoffed as they reached the space that passed for a maintenance room. Two ladders had been hung on the wall. He lifted one down. "The first thing I'm gonna do when I blow this place is go to New York City and start my band."

Ethan took the other ladder. Shouldering it, he turned back to the doorway. "Trust me, kid. Running doesn't fix you."

Before Colin could answer to that, Ethan stalked moodily out of the room.

****

The morning of the fire house dance arrived in a wash of golden sun and delicious autumn air. Gypsy had taken the day off from work to help set up. Her assistant, Kayla, would hold down the fort at The Holistic Mystic for her. Studying her tin-tiled bedroom ceiling, Gypsy smiled to herself. One of these days, she would have to make that young woman a full partner.

Unaccountably cheerful, she slid out of bed. Burt had disappeared from the rag rug, probably already outside on his morning rounds of scaring off the squirrels. She went to the window to soak up the sun spilling through the curtains.

Thanksgiving would be here soon. She could feel it in the slant of the light and see it in the blazing colors of the late-turning maples in the woods surrounding her property. One of Pickering's most wonderful holidays, when it seemed even nature celebrated along with them. This year, it even seemed to want to lengthen the show. The days had been warm and full of sun, and the nights cool enough to slow down the leaf-drop without being too chilly. Almost as if the world wanted her to stop worrying about money and men, and just be.

Well, it was always best to listen to nature.

She moved to the closet and selected a pretty black vintage dress she'd bought from the thrift shop in town. That would do for tonight, along with the pearls her college friend Paula had sent her for her last birthday. For now, she hung the dress on the back of the closet door and selected a pair of jeans and a tattered but comfortable sweatshirt. One last mow of the lawn before the frost, and today was a day that simply couldn't be wasted indoors.

She met Burt on the way to the carriage house. The dog barked and gamboled around her, then rushed to something that lay on the gravel beside the building to snap it up and trot it proudly back to her.

"Oh, goddess, please don't let that be a squirrel," she murmured.

Burt dropped his prize in front of her. A tennis ball, much-chewed and well-slobbered. "Where did you get this?" she wondered, picking it up.

"Me," Ethan said from the carriage house doorway. He was wiping his hands on a rag. "Do you know you have an old schoolroom teacher's desk up there in the loft? This carriage house is full of great stuff."

"Are you a fan of antiques?"

"I'm a fan of a better time. People were nicer, things were cheaper. Things were…easier."

She beamed. "You have an old soul."

He raised a brow at that. Since Gypsy hadn't thrown the ball, Burt was dancing back and forth between them. Ethan took the tennis ball from her hands, then threw it with admirable skill, so far into the field before the woods that she lost sight of it. With an overjoyed bark, Burt bounded after it.

She shoved her hands into her back pockets and watched the shepherd arrow toward his new toy. "That was nice of you to get him something to play with. Where'd you find them?"

"General store in town. They had a can of them on clearance."

He stood beside her, so close that his very nearness took the chill off the morning air. Gypsy sensed something on the tip of his tongue. When he said nothing, she stole a look. He was watching Burt, too, but something in his posture said he was distracted. "You know," she ventured, "'then' isn't necessarily a better time than now. Just different."

"If you say so."

"I say so." They stood in silence for a while. Gypsy listened to the wind whistling through the distant woods. Mostly hardwoods out there, dressed in their autumn finery, but enough pine and spruce mixed in to keep Aegis happy. The little owl could be found flitting back and forth between her carriage house—which, Gypsy had to admit, probably housed enough mice to keep Aegis occupied anyway—and the forest. Right now, she felt sure the owl would be drowsing in some hollowed-out tree.

Ethan, on the other hand, stood with an uneasy alertness that transmitted itself to her better than a telegraph. "Thanks for going to this dance tonight," she said.

He shrugged. "Someone's gotta stop Officer Friendly from hanging on you, I guess."

"Thanks for the vote of enthusiasm."

His cat-gold gaze slid toward her. "I don't want you to get the idea I'm putting down roots here. I'll help you around your place, maybe do a little at the fire station…but it's not permanent. I'll be out of your house as soon as those bike parts get in."

"You're not a trouble," she protested. His too-easy tone bothered her—and oddly, not for her own sake. Maybe he wanted roots, and the risk was what worried him. When he didn't speak, she decided on a more neutral topic. "What have you been doing out here?"

"Sanding. Painting the porch," he responded, and now she noticed a smattering of sawdust and paint across the front of his shirt. "Cutting some balusters."

"You don't like to sit still, do you?"

"I've only got a week or so here to finish this work, right?"

She studied him. Sitting still was also for people who didn't mind being alone with their thoughts. She considered asking him if he'd seen her spell book, but she knew he'd only shut down if she tried. And if anyone needed healing, it was him. He radiated tension. "How would you like to walk to the diner for breakfast this morning?"

He shrugged. "I could eat. Let me get a shower first." Burt came back with the tennis ball, but when he dropped it, he didn't seem inclined for another go. Ethan scratched the dog's head. "Do I have to wear anything fancy to this function?"

"Just bring yourself. Nobody's going to mind." She

ventured a smile. "You're thinking about being a fire volunteer, so that practically makes you a Pickering hometown hero."

Whatever she'd said put him on edge again, and she gave herself a silent scolding. His eyes darkened, and he started back for the house.

She was left watching his back and the long-legged swing of his stride. An amazing view, in a town known for amazing views.

Burt nosed her hand. She patted him. "Don't know what's bugging him, boy, but we'll find out."

****

Black jeans and a dark red, long-sleeved Henley shirt. He carried his leather jacket under one arm. That was about as dressy as he could get, when choosing from among the clothes he had that weren't riddled with burn holes. He'd checked them over before they left the house that evening, and found no sign of his frequent, must-be-insane trips into buildings consumed by fire.

Why the hell did he still bother doing it? Why had he been dumb enough not to give an outright no to fire volunteering? He could take the clothes on his back and walk out of this damn town right now without anyone the wiser. Instead, he'd posted a big, flashing advertisement of his ability on his back. Sooner or later, people would find out.

He could just stop doing it.

No, he couldn't. Staring at the façade of the fire house as they neared it, Ethan ground his teeth. He liked his privacy, but he didn't want the self-reproach that would come with letting people die in a fire when he had the ability to stop it. That sure as hell didn't make him a hero. Heroes did what they did because it was right.

He did it to avoid a guilty conscience.

Gypsy walked beside him, unaware of his inner argument. She wore a dress that screamed Fifties, black with no sleeves and a subtle floral pattern. The scoop of the neck left a tantalizing sweep of her pale skin visible, and the cut of the dress alone was enough to emphasize every slender curve he remembered all too well from their night in her living room.

She rubbed her arms. Over the dress, she wore a black cardigan that he doubted did much to protect her from the cooling evening air. She'd freeze on the way home. Only half conscious of it, he moved closer to her as they walked.

A knot of firemen stood at the entrance to the fire station. Among them were Colin and a girl Ethan didn't recognize, as well as Rich and Hollis.

Gypsy groaned softly. "He has flowers."

Ethan bit back an I-told-you-so behind a smile. "I got this." As they reached the door, he drew himself up to his full height. "Evening, Officer."

Hollis gave him little more than a grunt of acknowledgement. To Gypsy, he presented the bundle of flowers. "Glad to see you here, Gypsy," he greeted. He'd dressed better than Ethan—a nice button-down shirt and pressed slacks with a matching blazer.

She took the flowers with a blush rising on her cheekbones. "Thank you, Hollis, but this wasn't really a date."

He didn't seem put off. "Maybe since you came this year, you'll save me a dance, eh?"

"Her dance card's gonna be full this evening,

Hollis," Ethan said.

Hollis passed him a genial smile that Ethan doubted contained a shred of sincerity. "I'm sure you can spare your cousin for one or two trips around the floor."

"Only if she promises them to me," interrupted Rich. He winked at Gypsy then slid Ethan a grin so quick that Hollis missed it.

Ethan took Gypsy's hand and led her past the group. "'Scuse us," he said smoothly, ignoring the scowl on Hollis's face as he and Gypsy swept inside.

The fire house had been transformed. The engines were out of the three bays, parked in the side lot. One bay had been cleared completely of anything but the deejay's equipment. In the remaining two, round tables covered with white cloths dotted the floor. In the center of each table stood squat little pumpkin vases, filled with flowers in vivid reds and golds and looking like miniature flames themselves.

Ethan shook his head ruefully. He wouldn't be able to avoid reminders of his power tonight. He looked at Gypsy to see her reaction to this civic-establishment-gone-festive.

She beamed and twirled in a circle to sweep a look at the balcony of the upper floor. Streamers festooned the railing. At each corner, they'd tied bunches of balloons in autumn colors. "It looks beautiful! Better than I pictured it."

Ethan hardly glanced at the decorations. "You did good," he agreed.

She shook her head. "It wasn't just me. I came up with the plan. The volunteers are the ones who did good. They do a lot for this town, and we appreciate it."

She gave him a sidelong smile. "And even if it's only temporary, you're one of them if you decide to volunteer."

He shied away from the admiration on her face. "I haven't said anything yet."

"Mister Sutter!" cried a voice. The drumming of footsteps on cement heralded a young boy rushing toward them.

Ethan looked up to find the boy from the Buswell fire. Behind him, the older man ambled toward them, supported by a cane.

"I just wanted to say thank you," the boy said. "We got out, and the firemen stopped the fire and saved my baby brother and my baseball card collection, and my great-grandpa's pocket watch that Grandpa said I could have, and my cat, Spooky, and…"

Ethan stopped trying to follow the speed chatter and looked helplessly at Gypsy.

She was giggling. "You've clearly made friends with Paul."

"Clearly," Ethan echoed.

The boy's grandfather reached them. Ethan turned his attention to old man Buswell and found an unnerving gratitude in the man's eyes. "We do want to thank you, Mister Sutter. That house has been in my family for five generations. Six, now," he added, laying a hand on the boy's shoulder. "There's enough left of it—and us—to make it worth rebuilding, thanks to you and the Pickering VFD."

Ethan's jaw clenched. If everyone would just stop thanking him, he could probably forget the whole incident.

The gratitude mirrored in Gypsy's eyes left him no

room for retreat. "See?" she murmured. "One good deed."

Doesn't erase a lifetime of being me, he added silently.

She led him toward one of the tables, saving him from adding anything to her comment, or to the Buswells'. He nodded to them both by way of a goodbye, to which old man Buswell assured them he'd see them before they left for the evening. Young Paul waved enthusiastically, then took his grandfather's hand and headed away to talk off someone else's ear.

It seemed all of Pickering had turned out for this fire house dance. The chatter in the high-ceilinged building would have echoed painfully in his ears if it hadn't been for the muffling influence of all the stuff in the room. He wondered what it sounded like when the siren went off.

A swish of long, curling hair caught his eye and brought his attention back to Gypsy and her lithe figure. He let his stare travel over a slim waist, generous hips, long legs, and tiny feet wrapped in strappy black heels that only accented the swish of her hips as she walked. Hunger jolted through him. Then again, maybe the sirens were already going off.

They sat at one of the tables. A paper menu had been laid at each plate, describing the available food from the buffet. Ethan, who was starving after a morning of working around Gypsy's house, skipped right over the salads and appetizers and decided he'd hit the main course.

Every few minutes as he scanned the page, someone came by to wish Gypsy a good evening. After the fifth time, he looked up and really soaked in how involved his "date" was in the workings of Pickering. She had a smile for all of them, even for Hollis, who came by to check how she'd enjoyed the cake he'd brought to her house. She slid a glance at Ethan before thanking Hollis in a perfectly civil fashion that conveyed her gratitude for the thought…but Ethan knew for a fact he and Burt had eaten most of the offering. She hadn't touched it. Whatever Ethan may have thought about Hollis, the man's sister was a pretty good cook.

When Hollis left, Ethan gave Gypsy a brief, conspiratorial smile. "It looked nice there on the kitchen table for a couple of days, anyway."

"Shhhh!" she hissed.

The deejay's voice boomed out over the loudspeaker. "Good evening, Pickering, and welcome to the seventh annual Autumn Blazes Fire House Dance. We'd like to thank the town board for their assistance in organizing tonight's event, and especially our firefighters, many of whom volunteered to help with the banquet. We'll start with a little dancing now to help you work up that appetite. Here's a newer number for the young folks and the young at heart." He launched into one of the pop songs that had been all over the radio.

Predictably, most of the teens and twenty-somethings filed onto the floor. Colin was among them, towing the young woman who'd been standing with them at the fire house door. He passed Ethan with a broad grin, as if he thought he'd nabbed the prettiest girl there. Ethan smiled back, but as he looked around the fire house, he had to admit no one else caught his eye the way Gypsy did. In her dress, with that glossy, impossible mane of hair, she shone like volcanic glass.

She didn't show any inclination to head for the dance floor. When she caught him looking, he tilted his head toward the throng there. "Not interested?"

Her lashes fluttered. "I didn't think *you* were."

"Not in Top Twenty, no," he admitted.

She gave him an enigmatic smile. "I can wait."

They were joined at their table by a family of four and a younger couple. Gypsy seemed to know them well. There was a flurry of smiles and small talk all around.

Gypsy made wrist decorations for the family's little girls out of the flowers Hollis had given her. They beamed with obvious delight, and even Ethan couldn't deny her artistic talents. Should I have gotten her flowers? No way. Too…something.

When the chatter turned to New Age remedies, Ethan perked up his ears. The woman from the young couple was describing some sort of cleansing ritual. Ethan couldn't have said what a cleansing ritual was, and doubted he wanted to know—it sounded sketchy— but then they began discussing something called a "purge" to rid oneself of negative energies.

That sounded a lot like the little book he'd stashed in his dresser drawer. He paid a bit more attention without letting on he cared all that much. Gypsy and the woman were ping-ponging back and forth about this or that ingredient, and which made the best catalyst for the ritual, and did they have problems when using fresh versus dried herbs, and what color candle did they use… Ethan's head began to spin until Gypsy mentioned a white candle she kept in her bedroom at home. Apparently, it was infused with a blend of oils that she believed purged negative energies from the body.

Jackpot. If Gypsy believed it, he'd believe it, as long as it damn well got the job done.

The deejay rattled through a handful of other songs Ethan had heard on the radio just long enough to change the station. The younger people packed the dance floor. He watched them, thumbing the corner of his menu absently.

He'd been to exactly one real dance, in junior high. He had ignored most of it in favor of a classic car in the parking lot. He and some of the boys from shop class had been wondering how fast they could boost it and take it for a joy ride when a boy stormed out of the auditorium covered in chocolate sauce. His hair stood in sticky, dripping spikes, and the stuff ran down the front of an expensive-looking dress shirt.

Elsa had stomped outside behind the boy with a face full of outrage. "Slimeball!" she screamed. "I should've dumped the whole thing on you!"

Ethan snagged the boy's shirtfront as he passed, and jerked him around until the kid was face-to-face with him. "What did you do to her?" he snarled.

"Nothing, nothing, I swear, nothing!" the boy squeaked.

Ethan looked to his foster sister.

"I caught him cheating on me," she snapped, "with Susan Pitcher."

Any thought he'd ever had of hot, cheerleading-squad Susan Pitcher flew out of Ethan's head on a wave of rage. He yanked the boy still closer, ignoring the chocolate sauce smearing onto his own T-shirt. "There's not gonna be anything left of you to scrape off the pavement."

"Ethan, it's okay," Elsa protested, laying a hand on his shoulder. "He's not worth the trouble."

Ethan fisted his hand in the neck of the shirt. The boy gagged and coughed. Ethan tilted his head toward his sister. "Your loss, punk." He shoved the boy away. The shop kids laughed as the boy stumbled away in a cloud of what Ethan hoped was total humiliation. Ethan glanced at the T-Bird then grinned at Elsa. "Want to help us wire this bad boy up and take it for a spin?"

She put her hands on her hips. "And get arrested?"

"Buzzkill." Seeing the barely-restrained trembling of her lower lip, he softened. "I'll walk you home."

"Hey," called a voice, shattering his memory.

Ethan came back to the present. "Hmm?"

Gypsy smiled. "Where did you go?"

He smirked. *Someplace where I was a better man.*

His funk lasted through dinner and dessert. Gypsy must have noticed his mood, because after the cranberry-glazed turkey, she grabbed his hand and rose from her seat. "Come on."

"Come on, where?"

The deejay returned to his post. "This next set is for the old souls among us." The man waved toward Gypsy, and with a sinking feeling, Ethan followed her where she towed him.

Right into the middle of the dance floor, and the deejay was firing up something vintage that reminded him all too well of their interrupted evening on her rug. Wary, he eyed her. "What are you doing?"

"Apologizing," she said, taking one of his hands in hers and laying her other on his waist.

Ethan had no choice but to echo the posture. He

was a sonofabitch, true, but the thought of leaving her there on the dance floor, no matter how he wanted to retreat, just turned him off. Her waist was tiny under his hand, too easy to sense under the thin fabric of her dress. He sucked in a breath, only to regret it when her spicy perfume filled his lungs. Awash in her, he froze where he stood.

She gave him a gentle smile, as if she knew he was ready to bolt. "Thank you," she said.

"For what?"

Instead of answering, she stepped into his space and turned. And they were off, circling to the sensual voice of a bygone era.

His younger self would have thought him the most complete of idiots, listening to outdated music and acting as if he were any other guy, one who was free to go around like his life wasn't a total charade. What a farce.

Ethan stared into Gypsy's dark eyes, shining in the dimmed fire house lights, and made a decision. For one night in his miserable lie of a life, he was going to be that guy.

Chapter Nine

Sooner or later, she's gonna see this guy's too good to be true. He keeps worming his way into her life, but he's gonna make a mistake, and when he does, I'll be there. I can wait.

****

Gypsy couldn't find her breath. She'd thought the fire house a little cool with its high ceilings and cement floor, but in Ethan's arms, she couldn't feel a chill at all. After that first surprise when she'd pulled him onto the dance floor, he took the lead and turned her into the throng like he'd been dancing all his life. She beamed up at him, more pleased than she could say at the way he seemed to accept her apology for her behavior the night before.

It wasn't just the way he shut down after she'd—well, not come to her senses, because she still trembled inside with the memory of his gifted hands and incredible kisses. She still hadn't come to her senses.

Hesitated. Hesitated because of that Tower card—something on a piece of paper that she'd always trusted to guide her through her life. What if the cards were wrong this time?

What if, after all the heartbreaks of the past and his departure in her future, she just didn't want to admit she was afraid to take the leap?

No fear, then, she told herself. But when she

139

looked into Ethan's cat-gold eyes again, the trembling deep in her bones rose to the surface.

"Are you cold?" he asked. He pulled her gently closer until she brushed up against his chest. He slid his arm farther around her back, and though his motion did little to stem her shivers, a lovely warmth spread through her.

She shook her head, and when he made to step back, she tightened her grip on his hands. "Don't," she urged. "This is…nice."

His lips curled up at the corners just a little. "Yeah."

They crossed the floor in slow circles. Gypsy folded her fingers over the top of the hand holding hers, wondering at the warmth of him. As if he were so real, so intense and vital, that he burned from the inside like a candle. She wished he could simply chase away her shadowy doubts once and for all.

"May I cut in?"

Ethan paused and arched back just enough to allow Gypsy to see Hollis standing beside them with a benign smile. "She's spoken for tonight."

Hollis guffawed. "Knew you weren't cousins the moment you strolled into town, Sutter."

Ethan stiffened in Gypsy's arms. "It's all right," she murmured, already regretting the spoiled moment. "I can spare him one dance."

Ethan raised her hand to his lips, then brushed a kiss across it, renewing her shivers. "Don't go far," he said.

After the heat of Ethan's embrace, being transferred to Hollis was like stepping into a snow bank, but the man's smile was friendly, and his grasp on her hand gentle. "Listen, Gypsy, I'm real sorry if I've been coming across too forward. I don't mean to push. I'd just really like the chance to get to know you better."

The earnest look in his eyes thawed her frosty sensations. She smiled. "Hollis, you *do* know me."

"As much as anyone else in town," he admitted, "but I mean better. On a personal level. Would you let me take you out some time?"

She hesitated. Ethan was right. If she didn't want Hollis, it was best for them both that she told him so right away. She glanced toward their table.

Hollis's voice picked up a note of impatience. "Is your new friend making your decisions for you?"

She snapped her gaze back to him. "Of course not. And I'm sorry I let you think he was my cousin."

"I didn't." Hollis bent closer to murmur, "I'm concerned about you, out there in that farmhouse by yourself. With him."

"He won't hurt me, Hollis."

"I've heard some funny things. I'm starting to think he didn't just happen across the fire at the Buswell house."

She arched back enough to fix Hollis with a stare. "What are you saying?"

"I'm saying, I've started a paper trail on our vagrant visitor, and he makes me worry for Pickering's safety. I reckon he's not as harmless as you think he is." He frowned. "This is all off the record. Don't say anything until I know more, all right?"

She tried to ask Hollis what he meant, but the song had ended. He led her back to her seat and handed her into it. "Just be careful, Gypsy. You know my number."

He left her in a turmoil of nerves.

Ethan returned to the table with two plates of pumpkin cake drizzled in caramel sauce. "What did Officer Friendly want this time?"

She kept her eyes on the dessert he placed before her. "More of the same," she lied.

Ethan sat and reached for his dessert fork. "Told you," he said lightly. "You give him an inch, and he'll take Vermont."

She slid a sidelong look at Ethan as he dug into his cake. What if Hollis were right? What if the Tower card meant trouble, not for herself, but for the town? But then, what did that Chariot card mean? None of it made sense.

The murmur of the crowd and the deejay's music filled the silence for a few moments, then Ethan put his fork down with his dessert only half-finished. "My table manners aren't *that* bad, are they?" He studied her, curiosity in that golden gaze.

Handsome. Oh, was he handsome. Gypsy had made enough bad decisions in love to stop trusting her own judgment…but the Buswells liked him. Colin liked him. Burt liked him, and even Rich did, too. Could they all be mistaken? Was Ethan Sutter much more than he let on?

She teetered back and forth like a metronome until at last, he swiveled in his chair to face her. "What's eating you?"

She pushed away her untouched plate, then leaned toward him and held out her hands. "Let's get out of here and go for a walk. I want to know about you."

He raised a brow. "What about me?"

"Anything. Anything you want to tell. Who you've

been, up to now. You know about me and where I come from. I want to know"—she shrugged and gave him a helpless grin—"what herding cattle is like. What's your favorite color? What do you do in Montana, when the snow is so deep and you're stuck inside all season?"

His raised brow evolved into an outright laugh. "What do I do in winter in Montana? Not much." He stood and reached for her sweater, hanging on the back of her chair. "Come on, then."

He helped her on with her sweater then shrugged on his leather jacket. He took her hand, waved goodbye to the fire volunteers, then led her outside into a night redolent with wood smoke and the lingering aromas of the fire house dinner. The din of the crowd lessened to a murmur as they walked down the sidewalk.

Away from the heat of the party inside the fire house, she rubbed her arms. That was the thing about Vermont. The nights had been warm up until now, but when autumn temperatures decided to arrive, they did so quickly. Even after a handful of years in New England, she hadn't quite adjusted to that.

Ethan slipped off his coat then laid it over her shoulders before she realized what he was doing. The body heat he'd trapped inside it spread through her, along with a giddy swell of pleasure. "Thank you."

"No big deal." He didn't look at her, just walked alongside with his hands in his pockets.

She studied him. "You're nicer than you think you are."

He quirked that charming half-smile. "Am I?" he rumbled in a tone that made his skepticism clear.

"I may not know much about you—so far—but that, I know."

"Yeah?" he challenged lightly, watching the drift of falling leaves through the air instead of her. "What else do you know about me?"

"I know you must have incredible courage to go into a burning building by choice and without safety gear. I know you care about people, even if you don't want them to know it."

"All that from a few days of knowing me?"

"I'm not blind, Ethan."

He paused to eye her. The skepticism in his tone had spread across his features. She wondered for a surprising moment whether that doubt was directed, not at her, but himself.

She reached silently for his hand, not trusting herself to speak. They continued walking, and she tried to content herself with the sleepy chirp of the season's last crickets. A few cars cruised past. Somewhere, a dog barked, and a child called to it.

As they left the town proper, she saw the stars dusting across the sky. "I know," she added carefully, "that there's something special about you that you don't want to tell, but please don't discount it."

His gaze shot to her. She'd hit a nerve, no question. She held his wary look with a head full of things she didn't know how to say. "Yeah," he muttered. "Everybody's special."

"You are."

"Y'know what? Let's not ruin tonight by talking about me."

"Would you rather know more about me first?" She slipped her arm through his, ignoring the way he stiffened. "My parents are accountants from Texas. They love me to death, and they hate it just as much that I make a living crushing herbs and making candles. I live in a big house with a dog and an owl for company, and you're the first person in eleven years who's taken me out for a bona fide date."

He tilted his head at her. "You're just gonna wear it all right out there on your sleeve, huh?"

"Why not? If you keep your heart shut, you might keep hurtful things out, but you can't let the good stuff in." She spoke lightly, but she ventured a look at him, expecting him to shut down at her implied offer to respond.

He didn't speak for a while, and she thought their conversation was over, but as they reached her gate he said, "My father was a crook and a drunk who liked to hit things. When he ran out of things, he hit people. My mother left him eventually, but not before I was put into the system. She didn't seem to care about finding me, so I wound up at Hope Creek with Cade and Elsa and Morgan. The Rathbones were all right. Better than my birth parents, anyway. I learned to read, got a life..." He trailed off to pat Burt, who greeted their return with joyous barks. "Sort of a life."

Gypsy feared to speak, feared it might break whatever spell had drawn the words out of him. She keyed open her front door to let them in, all in silence. For a few moments, he simply stalked into the house as though he weren't quite sure how he'd found himself there. He circuited her living room then stopped to touch a framed photo on the mantel. "Is this them? Your parents?"

She slipped off his coat then hung it on a peg by the door. "Yes."

"Your mom looks like you."

She smiled, but remained silent.

Ethan strolled along the mantel to a little statue of Gaia, the Earth Mother. "How'd you get so different from them?"

"An open mind and a lot of determination," she answered. "I'm guessing, the same way as you."

That look again, a wary spark deep in those hazel-gold eyes that said he wanted to disappear the minute someone got close.

She crossed the floor to his side. "It isn't hard once you've found people who accept you for who you are," she added, eyes on the statue. "Pickering has been kind to me in ways my hometown wasn't."

"Even with your track record with guys?"

"Even with that," she insisted. "My store would never have made it back in Lubbock, and I have a lot of friends here. I'm a part of things."

"I know what you're doing, Gypsy. You think you're gonna spread your good karma to me just by hoping for it." He tapped the statue, then shoved his hands in his pockets to stare at the dead hearth. "Some things, you can't fix."

She looked at him from the corner of her eye. "Why do you think you need fixing?"

Instead of answering, he moved to the stereo then turned it on. Jazz music filtered softly out of the speakers. She watched him build up a wall, brick by brick, and it bothered her more than she thought possible. "Ethan."

He tensed.

She approached him, step by careful step. Hollis's warning echoed in her ears. "Do you want to know the reason most people are unhappy with who they are?"

He sighed, and she knew he was about to tell her he couldn't care less what people thought when he so obviously did. In a crowd of people as he'd been tonight, he'd drifted on the fringes, skittish as a stray dog—there, but not connected to anything or anyone.

Except her…and that, with the barest of threads.

"The reason," she said, laying her hand on his arm, "is that they keep trying to change themselves to chase other people's expectations of them. They let other people—people who may hardly even know them—be their judge, jury, and executioner." She slipped her arm through his and around his waist. "That's an awful lot of power to give away."

He scoffed and shook his head. "You have no idea."

"I would if you wanted to talk about it." She urged him into a gentle sway with the rhythm of the song. "But *only* if that's what you wanted."

He took her in his arms, and his gaze warmed her as nothing in a New England autumn could have done. Her insides quivered with anticipation. "What I want," he murmured, sliding both arms around her, "is to forget trying to analyze me, and think about how we want to spend the rest of this night."

****

I hate that sonofabitch. I've spent my whole life here, serving this town. Serving her *town. What do I get for it? A constant brush-off. Sutter just waltzes into her life, and after a few days, she's all starry-eyed like he isn't going to turn out just like all those other sonsofbitches. What does he have that I don't?*

****

Ethan had distracted her on purpose. A cop-out

move, and he knew she recognized it…but the moment his mouth came down on hers, he silenced any possible protest. He slid his tongue along the seam of her lips. She opened for him without hesitation and stoked to life a rush of heat and eagerness. Her entire body answered yes to his unvoiced question. Ethan crushed her against his chest, more than willing to oblige.

Her arms snaked around his neck. She threaded her fingers through his hair as though he'd even thought about backing away.

Not a chance. His body made the decision for him, too long denied the privilege of a gorgeous woman. He drew her toward the sofa then sat, pulling her down without breaking the kiss. If he gave her a chance to come up for air, she would undoubtedly run like she had last time. She knelt over him on the cushion with no sign of retreat, and he wanted to growl in feral triumph.

He cupped his hands around her backside, firm and oh, so sexy under the thin, silky cloth of her dress. He'd noticed earlier tonight that she wasn't a pantyhose woman. Her legs, folded one on either side of his thighs, were beautiful without the help of artifice. He slid his hands back to stroke the smooth skin of her knees. Higher they went, in unhurried circles that brought a whimper from her lips, quickly swallowed in his kiss.

When he reached the crease at the tops of her thighs, she let out a thoroughly charming squeak and arched backward, giggling.

He grinned. "Ticklish there, huh?"

Her eyes danced, but she dove back down for more kisses. The motion ground her against his lap. Ethan reached under the skirt of her dress to grab her hips and pull her down still harder. His fingers brushed the tiniest scrap of lace, hardly any barrier at all as the heat of her pressed against him. He gave a tormented groan and wished he'd torn all their clothes off before sitting down.

Gypsy seemed to have the same thought. Whatever reservations she'd had at the beginning of the night, they'd fluttered away like dying leaves. What remained was a woman so sensual and lithe and responsive to his touch that his self-control blew to pieces. He slipped his hands out from under her skirt—regretfully—to reach for the zipper at the back of her dress with just enough presence of mind not to tear at the delicate fastening.

She reached back to help him. With a wicked smile against her lips, he stilled her fingers. "I can think of a better use for those hands."

Her dark eyes glowed underneath long lashes, enticing in their impishness. She slipped her hands back around to tug at his shirt and the fly of his jeans. With an eagerness that only drove his hunger deeper, she slipped off his Henley then flung it over the back of the couch. The button of his fly popped open. Her searching fingers found the zipper.

Unable to resist with her hands so close to his cock, he groaned and arched his hips. The backs of her knuckles brushed him through the coarse denim. He bit out a low curse. Still kissing her, he heard the telltale jingle of metal on metal. "Dog," he murmured by way of warning.

As he unzipped her dress and slid his hands inside to her silky skin, she gave a soft moan and arched her back. That long, curly fall of gloss-black hair slid over his arms as she tossed her head back. For one mesmerizing second, her lips opened on an indrawn breath that made him wonder what she'd look like riding him in the middle of an orgasm. His cock hardened painfully. He struggled against the need to flip her onto her back, strip her panties off, and bury himself inside her. She came back to him to nuzzle into his neck. Her lips were a cool ping of sensation against his heated skin. "Go upstairs, Burt," she murmured.

Ethan didn't bother to look, merely heard the dog's tags jingling as he disappeared. Ethan slid Gypsy's dress down off her shoulders, revealing a hot little swish of bloodred lace that barely covered her gorgeous breasts.

He liked this Gypsy. What the hell had he done to deserve her switch from demure to devilish? He buried his mouth in the hollow between her breasts, relishing the gift. She clutched his shoulders and then tried to go for his zipper again, but he swooped onto his feet with her in his arms.

"What are you doing?" she whispered.

"Making sure Burt doesn't get a second chance to tear my face off. Put your legs around me, honey. We're going for a walk."

She wrapped her long, beautiful legs around his back. He carried her toward the little library-slash-sitting room he'd discovered at the back of the house. He'd searched the dark-stained, ceiling-high bookshelves after scouring the stolen spell book, but this library had little in the way of books that might help rid him of his power.

What it did have was a narrow, high-backed, upholstered couch, a thick braided rug, and a sturdy walnut desk. A visitor might observe the room and see a tidy office or reading space. Ethan looked around and saw all the places he wanted to lay Gypsy down and spend the rest of the night blowing her mind.

He kicked the door shut behind them then carried her to the couch. He sat and arranged her in a kneeling position on his lap, the way she'd been in the other room. "Now that there's a door between me and certain mangling, where were we?"

She smiled, at complete odds with the total seriousness of her being half-naked and extremely sexy in the moonlight filtering through the room's two windows. "He's not mean, really. Not with people he likes."

"He likes me when I sneak him treats and when I'm not pawing you."

"He wouldn't have let you in the house if he didn't like you." Her eyes went smoky. "Neither would I."

Ethan arched a brow. He slipped the fingers of one hand up under the lace at her breasts. They skimmed the smooth swell, then circled the puckered tip. "I like you liking me better. No offense to Burt."

She wriggled closer to reach for his zipper. "None taken."

A rush of heat followed the sweep of her fingers, straight to his groin. Underneath it pulsed a disturbing uneasiness—not for himself, but for her. "Gypsy," he said, stilling her hands with his own, "are you sure about this?"

Her gaze came up, soft but somehow more intense than any fire he'd ever faced. "I'm sure. Aren't you?"

Not by a long shot, but not for the reasons she thought. He nodded because he didn't trust himself to answer. If he spoke, he might say something rational to stop this…and heaven help him, he didn't want to stop this. He reached a hand behind her head to draw her close for another kiss.

Her fingers resumed their motions and released him from the tightness of the zipper. In her hands went. He snarled deep in his throat at the obliterating pleasure of her hands on him. "You feel amazing," she said.

Eyes closed, he nuzzled his way to her breasts. "*You* feel amazing." He reached around her back to unclasp the bra, slid it off, then pushed the top of her dress down to her waist. She whimpered as he skimmed her delicate skin lightly with the stubble of his beard. God, that sound. He could live on it.

She pushed at his pants, trying to get them down. He raised his hips just enough to help her. Exposed to the air, only a thin wisp of lace away from being inside her, he stifled a shudder as adrenaline rushed through him. "Condoms?" he whispered, wishing he hadn't thought of them so late. The heat of her against his lap drove him mad.

"Pill," she said against his neck.

"Thank God." Unable to wait any longer, he didn't bother removing her panties, just slid the tiny bit of lace aside and lowered her onto his throbbing erection. She gasped and clutched at his shoulders, her eyes wide and unspeakably gorgeous with passion.

Tight. Oh, so tight. He wanted to snarl in possessive satisfaction. He wanted to flip her onto the back on the couch and plunge into her like a madman. He wanted to hear her shouting his name again and again until she went boneless in his arms.

But no. Not yet. He didn't want this to end. Not for

years.

He raised his hips again, driving gently deeper in an agony of control when he wanted all of her at once. She arched against him like a cat, exploring his shoulders and back with cool hands. "Oh, Ethan," she said, nuzzling him. "Oh, goddess, I've been stupid."

Stupid? Not very complimentary. He lifted his head to fix her with a wry look.

Seeing his confusion, she smiled. "I don't know how I thought I was going to keep away from you. Away from this."

That sounded much better. He allowed a slow, smug, lazy smile to cross his face…even though he was feeling anything but lazy. She shimmied her hips and sank a little farther into his lap. Ethan gave a soft groan, at which she only smiled wider.

Little minx. Well, if she wanted it that way…

He gripped her hips and pushed to the hilt. She gave a thoroughly satisfying moan and dug her fingertips into his shoulders. Dropping her forehead against the hollow of his neck, she pressed close. Her breath rushed out against his cheek.

Ethan slipped his hands up under her dress. "Raise your arms." She did, and he swept the dress off over her head to drop it on the carpet. "Looked good on you. Looks better on the floor."

She met his hungry stare with glazed eyes, then looked away to where they were joined, the little wisp of her panties pushed aside to allow him entrance.

"You want them off?"

"No," she murmured. A tremor ran through her, and a high flush bloomed across her cheekbones. She kneaded at his pecs, and her breath rushed faster in her throat.

If it were possible, he got harder just looking at her, looking at them. "You like having a few clothes on, huh? Should've had you keep the shoes."

"Next time." Before he could process that there might *be* a next time, she threw back her head. "Oh!" Her nails dug in as he hit her sweet spot.

Never too much of a good thing. With a wicked smile of his own, he bucked his hips exactly the same way. A whimper escaped those delicious lips. He swooped forward to catch it with a kiss. Cupping her hips, he angled her so that every thrust ground him against her just right. She rewarded him with a long, low moan and rode him faster.

Sparks of pleasure shot through him from every point where he touched her. He dragged his tongue down her graceful throat to flick it against the hollow between her collarbones. The little sounds she made deep in her throat told him he was on the right track. He smiled against her skin. If a thing was worth doing, it was worth overdoing. He took his cues from every moan, every sigh, every little gasp. He grazed each breast with attentive nips, finally cupping one to suckle hard on its tip. Ah, that was it. She tensed and clutched at his shoulders. "Ethan... *Ethan!*"

The sparks converged in an involuntary rush, so searing-hot he wondered for an instant if he'd punched his power. But no. It hovered, threatening, but didn't surface. He teetered on the edge, unable to catch his breath as he watched Gypsy careen over the precipice herself. Her inner muscles gripped him hard and blasted his control to pieces. A groan tore from his throat and he plunged all the way inside her, giving himself up to the climax. It blasted through him, stronger than his power had ever been, wiping everything out of his head but the sight and feel and smell of her. He crushed her against his body and buried his face in her hair while shudders racked him. For several moments, he could only gasp for air.

Oh, God. He was wrecked for anybody else.

Minutes later? Hours? Days? He manned up and raised his head. He brushed her tousled hair out of her eyes to find her staring at him with just the same sort of surprise that must have been on his own face. "Doing all right?" he murmured.

When she spoke, it came out breathless. "I think, right now, I'm off-the-charts all right."

He quirked a smile, though it was an effort past the increasing rumblings in the back of his head. "That's what I like to hear."

Her lips curled upward in an unbearably sexy answering smile. With a sinking heart, he realized he wanted to start all over again. "Particular about the quality of your efforts?" she asked.

This time, he had to force a grin. "Yes, ma'am."

"Oh, Ethan." She kissed him. "You have *nothing* to worry about."

She unfolded her long legs and rose off him. He watched her as she moved around the room, gathering up her clothes. Her long, raven-black hair swished at the small of her back above a shapely ass that almost made him jump off the couch.

Almost.

"I'm going to get in the shower. It's a little too small for two," she said, "but if you're hungry, I can make us something to eat while you shower afterward."

"I'll get it," he answered.

She hurried back to kiss him again. "Thank you."

He gave her his most wiseass grin. "Anytime."

She lingered at the door, looking like she didn't want to go, but then left the room.

And none too soon. Ethan let out his breath in a rush. Nothing to worry about, his ass. She'd hooked him good.

That was *everything* to worry about.

Chapter Ten

Gypsy had never been accused of having a beautiful singing voice. In high school, she had tried out for choir. It was apparent from the start that she'd be a dismal addition to their group, so she had withdrawn without a squeak of protest.

Tonight, she didn't care. She stepped into the shower, humming the tune to a song from the fire house dance. In her mind, she replayed the amazing experience of whirling around the floor in the arms of a man who wouldn't end the night with a screaming match—or worse, his fists. Her song faltered, but she pushed the memories aside with a better one—how they'd *really* ended the night. Was Ethan actually that giving—seeing to her pleasure more than his own? Had she lucked out in relationships at last? Maybe it was best that she'd gone against her own judgment for a change. It had never served her well before.

Still singing, she toweled off, pulled on her bathrobe, then sauntered into the kitchen with half a thought to coaxing him back to the study.

He'd pulled on his pants, and was at the stove watching over a pan of scrambled eggs. Her gaze landed on his bare back and arms, and even though he couldn't see it, her playful smile faltered.

So many scars. One of them, clearly recent, crossed his shoulder blade, pinkish and glaring. Too old to have been from the Buswell fire. She'd nursed those injuries, and they were healing, but only just.

She approached him with a twinge of misgivings. "Does that hurt?" she asked, touching his shoulder as near the scar as she dared.

He tensed, as she expected she would. "It's fine."

She thought about his fireproof boots. "Didn't you have safety equipment?"

He didn't answer right away. The eggs had finished cooking, and he turned off the burner then loaded them onto a plate already supplied with toast. He handed her the dish. "I don't wanna talk about fires."

She laid the plate on the table, picking her words. He said nothing more, but his edginess telegraphed itself across the space between them. Fireproof boots. A willingness to dive into a house fire with no protection on his back, no breathing gear for his face. Rich had said that smoke inhalation was often a worse worry than the fire itself, damaging lungs with heat and pollutants. How did Ethan emerge from that with little more than an irritated cough?

Oh, goddess, what if she said the wrong thing and he bolted out of her life?

She avoided his gaze, giving him as much space as she could. "When—when and *if*—you want to talk…I'll listen."

The silence that followed was agonizing. Finally, he gave a gusty sigh. "This was great, Gypsy. Believe me. But I'm gonna be gone in a few days. Please don't think I'll stay."

Why not? she cried inwardly…but the words crashed to a stop behind her pride. She almost didn't hear the torment in his voice.

She looked then. He was at the sink now, half turned away, but he'd looked toward her. What she saw in those hazel-gold eyes squeezed at her heart.

He was sorry. Damn it, he was sorry for the most beautiful thing that had happened to her in the last five years. "Don't do that," she said, her eyes stinging.

He stepped toward her. "Gypsy, come on."

"No," she said, backing up, blinking furiously. "You've made your point. Ethan, something's going on with you, something that's chewing you to pieces from the inside, and all I want to do is help—"

"I don't need your help!" he shouted, darting into her face. His broad shoulders blotted out the rest of the kitchen, and his eyes blazed.

Terror strangled her throat shut. She cringed backward with a pathetic, choked-off yelp and fled the kitchen.

"Gypsy!" he called after her.

She ignored him and pounded upstairs. Burt met her on the landing, all canine concern. Shaking, her eyes now burning with overflowing tears, she shot past him to her bedroom, where she slammed and locked the door.

There, where she felt safe enough to do so, she burst into sobs, muffled viciously in the sleeve of her robe.

****

Ethan closed his eyes and listened to the refrigerator cycle on and off twice before the tremors under his skin subsided. His heartbeat banged in his chest, and it took even longer to get that under control. His power tugged at him, demanding to be let out. One breath, two, three. Maybe six before he could stuff it back into the hellhole where it belonged.

She thought he was going to hit her. Jesus, that look on of fear on her face had even scared *him*.

Burt loped into the kitchen, sniffing at him, staring at him as if he had the answers to what had just happened. Ethan dropped into a kitchen chair, then leaned forward with his elbows on his knees to rub the dog's face between his hands. He pressed his forehead against Burt's. "How do I fix this, bud?" he murmured. "You can't be the only man she ever trusts…and I can't stay. Not how I am."

Burt slurped at his face. With a last scratch of the dog's chin, Ethan sat back. The plate of eggs still sat on the table, cooling. With a sigh, he laid it on the floor. Burt dove in with a wagging tail while Ethan stared into space, thinking.

His gaze landed on the little rack of keys on the wall by the doorway. Gypsy's shop key dangled from the first hook, its silver, stylized-tree fob glinting in the light from the overhead fixture. He thought of the spell book in his room, the ingredient list clear in his mind. Then he thought of the wealth of kitschy herbs and incenses in Gypsy's shop cellar.

So. He'd be going from stealing to breaking and entering. Maybe he really was as bad as all of Gypsy's ex-boyfriends.

Or maybe this was how to be better.

He swooped out of the chair to grab the keys.

****

Gypsy woke to a faint scratching at her door. A whine followed it. After a few seconds, the scratching resumed.

She levered herself out of bed then went to the

door. She'd slept in the robe, too tired to trade it for pajamas. If you could call it sleeping. Most of the night, she'd tossed like a pancake. Exhaustion weighted her limbs.

Work today. Normally, the prospect of going to her shop, full of the scents and character she loved, lifted her spirits. Today, she felt leaden.

She opened the door to Burt, wagging his tail slowly and giving her the most reproachful look ever to come from a dog. "I know. I shut you out last night. I'm sorry, sweetie." She bent to hug him. His tail thrashed the air, and all was forgiven.

Maybe a little dog therapy was in order today. "What do you say we take a walk to the coffee shop before work, and you can spend the day with me?"

He barked—clearly hearing that word *walk* in between her banter—and ran down the stairs.

"I have to get dressed first!" she called after him, then laughed.

She descended to the kitchen in a warm sweater and her favorite slacks. As she crossed the floor, the toe of her fashion boot bumped an empty plate. The edge had a little chip, and she recognized it as the one on which Ethan had set her ignored early breakfast. A little pang darted through her chest. She forced it away and picked up the plate. "I see you've eaten." Burt wagged, unrepentant. Only then did Gypsy realize how silent the house was this morning. She twisted around, searching for…what? Signs that Ethan had up and run? She felt hollow.

Maybe she should have listened to her instincts in the first place. Maybe she should have left him on that park bench. All her past relationships had started out wonderful: flowers, compliments, kisses. Then came the insults, the hitting, the false apologies that sucked her in, time and again, until everything crashed into a burning hulk of rubble.

Her throat tightened into a knot so hard, it hurt. She crouched in front of Burt, hugging him and squeezing her eyes shut. "Well," she whispered, "you'll never hurt me."

Burt licked at her face. When she let go, he trotted to the front door. She looked to the key rack.

Her spare shop key was missing.

A chill rushed through her. She'd let him into her house. Into her life. She'd trusted him far too much. With a sinking heart, she grabbed her usual set of keys and hurried after her dog.

The day called for a lightweight jacket over her sweater. On the way to the coffee shop, she tried to calm her buzzing nerves. The sun filtered through the last fiery leaves, and the smell of fall mums lingered in the air from the profusion of pots outside each shop doorway. Pickering loved its seasons, and autumn more than most. Burt's claws ticked against the sidewalk. Instead of soothing her, the sound reminded her of a countdown clock rigged to an explosive. She reached her shop door with an amorphous sense of foreboding.

The door was unlocked. She pushed it open as slowly as possible to avoid the ringing of the bell. Even so, it swung open on a creak that sounded as loud as a circular saw. She winced and stood for a moment on the doorstep. Burt looked up at her with as human an expression of "What on earth are you waiting for?" as she'd ever seen on him. She wondered the same thing.

This was her life, for goddess's sake. She *ought* to

defend it.

Straightening, she stepped over the threshold.

Her shop looked just as it always did, though there were no lights on. She thought of her cell phone, in its pocket in the tote on her shoulder. If she dialed it now, Hollis would come. He'd warned her of his suspicions about Ethan. About the fire at the Buswells'. She set her takeout breakfast on the counter.

Oh, goddess, what if he was bent on arson? She let go of Burt's leash.

The dog trotted directly to the back of the shop. Gripping her tote harder, she hurried after him.

Down the cellar stairs he went, with his happy bark echoing off the old brick walls.

"What are *you* doing here?" came Ethan's voice, sharp with the ring of surprise.

Gypsy froze at the top of the stairs. The light of the naked cellar bulb spilled weakly onto the cellar landing. The only smells that drifted up to her nose were those of the herbs and oils she always smelled in her shop.

But still...

Turn around. Turn around and go, as fast as you can. She whirled on her heel.

"Gypsy?"

Her heart smashed against her ribcage. "Yes?" she called, breathless over its frantic attempt to get out. Shaking, she turned back, wondering how fast she could dial 911 before he charged up the stairs.

Ethan appeared at the bottom landing, dusting his hands off on his jeans. Whatever he saw on her face transformed his own. His forehead creased in a frown. "You all right?"

Your shop. Your life. No one can take it away from

you, she thought. "What are you doing here?" Her voice came out little more than a whisper.

"You look like you've seen a ghost." His eyes crinkled briefly at the corners. "You can't, can you?"

"D-Don't change the subject." She bit off the end of her sentence in a desperate attempt to stop her teeth from chattering. She heaved a breath to fill her starving lungs and tried to reassemble her scattered nerves. "I asked what you're doing here, and I w-want to know right now. Why did you take my keys?"

Burt appeared on the landing beside him, a traitor from his nose to his furry tail.

"I haven't wrecked anything. You can come and see for yourself." He stepped to one side of the landing as if allowing her space to come down.

Down there. Into a basement. With him. The trembling started all over again. Her hesitation stretched into a century of awkwardness.

His frown deepened. "Gypsy, I didn't mean to scare you." He started forward.

She backed off a corresponding step.

He spread his hands. "I'm sorry."

They always said that. Always. She folded her arms over her chest, trying to look indignant when she only felt like a cornered mouse.

Ethan stopped with his foot on the bottom step. He looked down, and his jaw muscles worked. When he raised his gaze to hers again, it was full of such repentance she almost believed him. "Look, I'll go. Right now, if you want. I'll find somewhere else to stay until my bike's fixed."

She stilled her shaking by main force of will. "Just like that?"

"If it's what you want." He dared another step upward, then stopped when she jumped back another step. "I've never hit a woman in my life, and I don't intend to start." He shoved his hands in his pockets. "But I'm sure you've heard that before."

He certainly *sounded* like he was sorry. Burt liked him. And he hadn't actually laid hands on her.

Not that way.

"What *are* you doing here?" she asked again.

He brought one hand up to knead the back of his neck. To her surprise, instead of approaching her again, he sank to the bottom step and petted the dog's head. "If anyone was gonna believe me, it'd be you. But I don't want to share."

The oddity of his response brought her down a few steps. Her skin tingled, and she couldn't distinguish it between premonition or fear. She didn't want to know. "I'm not trying to push," she murmured, "but last night, I did want to help you."

His broad shoulders hunched under his thin shirt as he propped his elbows on his knees. He hung his head for a minute, and she stared at the way his rust-colored hair gleamed in the weak basement lighting. She'd run her fingers through that hair just hours ago, like fire in her hands.

Fire. Arson.

His motion interrupted the darker turn of her thoughts. He leaned back to pull something from his pocket. A jingle followed the movement. "Your keys."

She didn't take them. With a sigh, he laid them on the step. The silence spun out so long after that, she doubted he was going to say anything more. His long, square-edged fingers threaded into Burt's fur. The dog wriggled and leaned into him.

She could only see the side of his face, but she caught the lift of Ethan's cheek as he smiled at the dog. The sight of them tugged at her. Could anyone who liked animals so much be cruel to people? Her reservations began to melt. She folded her knees, intending to sit on the step above him and wait as long as he needed until he wanted to talk.

The shop bell jangled. "Gypsy?" shouted a voice. "Gypsy, come quick!"

Gypsy shot upright to rush upstairs, expecting her shop to be in ruins. Instead, she found Kayla dancing in place in the middle of the floor, looking fit to burst. "What? What is it?" she asked, more than a little breathless.

"I'm getting married!" Shining-eyed, Kayla thrust her hand out to show Gypsy the diamond ring gleaming on her fourth finger.

Troubles forgotten, Gypsy seized her shop assistant in a hug that surely crushed the breath out of her. "Kayla! Oh, my goddess, Kayla, I'm so thrilled for you! That's wonderful!"

"He surprised me last night. He took me to Chaffee Art Center in Rutland, and right there in the middle of their new sculpture exhibit, he proposed to me. He said he wants to spend the rest of his life looking at beautiful things, and me, most of all. I cried all over him."

Kayla didn't look at all tearful now. Pretty before, she'd been transformed by adoration for her artist boyfriend—no, fiancé, now. Gypsy clasped Kayla's hands in her own with a huge smile…and only a tiny bit of envy. Her assistant—her friend—was going to be deliriously happy. After all, Kayla didn't have Gypsy's kind of luck in love.

A thumping on the old, wide floorboards, followed by a *Ruff* of greeting, reminded her of her unfinished business.

Ethan entered the main room of the shop. When he saw Kayla, so radiant with engaged happiness that her very aura filled the shop like sunshine, he paused. "Hi."

"Hi. Ethan, right?" Kayla slid Gypsy a bright-eyed look that could only be called matchmaking fever.

Oh, no. Please, no…especially not now.

Ethan sauntered forward and extended his hand. "Yeah. Sutter."

"Kayla Remsen. Soon to be Wolcott." She beamed again.

"Congratulations," Ethan responded. "Nice ring."

He sounded cordial enough. Gypsy would've given her right arm to know what was going through his head as he looked at that shining stone and the equally shining young woman wearing it. He had the perfect poker face. Now that she'd looked, she couldn't stop. Did he think marriage as unreachable and mythical as she did?

She tore her attention away. "Is Andrew home this week?" she asked Kayla.

"Just until the gallery in Manhattan opens with his work. He leaves on Sunday night."

"Well, what are you doing here, then? Go be with him!" Gypsy said, urging her assistant toward the door.

"Are you sure? I can work—"

"No, you can't. I forbid it. I want you to spend all your free time with your sweetie today. You're too young to waste this gorgeous day when he's in town."

Kayla's gaze shifted to Ethan. Drat. The girl was

too perceptive for her own good. Gypsy often suspected her assistant had a true sixth sense. "I could bring back lunch later, if you like," Kay added.

"I'd love that," Gypsy murmured over the rising sense of stress in the air. She kissed Kay's cheek. "Go. You're off the hook for today."

Kayla hesitated only a second before letting out a little squeak of excitement. "Thank you!" She darted out the door, no doubt rushing toward home and her fiancé's arms.

Gypsy stood where she was, watching the swing of the curtain cord on the door. How wonderful it must be to be in real love, and have it returned.

The negative sparks in the air sharpened as Ethan approached her. "Aren't you supposed to be open for business?"

"Not for half an hour. I was going have my coffee and breakfast while I do the books…but the books can wait a little." She didn't dare look at him, instead moving behind the counter where her coffee and the paper bag containing her cinnamon bagel rested. "I bought a large with cream and sugar. Do you want some of it?"

"No."

She sat on the stool behind her compounding bench. Burt made himself comfortable on the shop floor in front of the counter.

Ethan reached toward her to set her shop keys on the piece of marble that stood in as her compounding slab. His gaze finally met hers. "I am sorry."

She believed him. Seconds went by. When he didn't speak further, she decided she'd have to be the one to break the silence. "I don't judge, you know."

One eyebrow arched, but he nodded. She could almost hear him thinking she'd better not swear to that before she heard him explain.

"There's another stool back here, if you'd like to sit. You're welcome to stay as long as you want." She forced back a pang. Stay, she'd said. In her shop, or her life, or both? Her breath came short at the memory of his mouth on her bare skin.

To her surprise, he sat, though he didn't speak for a very long time. He looked around her shop with an expression of detached curiosity, as if he'd landed here without knowing how. She'd given up on him speaking and started on her bagel when she heard him clear his throat. "I'm on the move a lot for a reason."

She waited to see if he'd add anything. He didn't, so she ventured, "Most people are, when they are."

"Most people aren't trouble."

The self-loathing in his voice surprised her into setting down her breakfast and looking at him across the few feet separating them. What she saw in those cat-gold eyes jerked her heart out of her chest. The air in the shop turned thick with his self-disgust, and she shivered as if she could shake it off. *She* had no sixth sense, but she didn't need it to feel the turmoil coming from him like bursts from a sputtering electrical wire. "What kind of trouble are you?"

A muscle twitched in his jaw. He raised his head, watching something across the shop, then waved a hand in the air. "How much of this stuff do you really believe in?"

She canted her head, refusing to be baited by the scorn in his voice. "All of it."

He grunted, the picture of impatience.

"Really," she said. "Just because you can't see or touch or measure something, that doesn't mean it isn't so."

"Seeing isn't the problem."

Tension crackled. She shifted on her seat. "What is the problem?"

He set his hands on his knees as if he thought that the only safe place for them to go. She stared at them—masculine, warm, capable. Gentle, when he wanted them to be. A wisp of longing curled through her.

"I don't…" he began, then ground to a halt with a sneer. "To hell with it." He shot off the seat and across the shop, pacing, a tiger walking the limits of his cage. He paused at a shelf of metaphysical books. Whatever caught his attention wasn't enough to keep it. After a moment's hesitation, he turned toward the door.

Gypsy rose to her feet, her heart squeezing with worry for him without knowing why. "Please don't go."

"Where could I go? I'm stuck in this town. I'm stuck in my life."

His bitterness sliced the air with savage ease. She flinched in sympathy, but stood firm. *Carefully,* she warned herself. "What would you change, if you could?"

He fisted his hands then shoved them in his pockets. He glared across the shop at her, but the hostility in his posture no longer frightened her. Too foolish for her own good, maybe—but her concern for him overrode her common sense.

"Everything," he said. "Go downstairs and see for yourself."

She put down her bagel to do as he suggested. He made no move to accompany her, no threatening gesture. She told Burt to stay upstairs, and down she went.

There on the cellar table lay her missing spell book, open to a page on restoring balance. The sheets were lightly stained with an oily substance. She sniffed it. Woody, with a hint of citrus. Frankincense. Well, he'd been doing his reading. But what sort of imbalance was he hoping to correct?

She scanned the table. Measuring bowls and a set of weights rested at the end. A few bits of herb had been tied in a bundle that looked like a smudge stick.

For a man who didn't believe in magick, he'd been awfully diligent.

In the center lay a heavy marble bowl with ashes at the bottom. Passing her fingers cautiously over it, she noted they were cool. She picked up a pinch and rubbed it between her fingers. Not herbs. Paper, maybe? What did it mean?

"It didn't work," came his voice.

She turned to face the stairs. He'd paused halfway up. Only his boots were visible.

He thumped down the remaining steps with his hands still in his pockets. The defeat in his posture saddened her. "I'll pay you for what I used, and I'll tell you what you want to hear. You deserve it after last night, I guess."

She left the supplies where they lay. Her heart beat louder. He must have been able to hear it. It pounded through her head, through the stagnant basement air, like a huge, concussive blast.

He fixed her with a laser stare. "You can't tell anyone else. You've got to swear it. Not for me. For my family."

His siblings' names rushed through her thoughts: Kincade, Morgan, Elsa. He didn't talk about them much. She'd thought he didn't really care about them, since he mentioned them so little. But now... "All right."

"Turn the light off," he said.

"Why?"

He scowled and waited. Curious, she tugged on the string by the bulb. It clicked off, throwing the cellar into gloom.

She heard the scratch of flint on steel. His hand appeared out of the darkness, holding a lighter. It cast a weak glow across his frowning face. He reached his other hand toward the flame. She jerked forward to stop him from burning himself.

The flame danced across to his other hand, then flourished in his palm until the cellar filled with light.

Gypsy sucked air into her chest and froze in mid-step. "Oh, my goddess," she whispered.

He had looked away. Away from her, away from the flame in his hand. The glow threw sharp shadows across a face gone hard with bitterness. "The problem," he said, "is getting back to when I *didn't* believe in any of this."

Chapter Eleven

She couldn't move. Gypsy stood there in the middle of the basement floor, halfway to him. A little voice was shouting inside her to do something, to acknowledge him before he disappeared from her life altogether…along with a miraculous blessing that he thought a curse. But she couldn't move.

This was why he braved burning buildings. Because in spite of the fact that he thought it a curse, he recognized his power's value in saving lives.

How had she ever thought him dangerous?

Her tongue unfroze. "Oh, Ethan," she breathed.

He fixed her with a glare as if he'd been waiting for a target for his bitterness. "What? You think it's some wonderful gift from Mother Nature? It's not. It's a bullshit freak show, and I can't go anywhere and have a life because of it."

"No," she protested, finally hurrying toward him.

He snuffed the flame before she got close. The cellar plunged into darkness once more, but light spilling from the stairwell outlined his silhouette. She reached for him.

He stepped back.

"Ethan, it's okay. You're not going to hurt me. You're not going to hurt anyone."

"Don't patronize me like I'm some snot-nosed kid."

"I'm not." But she stopped short of laying her hand on him, fearing he'd bolt. "How many fires have you gone into?"

She couldn't see his face, but his tone left no doubt of his self-hate. "Thirty-six...seven."

She remembered the scars all over his body, too vividly. She hurt just thinking of them, of what he'd been through to get them. The Hanged Man, indeed. He must feel his entire life was upside-down. "Were there people in all of the fires?"

"Yeah."

She dared to close the distance between them. He stood on the bottom of the landing, stiff, unresponsive. She stepped up in front of him. His arms hung at his sides. The smell of the flame—hot and smoky, but not unpleasant—lingered on his skin. At last, she reached for his hands then raised them in her own. With her fingertips, she traced small, ridged scars across his knuckles. For a long time, she didn't speak, trying to find a way to put her wonder into words.

Finally, she looked at his face. "How?"

He seemed to know what she was asking. He sighed. "Cade wanted us to go hiking. An adventure, he said. I didn't want to go, but he insisted, made it a dare. We found an abandoned mine by the river, and he pushed us all to go inside." Ethan lifted his hand out of hers to make a fist, as if he could clench the power out of it. "Couldn't see much. He asked me for my lighter. I used to steal smokes, back then." Ethan didn't seem to know what to do after that, because he started to let his hand fall. Gypsy grabbed it, sensing he needed to hold onto something even if he'd never admit it.

"The lighter did it," Ethan went on. "Chemicals in

174

the mine, stored, forgotten, who the hell knows? The explosion burned my arm. It caused a cave-in on top of Kincade. The river poured in, and I thought Morgan was going to drown in it. I think Elsa got knocked back out of the entrance by the blast. She was too smart to go all the way in."

Reeling, aching for him, Gypsy stood mutely, waiting for him to go on if he wanted.

He stood like a statue, as if he expected her to tire of listening to him. Or more likely, he hoped it. She waited until he gave up and met her gaze. "I know what you think you're doing is punishing yourself," she murmured, "but I'll bet the people you've saved think of it as a second chance at the rest of their lives. *That* is the gift, Ethan. And whatever you might think, you gave that to them."

In the light from upstairs, she saw one of his eyebrows arch upward. "And this is what *I* get out of it."

She threaded her fingers through his, noting the familiar warmth of his skin, but no burns from where he'd held the fire in his hands.

It wasn't the surprise of not getting burned that did it, but the familiarity of touching him. The familiarity of his skin on hers, of the smell of him. The way the warmth of him drove away the New England chill that she could never get out of her bones. The way she knew, somehow, that no matter what happened, Ethan was hard-wired for protecting people, not hurting them. There in a dusty basement, where romance was the last thing on her mind, she fell hopelessly in love with him...and as exhilarating as it felt, it scared her to death. She took a deep breath. A swarm of hummingbirds beat their tiny wings against her insides.

"Let's go upstairs," she said.

He didn't resist, but neither did he show much willingness to follow. Burt waited for them at the top, wagging. She returned to her stool by the compounding bench as if her world hadn't just turned over. Shock, she supposed, but not at the discovery of his power. She believed in such things, even if she'd never seen an example with her own eyes until now. The world was big, and she'd only ever explored a tiny part of it. Who would she have been to say a thing couldn't exist?

No, the shock was something else entirely. She'd never had something to lose before. Not like this. Not to someone who, for once, deserved it. She shook, fighting the urge to scoop up her emotions and stuff them back inside in blind panic.

"I should go," he said, taking up Burt's leash.

She shot to her feet. "Ethan?" Her voice came out breathless, a little too desperate.

He paused, studying her as if he thought he had somehow hurt her. Or maybe he expected he would, sooner or later. If he walked out that door now, would he keep walking until he disappeared from her life? What could she possibly say to stop him? Seconds trickled by in ringing silence.

He shifted on his feet. "I'll see you later."

He left. She watched him walk out as if she were another person in another life, stymied by the turmoil in her heart.

If he wanted to be rid of his power—if dispelling it would bring him the peace he needed—she had no right to stand in the way. Her entire adult life had been about helping others find their tranquility, even when she couldn't find her own. Ethan needed it more than most.

She crumpled up the wrapper containing the rest of her breakfast to drop it in the trashcan. "All right," she said, striding to her bookshelves. She pulled down a volume on the elements, then realized with a start that this was exactly where Ethan had been looking earlier.

Everything fell together. She shot a look toward the shop door, even though Ethan was long gone.

He needed her. Unlike anyone she'd ever known before, Ethan Sutter needed her without any intent to take something from her. And that was why she decided to give it.

Her fears crystallized into a new resolve. She opened the book. "This calls for a little research."

****

Hollis hung up the phone with a frown. "That was Chief McIntyre," he announced to the deputy sitting on the other side of the desk.

The clicking from Knox's keyboard paused. "Yeah?"

"Buswell fire report's coming over on the fax. Wiring."

"Too bad. House wasn't a total loss, though, was it?"

Hollis grunted. "Insurance is still looking at it, but the Buswells will have a time of it fixing her up." After a long enough pause where he thought Knox wouldn't connect any dots in the conversation, he said, "Get anything back on that plate from Sutter's bike?"

"Ran it, but there haven't been any tickets or anything," Knox reported. "You got suspicion?"

"Nah, just a hunch about him."

"The way he worked himself into Gypsy's life, I'm

not surprised," said Knox.

Hollis shot him a glare around the computer terminals.

Knox only shrugged. "Anybody with eyes knows you're soft on her. Of course you'd feel…protective."

"Shaky ground, Knox. Do something useful, like filing those reports you've been hoarding in your inbox."

The fax chirped its receipt of the fire report from Chief McIntyre. Hollis scooped it off the machine to flip through it. Wiring, it confirmed. No trace of accelerant, as far as the preliminaries went.

Good. Still, one should be thorough.

Hollis turned back to his computer to search the databases for Ethan Sutter. Nothing came up. He sat there, tapping a pencil on the blotter. An idea sparked, and he typed *Fires, investigation open or unsolved,* then pushed his rolling chair away from the desk. He usually left it to do its search while getting a coffee from the shop down the street. With an open-ended search like that, it'd be a while.

But the computer chirped right away. Hollis stared as the screen filled up with entries.

Burlington, Vermont. Unknown white male present.

Stowe, Vermont. Unknown, red hair.

Montpelier, Vermont. Unknown white male, six feet tall, 190 pounds.

Staring at the monitor, Hollis showed his teeth. Then he opened a screen with a map to begin plotting cities farther afield.

****

Ethan rarely asked Morgan for more of his money

than he absolutely needed. When he called her, it was no surprise she sounded like he'd announced an intention to join the circus.

"You want *how* much? What are you buying—a mansion in the Hamptons?"

He gripped the phone and circled the small space of Gypsy's kitchen. "I found a use for it."

There was a long, uncomfortable pause. "Is it a woman?"

"Christ, Morgan, I don't need a babysitter. And I shouldn't have to beg for my own money."

"All right, all right. I'm not criticizing. It's your money."

"Yes, it is."

"And you can do what you want with it."

"Yes, I can."

"And if you were in trouble, you'd tell me."

Ethan clamped his mouth shut long enough to count to ten. "Babysitter," he scolded her.

"Okay, I'll stop fishing." She paused, and in his head, Ethan saw her brow wrinkle in that familiar expression of concern. It annoyed him, but in a little corner of his heart, it made him smile that she still thought she needed to look out for him. After a minute, she added, "I'll wire it around lunchtime when Trent and I go into town. Love you."

He stifled a grumble. Affection from Elsa was one thing. She was a big ball of it. Affection from Morgan usually meant *I care about you and I've never outgrown feeling protective of you.* Ethan doubted he'd let the word "love" pass his lips since he was in footie pajamas, even when he did feel it. "Yeah," he said, letting it slide. "You, too."

They hung up, leaving Ethan the rest of the day to stew on what had happened that morning. If he *really* cared about his foster family, would he have revealed his power? Gypsy might believe in the supernatural, but he doubted she'd ever seen an example of his ability firsthand, let alone seen an entire family of Elementals. At least he hadn't brought them into it.

He'd been down to the garage to check on his bike's progress, only to be told there was a problem with his parts order. The clerk who had filled it entered the wrong product number, or some such crap. The fix would take a few additional days. Karma was kicking his ass all over town, and he hadn't helped his cause by showing Gypsy his ability.

On the way to his bedroom, he passed the living room. A look at the rug reminded him only too well about what he and Gypsy had been doing when lying there last. He whirled away from that to the sagging bookshelves. Simple, rectangular cuts. Nothing that flipping the boards and installing a shelf bracket couldn't fix. She had a lot of books and knickknacks weighing down that wood. He had some scrap left in the garage from the porch project.

Well, it was either this, or continue to ruminate for the rest of the day on his colossal stupidity.

Burt kept him company in perfect canine fashion— there, but uncritical. Ethan cleared and flipped the shelves in mostly comfortable silence. He was preparing to cut the brackets on the sawhorses outside when the crunch of gravel announced a vehicle rolling into the drive.

Ethan recognized Gypsy's friend, Rich Pettit, behind the wheel of his rescue truck. It pulled up outside the gate. "Hey," Rich called. "You hungry?"

Ethan wiped a sweaty film from his forehead. "Sure."

"Good. I got some fried chicken here that even I'm not gonna be able to eat all by myself." Rich climbed out of the truck, loaded down with a big bag of something that smelled like heaven.

Burt trotted toward the man, sniffing at Rich and the bag of food with equal enthusiasm. He danced back and forth, barking.

Ethan grabbed the dog's collar. "Down, you big moose." He led the way into the house. In the kitchen, he pulled out plates. Shooing Burt out of the way, he hooked a pitcher of tea out of the fridge then poured two glasses. "Don't sit in that one," he said, indicating the chair pushed against the wall. "Burt broke it, and I haven't fixed it yet."

"Saw the shelves. You're pretty handy. That what you do when you're not cross-country traveling?"

"I lived on a ranch. You don't learn to fix things, pretty soon you're up to your ass in rubble." He handed Rich a glass of tea, then he slid into a chair with a smile. "Haven't had a decent piece of fried chicken since I left Georgia."

"You're not gonna get one now," Rich responded. "This is from Lolly Hammerfield. She lives in town. Widowed. Young. Cute. Not the best cook, but I let her keep trying." He portioned out a plate of chicken with a grin of his own. "Don't have the heart to tell her any different." He slipped a few bites of chicken to the dog, which made Ethan smile. *Furry pushover,* he thought again.

Whatever Rich thought, the chicken tasted pretty

damn good after a morning's hard work. A little bland, yes, but the made-from-scratch taste made Ethan miss Morgan's cooking.

His money should be wired in by now. He could walk Burt back into town later to pick it up. Better yet, he could get the materials for fixing those roof tiles. Much more waiting, and the winter snow and ice would give Gypsy roof problems and water damage.

The least he could do was forestall that, if her help—and her silence—would rid him of this power. "How much is it to rent a truck in town?"

"You need wheels? I've got the afternoon off."

"Gotta get some roofing."

Rich fixed him with a calculating look. "You planning to hang your hat here for a while?"

The direction of Rich's suspicions wasn't hard to pinpoint. "It isn't like that." Was it?

"I'm not judging, brother. She's a nice woman, our Gypsy. A little out of the ordinary, but who doesn't like the adventurous?" His eyes crinkled at the corners.

"Pervert," Ethan rumbled.

Rich laughed and sat back. The old chair creaked a little. "To be honest, I'd be glad if you stayed awhile. You could save my ass some more."

The Buswell fire resurfaced in Ethan's thoughts. "Don't mention it."

"I'm gonna mention it. And I'm gonna hound you until you start volunteer training with us. You've got guts this town needs."

"Thanks," Ethan responded, though he felt anything but thankful. They moved on to other, safer topics after that. After their meal, Rich helped him cut the brackets for the shelves. Ethan found himself glad of the company, and Rich was no slouch at hauling bulky wood pieces from carriage house to yard to living room. By the time Gypsy arrived home that afternoon, they had dry-fitted the new brackets and readied them for painting.

She pulled into the drive on her bicycle. Burt greeted her with sloppy licks. Uneasy as he was, Ethan smiled. Must be nice to come home to someone who was glad to see you.

She didn't seem glad, herself. Faint worry lines creased her brow.

Rich beat him to the question. "Something wrong?"

"Not important," she answered.

"Fixed your kitchen chair, too. Turns out, Rich had an old working lathe," Ethan said.

Rich grinned. "You start borrowing my tools, you gotta live here, Sutter. That's the rules."

Whatever bothered her, the expression cleared from Gypsy's features as they showed her into the living room with its improved bookcases. "Thank you. At this rate, I'm going to have a whole new house."

The faint blush creeping into her cheeks, and the look of pleasure on her face, made Ethan glad he'd decided to use some of his spare cash for house repairs. He liked the work, and carpentry came naturally, so it was nothing to him...but her reaction made it seem like he'd given her one of the ancient wonders of the world.

"Rich, I hate to ask it after you've obviously helped Ethan out so much today—" she began.

"Oh, you know it's no big deal, hon," Rich interrupted, then he pecked her on the cheek as he passed by to set an empty glass in the sink.

"Well, the thing is," she said, shifting from foot to foot, "I need to talk to Ethan."

Rich paused. The tone in the air changed abruptly to awkwardness. "Oh. Uh…yeah, okay. Not a problem."

Ethan's alarm sirens began ringing at the look on Gypsy's face. He shot a look toward her, but her back was to him, facing Rich at the sink.

Whatever was on her face, Rich's gaze went quickly over her shoulder to Ethan, his eyes full of confusion. Ethan stuffed his worries as far down into the pit of his stomach as they'd go. After a tense moment, Rich turned his attention back to Gypsy. "Are you all right?"

"Yes, yes," she said quickly. "It's just a little…private."

"All right. Call me if you need me." Rich said his goodbyes, and got out of there a lot more slowly than Ethan liked. Gypsy's tone had his skin crawling. What had gone wrong today?

When Rich was gone at last, Ethan leaned against the counter. "Tell me."

Her breath whooshed out, and she lowered herself into a chair, ignoring Burt's nudge for attention. "Hollis came by. He was pretty pushy."

"What did he do?" Ethan said on a growl.

She looked up. The expression in her dark eyes chilled his blood. "He's drawing up a paper trail on you. He's trying to pin you for arson."

****

By his expression, she half thought Ethan would bolt out of the house and not come back. He stood upright, every muscle in his body rigid. Burt picked up on it and turned to him with a whine, which Ethan ignored. Poor Burt came back to her, pushing at her with his nose in a new plea for acknowledgment. She patted him, soothing him, but coming nowhere near easing her own fears.

The Tower. Could this be that flaming building and falling man? Would Ethan spend the rest of his years behind bars, desperately trying to conceal the amazing ability that allowed him to save lives at the risk of his own? Once Hollis discovered a problem in his town, he went after it with both guns.

And if Ethan was out of the way, that would allow Hollis to resume his advances without obstruction.

"So," she said, choosing her words, "I guess the question is this: Do you really want to get rid of your power?"

He angled his head. "Not 'Did I do it?'"

"You're not capable of it. I know that much about you," she protested.

"You never thought your exes capable of being bastards, either," he shot back.

Stung, she stared at him.

His shoulders relaxed a little. "Gypsy, you aren't the best judge of people. You want to see their good sides too much."

"I see *your* good side."

"You're looking too hard."

"Are you trying to convince me you're a bad person?" She rose from the chair to approach him. She wondered if her advance would send him rushing out of the house, but kept on, riding a wave of hurt pride splashed up by his words. "I've had my belly full of bad people, Ethan Sutter. I may not be the best judge of character, but I've been with you for several days now, and you don't have a mean streak. So why do you keep trying to get me to believe you do?"

A flash of something that looked like regret went through his eyes. "Because I'm not gonna stay," he said softly.

Her heart clenched. She jerked to a stop as if he'd reached out to slap her, and tears sprang automatically to her eyes. The blow had come without any forewarning, and she cursed her soft heart and the way he'd worked himself into it. He would never hit her. Never. But this was so much worse. Struggling for calm, she said, "Even if I can help you get rid of that power you hate so much?"

Long moments of silence rang through air that felt unbearably stale after riding home in the fresh autumn breezes outdoors. He looked away first. "Even without it," he murmured.

She choked back a response prompted by pain, not wanting to perpetuate the negative vibes lying on the air like an oil slick. "I think I'll go for a boat ride," she whispered. "Come on, Burt." She left the room, not looking back, the tick of Burt's claws a counterpoint to the tomblike silence from Ethan.

Only when she got outside did she let the tears fall.

Chapter Twelve

She's too wrapped up in him, that's what it is. She's too close to him, all day, every day. I've got to save her from him. I've tried being nice. Now, I'm going to start playing hardball. I'm the better man, and I've got to show her that.

****

Ethan should have known. He should have known that if he stopped for any length of time in any one town, someone would link him to the fires.

Gypsy had been with the worst sort of men, drunks and abusive sonsofbitches that didn't deserve her in their lives. Did he deserve her any better when he could be branded a criminal and yanked off to prison? Even if the fires weren't his doing, his presence at each one would be enough to get him arrested on suspicion. And he couldn't prove otherwise.

He thought absurdly of the stack of roof tiles he'd ordered from Brandon, Pickering's nearest big town. Expensive as hell, since no one really tiled a roof with fish-scale anymore. He'd also bought some house paint out of his own pocket. What in hell had he been thinking, buying up home repair supplies when he was just going to blow out of town in days?

You don't want to go.

An all-too-vivid memory of her lips against his, of her soft skin and long, sensuous hair plowed through him. His body shook with it, and he fisted his hands. She hadn't needed to whip up some magic spell to bind him to her. She accepted him. She'd barely batted an eyelash when he showed her his power. She believed him—believed in such power—and moreover, she believed he was a decent man in spite of it. Who the hell did that?

Gypsy did—and because of that, she had him thinking about sticking around in one place for the first time in over two years.

He could go home to Hope Creek. Cade and his wife Allyson would always welcome him, but he hated the thought of crawling back there when Cade was the reason he was in this mess. Ethan clenched his fists tighter. Morgan and Elsa both preached forgiveness…but they had found ways to be satisfied with their damned power. Ethan doubted the same would happen for him.

Even if he did get rid of his hated ability, Hollis would connect him to the fires, and that would be the end of his choice to go anywhere. Gypsy would be pitied by her neighbors, that poor, eccentric woman who'd made her worst choice yet: a man who didn't stop at hurting her, but went on to endanger dozens of people wholesale.

Ethan couldn't absolve himself any more than he could save Gypsy from their pity.

No. Best to go. He'd get down to the garage and see how long they planned to make him wait for his bike, and what he could do to hurry things up. He'd have the roofing tiles shipped here, maybe stored in the carriage house until someone could fix the place up. She had friends in town. Some of them had to be the sort who'd come over on a Saturday and spend a few hours helping Gypsy patch the place up.

Ethan never felt like such a skunk in his life.

****

Gypsy pushed off from shore and rowed out to the middle of the pond. Burt lay in the bow, content to survey their progress. One of her favorite things about this property had been its serene pond, ready to welcome an afternoon boat ride or curious fisherman. It was just as serene now, with the last of the fiery maples and golden birches reflecting their fall splendor in the surface of the calm water.

The scene did little to soothe her. On the walk here, Burt had picked up on her mood and tried to jump up to lick her face. She pushed him down with a murmur to behave, and after that stifled her tears.

She didn't even know why she was crying. He had never made any secret about wanting to leave once his motorcycle was fixed. If she'd thought different at any point, she was only fooling herself. One night together—one beautiful night—didn't mean he loved her. She had no right to him, and no sense to get attached to a man who wanted only to let go.

In the center of the pond, she drew the oars in and let the boat drift, listening to the chirp of birds who'd decided to stay for the winter. She forced a smile, which no one was there to see. Once the pond froze, she always invited the neighborhood over for a day of ice skating. The seasons would go on rolling along, whether Ethan Sutter stayed in Pickering or not. Her throat tightened.

Burt, who'd stretched out with his head on his paws, now raised his head with a soft *Woof.* She looked around to see what had gotten his attention. A few ducks took wing from the water, laggers who'd not yet flown south ahead of the winter snows.

"Imagining yourself a hunting dog, just because you've taken a few runs after Aegis?" she murmured.

Evidently not, because he laid his head back on his paws with a canine snort that sounded as disgruntled as she felt. She heaved a sigh full of the rich scents of the season—leaves, damp earth, the smell of the water, and a faint whiff of wood smoke. Pretty soon, the heavenly smells of Thanksgiving feasts would join the seasonal bouquet. Who would she share that with this year? She'd been invited to Kayla's house, but after her assistant's engagement to Andrew, Gypsy didn't think she could bear to show up, especially without Ethan in tow. It would almost be like admitting defeat—that she really was that big a disaster in love.

Pick yourself up and dust yourself off, Gypsy, girl, she told herself. *Giving up now will only prove them right.*

She sat bolt upright, so fast the boat rocked on the still water. That was exactly it! Ethan wanted to leave, but after Hollis's accusations, wouldn't that only make it seem like he had something to hide? He needed her support as much as anyone who'd ever come to her shop seeking guidance. More so, because he actually had a problem which she was better qualified than anyone else to help him solve. He might talk a big game about wanting to leave, but what he needed was an all-clear to stay.

"I've got to go back to the shop. Tonight, and every night until I can help him fix this," she said, though no one was listening except Burt.

The dog lifted his head to regard her with a quizzical expression, as if to say, *What are you waiting for?*

With new determination, she leaned into the oars and pulled for shore again.

****

Ethan arrived at Clemens Automotive with a chip on his shoulder. He tried to remain patient, but the mechanic was strangely evasive when asked about the expected arrival of his bike parts. While they were bickering over the shipment, in walked Hollis.

Just as if he'd been on cue.

"Evening, Roy." Hollis tipped his wide-brimmed officer's hat to Ethan as he strolled up to the counter.

Roy wouldn't meet Hollis's stare. Instead, he dropped his gaze to the grimy computer keyboard in front of him and pretended to enter data, though Ethan noticed he didn't look at the screen to check that he'd opened a service ticket. The screen remained on a wallpaper picture of a classic car.

Suspicion pricked at the back of Ethan's neck. He rounded on Hollis to find the officer eyeing Ethan's fireproof boots. A charge of hostility flashed through him. "If you're here about a delay in repairs, you'll need to get in line," he said as pleasantly as possible.

"Checking on an order," Hollis said. He looked back to Roy as if that put an end to their conversation. "Roy?"

"A-Another week, maybe?" Roy offered. The tips of his ears went faintly pink.

"That's not gonna be good enough, Roy. Make it work."

"Yessir. I mean, I'll try."

"You do that. Evening," Hollis said again. He made for the door, but not until he'd shot another critical look at Ethan's boots.

Ethan's temper flared. He hurried after the officer, catching up once they were out on the sidewalk. "Hey."

Hollis fixed him with a look which could only be called disdainful. "Mister Sutter?"

"Must not just be me, then."

"Meaning…?"

"Meaning you like to throw your weight around. Bully innocent people all over town."

Hollis cracked a grin. "Tell you what, Mister Sutter. You stay out of my affairs until I need you. When I do, I'll come after you. Deal?"

"Aren't you supposed to have a deputy with you when you question people?" Ethan asked, in a tone that made it clear Hollis needed a leash.

"Now, what gives you the idea this is official business?" Hollis responded in the same tone. "If I were on an investigation, Mister Sutter, you'd know it. I believe I've wished you a good evening enough times tonight. Be seeing you." He swiveled around to walk toward a cruiser parked at the curb.

Clenching his fists, Ethan watched the cruiser pull away. He was used to stifling his power, used to keeping his fingers tightly folded until a spike in his temper passed and the danger of his power surfacing had receded.

He was also used to the smell of smoke.

A whiff of it drifted under his nose. Different fires had different scents, and he'd been in so many of them that each kind had as distinctive a smell as different flowers. Wood smoke from someone's hearth carried a far different aroma than that of the sharp, oily smell of a grease fire.

His power, pushed down just a moment before, bounced back in reaction to the scent. An instant later, sirens filled the air. Ethan bolted toward the diner.

Flames poured out the back as the fire engine pulled up to the building. "Is anyone inside?" he called to the firefighters as they jumped down from the truck.

The chief herded him back from the blaze. "Don't know, but you can't go in there. You haven't trained, and even if you did, you don't have gear."

A moment later, a gold sedan pulled up across the street. Out popped an older man Ethan recognized from the last time he'd been to the diner. The man hurried toward the diner, as close as the firemen's quickly established perimeter would allow. "Oh, God," he moaned. "My whole life, my whole life is up in smoke…"

Ethan swallowed back a response. He'd seen that look of desperation enough times to know the man owned that building. He could see, could sense, that they were going to lose the diner. Fire had a voice, a language. In it, he recognized a greedy intent to gobble up the entire structure and possibly even the buildings to either side.

Nothing he could do about the diner. They might stop the fire, but not before it ate up everything but a skeleton.

He could, however, slip away and prevent its spread. He took a step…and then, for the first time since leaving Hope Creek, he hesitated.

What if he were an ordinary man, just like the one beside him? What if he left the firefighters to handle it?

"Sutter, move aside, man!" called a voice.

A row of firefighters had begun lining up along the front sidewalk with axes, and another row were unraveling the hose from the truck. Rich stood beside him, staring at the flames now spreading across the roof as his fellow volunteers moved into place. "God, it's a mess. That went up quick. Kitchen, y'think, Laramie?"

One of the other volunteers nodded. "Betting so. Let's get in there."

Stepping well back, Ethan turned his attention once more to the flames. Even at a distance, the heat plucked at his power. He clenched his fists until they hurt. *I could walk away from this.*

A cry from across the street brought his attention around. A younger woman stood outside a minivan, holding a child's hand and gaping at the flames eating up the diner. "My shop!" she cried. Her horrified stare had locked on the florist's next door.

Yeah. The hell he could walk away.

For now.

He slipped around the corner. The increased distance did nothing to quiet the insistent throb of his power. Away from prying eyes, he ducked into a service alley behind the buildings and let it flow.

The gleam of his power rushed across his skin, reflecting in ripples on the brick behind the flower shop. Fire poured from a hole in the roof over the back of the diner. The heat had cracked some of the brick in the florist's building. Ethan held up his hands.

"What do you think you're doing now, Sutter?"

Ethan clenched his fists and snuffed his power.

Hollis stood behind him with his hand on his gun holster, squinting in the heat glare. "Get away from the building."

Ethan muttered a curse, leaving his hands well over his head and in plain view while his mind spun in circles. The fire would eat through the wall of the diner and start in on the next building at any moment. In spite of the passive protection of his ability, heat blasted against his skin. He glanced at Hollis then took a careful step back.

The flames licking their way down the roof reflected, demon-like, in the officer's eyes. He turned his glare on Ethan. "I've had enough of your crap, mister. You and I are taking a ride down to the station."

"I didn't do anything," Ethan protested. It sounded just as pathetic on his lips as it had in his head.

Hollis clamped a hand onto Ethan's shoulder. "And you can tell me all about how you didn't, down at the station."

Furious, Ethan let the officer steer him toward the police cruiser, standing at the ready across the street. A couple of the firefighters still battling the blaze from outside passed them a curious glance, but quickly resumed their work. Oddly enough, he wasn't bothered by humiliation at being herded to the officer's car like a common criminal. What got him was the look of desperation in the florist's eyes as she watched her livelihood go up like an inferno.

All because he'd hesitated.

****

Gypsy ran upstairs to the main shop at The Holistic Mystic to the insistent ringing of the phone. With her apron covered in oil stains, she cried, "Oh, shoot. Don't hang up, don't hang up!" She made it to the receiver and snatched it up. "Holistic Mystic. Can I help you?"

she panted.

"Gypsy, it's Hollis."

"Hollis. The shop's closed. How'd you know I was here?"

"I was in town tonight. The diner had a grease fire. Didn't you hear the sirens?"

"I guess not. I've been in the cellar with a radio on. Is anyone hurt?"

"No. Luckily, no, but the diner will be closed for a while. Do you have some time free tonight?"

Her gut squeezed in sympathy with the awkwardness now flushing through her. "Hollis, I don't really think—"

"This is important," he said, his voice suddenly hard with "cop" authority.

A pang of alarm rushed after the awkwardness. "What's the matter?"

"I'll tell you when I get there." He hung up without giving her a chance to reply, yea or nay, to his impromptu visit.

Silence hung heavy on the air. She replaced the receiver, then sat on the stool behind her compounding bench to stare uneasily at her fingers, stained green with crushed herbs.

A fire at the diner.

Guilt supplanted both the awkwardness and alarm. She fought a completely unreasonable desire to clean up her work downstairs, as if Hollis might somehow connect her spell with Ethan, and declare Ethan the arsonist Hollis suspected him to be.

He wasn't. She knew he wasn't, just as she knew Hollis would try to make her doubt that when he showed up. But Hollis had his own motive for that, which had nothing to do with his investigation. Ethan was right. She should have given him a definitive "no" ages ago.

Well, as soon as he showed up, she would. Enough was enough. She didn't want Hollis romantically, and never had. And now that she'd been with Ethan, she doubted anyone else would measure up.

She didn't have to wait long. Hollis must have been right down the street when he called. Not ten minutes later, she heard a knock at the door.

She rose from her stool to answer it. She flipped the lock and deadbolt then let him in.

He looked angry. A little chill ran down her back. "Something's wrong," she prompted again. "Tell me."

He removed his hat to rub a hand through his short hair. "Yeah. Gypsy, you better sit down. I'm sorry. I know you think he's harmless, but—"

The chill expanded into tendrils of frost rushing through her blood. "What happened?"

"You need to get Sutter out of your house before something bad happens to you."

She heaved a sigh. "Oh, Hollis—"

"He was *at the fire*, Gypsy. He was there. I caught him trying to get inside."

Dread stung at her like a bitter wind, but not because of Hollis's suspicions. What was Ethan doing, looking for trouble when she was trying to rid him of his power? "Why would he try to go in there?"

"Why does an arsonist do anything he does? Destroy evidence? Watch it burn? He's sick, and he's going to hurt you." Before she could react, Hollis took her hand in a firm squeeze, as if he could impress his doubts on her with a touch. "Kick him out, Gypsy, please. I don't want to see a fire at your house next."

She forced a light laugh and lifted her hand from his. "I know it's your job to protect this town, but you're going overboard." She backed away to rearrange some books on a table.

"Am I?" Hollis came forward. "Burlington. Stowe. Montpelier. All places where a building went up, a total loss, and a man matching Ethan Sutter's description was at all three."

Gypsy was suddenly disappointed with her fair skin tone, which she knew couldn't hide the heat creeping into her cheeks. Hollis was most likely dead-on correct, but not for the reasons he thought. Not that she could prove it. She opened her mouth to defend Ethan, regardless.

"Has he told you where he's been?" interrupted Hollis. "Maybe you should ask him some time." His pale eyes narrowed. When he spoke again, his voice had lowered to a quiet murmur that set her skin crawling with worry. "When he got here, you lied and said he was your cousin. Why would you do that?"

To stop you from bullying me into a date, she almost said. But the intensity in Hollis's searching eyes backed her up against the counter. She bumped against it, felt behind her with her hands, drew strength from the worn wood frame of the glass case.

Her shop. Her life. And no one could tell her how to live it. "Where is Ethan?"

He stuffed his hat back on with a disgruntled look. "He's cooling his heels at the station while we interview him about his undocumented road trip. We know he grew up in Sagerton, Montana after being pulled out of a bad family and put into foster care. Did he mention that?"

"Of course he did."

"Did he mention his father was a fan of prodding him with lit cigarettes? Did he mention his old house burned down three years after the state removed him from it?"

Her mouth dropped open, but the words she wanted to use to defend Ethan swept away under a horrible mental image of the damage Ethan's father had inflicted on him.

Hollis's eyes glinted the way they did when he was on the trail of a criminal. "I guess he didn't mention that part. Mysterious circumstances, and no clear cause to the fire. A lot like Burlington, Stowe, and Montpelier—or so I've been told by their fire departments."

Gypsy gripped the edge of the counter behind her until her fingers hurt. Her breath had deserted her.

She believed in Ethan. He was a good man. He wouldn't have started those fires. He'd just been there to stop them, to see that people got out safely.

Hollis mistook her hesitation for fear. He closed the distance between them to lay his hands on her shoulders. "I don't have hard evidence, and I don't have anything I can pin on him—yet—so I'll have to let him go. You need to get him out of your house and out of your life before he does something to hurt you. Something I might not be there to stop. I care about you, Gypsy."

She said his name on a forced breath of exasperation. "Hollis…"

He cut her off with a kiss.

Backed up against the counter, she had nowhere to

go. With a muffled sound of protest, she pushed at his chest.

Hollis backed up. The surprise in his eyes turned at once to a hard glare of clear disgust. "Don't tell me you *trust* him."

"I do," she insisted. "You don't know him like I do." She wiped at her lips, seething with her own discomfort and the tangible echo of Hollis's frustration. "I'm not interested in you that way, Hollis. You have to believe that. I'm sorry if you read something more into it—really, I am—but please don't make this any harder."

He looked for a disturbing second like he might appeal—disturbing because she had no idea how to respond. He saved her the trouble by jamming his hat farther down onto his head and whirling toward the door. He paused at the threshold, his face resolute. "All this evidence… It's got to mean something, and I hope for your sake it doesn't mean trouble. But I'm going to prove it, one way or another. Maybe then you'll believe me."

She thought he might slam the door behind him, his expression had gone so dark, but he merely closed it with a soft click.

Little tremors ran through her body. Fear? Of Hollis? Or fear that Ethan might be whisked off to prison and out of her life with no way to defend himself against the charges?

She went back to the cellar like a woman in a trance. Ethan wanted her to help him get rid of his power. She'd do it. She'd promised…but she worried that his ability to *stop* a fire might be the only thing standing between him and the accusations of him *starting* them.

****

An hour and a half in a hard plastic chair hadn't done Ethan's mood any favors. The air at the police station was stale with the stink of old coffee. The deputy's hunt-and-peck clicking on his keyboard was so loud it might as well have been a woodpecker hammering at a hollow tree. And that image just reminded Ethan of the mountain forests back home, which reminded him of Cade. Which reminded him why he was here in the first place.

Damn it. Damn his power, and Cade, too. If his power had never happened, he might have lived and died at Hope Creek without the slightest care in the world. Instead, he was staring across the desk at a pasty-faced man in standard-issue cop wear with a coffee stain on his tie. Deputy Knox had ignored him for the past fifteen minutes, affecting an air of intimidation that wasn't at all intimidating while he entered Ethan's information into the computer. Every few keystrokes, he hammered on the Enter key with a look of frustration.

Ethan considered asking the deputy if he'd like Ethan to dismantle his keyboard and fix that sticky key. Probably spilled coffee on that, too. Stifling a smile, Ethan sat back in the chair and stretched his legs out. Two could play at this waiting game…and after years of riding fence in nothing but silence, Ethan probably better at it.

The front door swung open. "Knox, go get us a sandwich," said Hollis.

Deputy Knox fixed him with a dumbfounded look. "It's the end of shift, and the diner's a pile of matchsticks."

"Then get a burger from the fast food place outside town," Hollis demanded. "Don't hurry back."

Knox hesitated only a second before scooting out the door like his pants were on fire.

So, this was how they'd play it: oblivious cop, bad cop.

Hollis lowered himself into Knox's vacant seat with a soft groan. He gestured to the half-filled coffee pot still sitting on the burner in a corner. "Get yourself a cup?"

Okay, maybe oblivious cop, pretends-to-be-your-buddy-until-he-gets-what-he-wants cop. Ethan studied him. How long had Officer Friendly been chasing after Gypsy?

What did she see in him that had made her reluctant to give him an outright refusal? Or was it that she was too softhearted to let the man down? She'd had her share of being pushed around. So far, Hollis had been nice about it. What would he do if she did send him over the edge with a final *no*?

Hollis gave him stare for stare, reminding Ethan forcibly of a pair of stallions sorting out their pecking order. Ethan wouldn't have cared…if it weren't for Gypsy.

"I'm gonna be downright honest with you, Sutter. I don't like you, and I don't like you sniffing around my town without knowing where you came from. So I did a little looking."

He reached behind him to the other desk in the small station room to pick up a folder. He opened it to slide a few photos and a typed list across the worn laminate surface. "I figure you'll recognize these places, if not by their names, then by the insurance photos. Yeah?"

Ethan leaned across the desk to examine the charred remains of three different buildings—the most recent of which, he'd entered to save a little girl named Sophie and bring her back to her nervous-wreck parents.

He sat back again. "Nope."

Hollis angled his head. "Where'd you get that motorcycle of yours? A real beauty, that. My brother was a big fan of bikes."

"Ordered it online through the dealer. You wanna see my receipts?"

Hollis's pale stare went positively icy. "Watch yourself, now. This is just a friendly conversation."

Ethan nodded at the photos. "Are you gonna charge me with something, or can I go home now?"

"Home's a long way off, or so I'm told. Hope Creek, Montana. You answer my questions, and I won't need to call Kincade Murphy to do my askin'."

Ethan bristled, even as he realized Hollis's whole purpose in dropping his foster brother's name was to rile him. He managed to keep his voice calm, but only just. "If you're looking for an arsonist, you're barking up the wrong tree, Officer Montgomery."

"Why'nt you tell me why you think that's so, Mister Sutter? Where were you on these dates?" He waved a hand at the photos on the desk, each neatly labeled with when the damage had occurred.

Ethan sat perfectly still, fuming. Cornered. He was going to end up in some dusty Vermont jail like a common criminal after spending his life using his hated power doing the only good thing he could do with it.

Now it had succeeded in ruining his life completely. He would never forgive Kincade. Never.

Chapter Thirteen

Sometime near midnight, Gypsy walked home. In any other town, a late-night stroll might not be wise. She would never have tried it back in Lubbock, but Pickering was a safe haven from the rest of the world, where neighbors still spoke to one another and were welcomed into each other's lives.

She entered her house to the sleepy canine grumble of Burt, who had stationed himself on the living room rug to wait for her. Seeing that she'd arrived home, he lowered his head and stretched out to sleep again. She smiled and continued upstairs to her room.

She'd just pulled off her sweater when a thump at her door made her jump. Hugging the garment to her chest, she opened the door a tiny crack.

Ethan's big frame filled the gap. "I waited up," he murmured. "We need to talk."

She spun around to shrug into her sweater—why, she didn't know, because he'd seen her without her shirt, and the memory slipped in to taunt her with all-too-enticing distractions.

But he was there in her doorway, looking like a dark storm cloud, and the memory evaporated. She finished dressing then turned to him. "What's wrong?"

"Hollis knows about me. Or he suspects, 'cause how the hell he'd know what I do is beyond me. The point is, I gotta get out of town, Gypsy, before whatever he's planning pulls you down with me."

She'd known this would come. She'd thought it would hurt…but his words washed over her without provoking the stab in her chest she'd expected to feel. Why?

Because she wasn't going to let him leave. For once in her life, Gypsy Ronan wasn't going to passively accept her lot. "What did he tell you?"

Ethan entered the room then leaned back against the door, letting it click shut behind him. He drew a long sigh, his gaze lowered to her rug as if in defeat. "He has a list of the places I've been, and he's trying to put it together that I started the fires at every one."

She searched his face. "Does he have pictures? Witnesses?"

"Nothing definite. Yet."

"So what are you asking, Ethan? That you want me to help you leave town?"

He exhaled again, more sharply, and threw his hands up. "I don't know. I don't want him to drag you into it. I should never… *We* shouldn't have—"

"But we did," she countered, approaching him, "and we can't take it back, and I don't want to. I like you. I like what we did together. With or without your power, I like who you are. You *are* a good man."

"No, I'm not—"

She gripped his hands and stared fiercely into his eyes. "A good man," she insisted. "And don't try to change my mind, because for once, I have it right. If you want help getting rid of your power, I'll do it, and gladly, because it's what will make you happy. But even with it—" He started to shake his head, but she gripped his hands harder and scowled at him. "*Even with it*, you are a good man."

He met her gaze then, and the extent of the torment in his eyes and radiating from his body stunned her. She had once thought that after years of abusive relationships and undeserving men, she was the wounded one. But there were so many people in the world who were more broken than she was. She had started her shop for that very reason.

And if healing wasn't her purpose, what was?

She stood there, silently holding his hands, knowing somehow that words wouldn't sway him, but maybe human contact could. The simple fact that, in spite of everything he was, another person wanted to be in his space and in his life.

Oh, goddess. Was that what was happening here? Had her heart somehow dared to hope, underneath all her self reminders about knowing his presence was temporary, that he'd stay? Had she finally dared to fall in love with a man who deserved it? She trembled and squeezed his hands harder, feeling suddenly cold.

Ethan seemed to sense the change and stepped closer. She pressed against him, marveling anew at how his body heat chased away the chill in her very bones. Holding him was like drinking down a cup of hot cider after a frosty day outside, letting it fill her every crevice with bliss. The extent to which she wanted that contentment terrified her. "Ethan?" she began, but the rest of her words fluttered away unsaid.

His hand came up to cup her cheek, large and rough and smelling as always of that faint wood smoke. She leaned into his touch, warm through for what seemed the first time in years. She looked up at him, unable to stem the flood of yearning.

His gaze fixed on her face. She went from warm to fever-hot at the intensity in his eyes. He pressed closer against her. She shook with eagerness as the ridge of his arousal brushed her belly. *Don't rush this,* she begged herself. *Oh, make it last. Make it last forever.*

Ethan raised her hand to his lips. He kissed the pad of each finger, slow and deliberate, his gaze still on hers. Gypsy couldn't catch her breath. He was fully clothed, and so was she, yet the look in his eyes was enough to melt her to her core.

Now, the trembling came from heat.

Just when she thought she couldn't take any more, he laid his hands on her shoulders and turned her gently, so she faced the cheval mirror and stood in front of him. "Enough about me," he murmured. In the reflection, she watched him bend his head, his rust-colored hair catching the moonlight from the window and turning him into a being of fire and ice.

Her boat neck sweater left her throat and most of her shoulders bare. Ethan pressed his lips to the naked skin where her shoulder met the curve of her neck. The contact ignited her. She whimpered and leaned against him, wanting everything he offered, for as long as he offered it.

His hands skimmed up under the sweater to caress her in unhurried strokes while he laid kisses along the slope of her shoulder. He found the front clasp of her bra and unhooked it with an eager-sounding growl. He cupped her breasts, enveloping her in heat. She whimpered again, unable to decide whether to push forward against his hands, or back against his body where the ridge of his arousal was plain against her backside. She reached back, desperate to touch him.

A chuckle rumbled deep in his throat and vibrated against her back. He nipped at her bare skin. "Greedy little so-and-so."

"Ethan," she pleaded.

He gripped her hips and pulled her hard against his body. She gasped at the insistent press of his erection. Tempted to boldness, she taunted back, "Greedy big so-and-so."

In response, he slipped his hand under the front waistband of her pants to cup the already aching spot between her legs. She gasped in surprise at the electric jolt of pleasure that rebounded through her body. "Damn right, I'm greedy," he said. "Told you I was no good."

Oh, you are so wrong, she thought, arching against his hand. She started to close her eyes.

"Open them," he whispered. "Watch yourself. Watch how beautiful you are."

She obeyed, but not to watch herself. She knew what she'd see: a woman who'd made all the wrong choices in love, who was good at advising others, but ironically failed miserably at finding her own heart's balance. She fixed her gaze on him, on the ethereal glow of moonlight on his skin.

No, not moonlight. His power. Open-mouthed, she watched the light ripple along his arms. Her skin vibrated with the echo of his power. His fingers found her center, and the waves of pleasure converged in that one, hypersensitive spot. She bit off an involuntary cry and bucked her hips.

"Beautiful," he said again. "Just a touch, and you're on fire." He held her hard against him and circled her bud with his fingers until an orgasm roared through her and tore a long moan from her lips. She shook all over, afraid to fall, but his embrace held her on her feet. "Look, Gypsy. Look at yourself."

Unable to help it, she stared at them both in the mirror. The sight that greeted her sent feverish ripples chasing the last of her climax through her body. She hardly recognized the woman with the passionate gleam in her eyes.

"See? See how gorgeous you are?" He held her there, gently, keeping her gaze fixed on the unbearably erotic scene of the two of them standing there. He raised her arms to slip the sweater off over her head and made her look again. He slid the thin silk bra off down her arms, then cupped her breasts in his large hands. His fingers kneaded her nipples. Sparks of ecstasy shot through her body at his touch. "I don't mean just the package," he said. "What's in it is every bit as beautiful as the wrapping."

She opened her mouth to tell him he was crazy, but stopped. He was trying to boost her self-image, that failure self-image she'd carried around with her since Lubbock. She knew that.

But he was talking as if he knew he wouldn't be around to do it anymore.

She tried to turn around, but his embrace prevented it. He ducked his head to press his lips to her shoulder again, kiss by unraveling kiss. When he cupped her face to turn her mouth to his, she let him. His tongue swept into her mouth, dipping and retreating in a sensual reminder of what was to come. His hands busied themselves undoing the button and zipper of her jeans. He eased them down off her hips, and her silk panties with them, with the same unhurried strokes of his hands. "Look again," he urged.

She did, drawn to their reflection, unable to deny the vision of herself wrapped in his arms. When he cupped her between her legs once more, liquid heat rushed to meet his touch. She trembled with eagerness. It was all too easy to push away the dread of his leaving.

She couldn't let him. She wouldn't. She drew breath to protest again.

Ethan pulled her pants all the way down. She stepped out of them and stood before him, utterly naked while he remained clothed. She stared back at the near-unrecognizable woman in the mirror—a wild goddess out of fantasy, waiting for a man who could match her passion. Could this creature possibly be her?

Taking her by the hips, he drew her back against him once more. The coarse fabric of his jeans ground against her backside in an undulating pressure that sent delicious tremors racing each other down her every nerve ending. At his urging, she let her head fall back against his shoulder. He laid a trail of kisses along her neck once more, suckling gently at the tender skin while his hands returned to creating their magick on the rest of her body. She'd never felt so positively alight with energy and power and joy. She hardly knew how one human body could contain it all.

"Stay here," he whispered. His hands left her for a moment that felt like an eternity. She remained standing at the mirror, breathless with excitement and anticipation. When he came back, he pressed a kiss to the thudding pulse at one side of her throat. "Eyes closed," he reminded her. He pulled her gently down to her knees. When he drew her back to him, she gasped at the heat of his naked skin and the sensation of his erection pressing against her center. His hands came up to cup her breasts once more, surrounding her in warmth. "Now look."

She did. The woman on her knees before the mirror, with her hair tumbling down and her eyes glazed with desire…

She was beautiful. Strong. Confident in who she was. Unafraid of her flaws or of what she would become. Unafraid to demand the same of anyone with whom she chose to be.

Kneeling behind her, Ethan gazed over her shoulder at the woman in the mirror, his hazel-gold eyes alight with passion and unmistakable admiration. "This is you, Gypsy," he said. "It was you before I even met you."

She smiled and kissed him. And when they joined, she made the first move.

****

Ethan nearly exploded apart when Gypsy welcomed him into her body. It took everything he had to avoid coming then and there. She was a lit match to a dynamite fuse. The heat in her eyes ensnared him past all desire of escape. When she leaned back into the cradle of his hips, he gasped out her name and pressed home deep, holding her hard against him.

Shaking. Shaking with the force of how much he needed her. His power snapped up and down his nerves. She must have felt it, must have felt how he balanced on the very edge of control. He wanted to make this last—this goodbye he couldn't say. What idiot would want to leave a woman like her, a woman meant to be worshipped with hands and mouth and body every single day?

And what about other things? whispered a voice inside him. *What about your heart?*

He crushed the thought almost by rote. He'd ignored that voice so long he'd assumed it was gone…but Gypsy had woken it with little more than a breath.

Maybe there was such a thing as magic.

She wriggled against him and reached back, whispering his name. Ethan rocked his hips forward, back, forward again in an undulating rhythm. He cupped her breasts once more, raising his gaze to the mirror only to find her staring back at him. The look in her eyes stoked his hunger to near madness. Light rippled along his arms, across the backs of his hands, then down his fingers to splash against her flawless skin. *Slow down, Sutter,* he reminded himself, fearing he'd burn her if he let loose his power. But Gypsy merely rolled her hips against him, demanding more.

Well. Far be it from him to deny such a compelling request. He reached between her legs to stroke her, then drove deep. She cried out and began to shudder in his arms. Her hair spilled forward over his arms. He thrust his hips in long, slow strokes as she came, and pulled her hard against his body, a possessive roar trapped in his throat. He gave it only the slightest bit of rein, his low growl a counterpoint to the soft, keening moan of his name on her lips. Oh, God, his favorite sound in the world, the sound of her wanting him.

Wanting *him.*

His own orgasm blasted through him with the force of an all-out house fire. Shock tore after it, and he let loose the roar he'd been holding back. At the last minute, he flung his hands free of her, terrified of harming her. With his eyes screwed shut, he tried desperately to hold onto his power, but it slipped its bonds and exploded out from his skin.

The instant it was over and his control began to seep back in, he withdrew and opened his eyes to scour her with an anguished look. In the mirror's reflection, her hair tumbled forward over her breasts and hid her face. He heard only her panting breath. "Gypsy!" he gasped. "Oh, God, I'm sorry. I didn't mean to hurt you—"

She raised her head, flushed, but with that same passionate glaze in her eyes. "Are you kidding?" She swiveled on her knees to face him, then cupped his cheeks and kissed him hard. Her nose bumped against his, and her breath puffed across his face. "Go again?"

Wait. What? Still catching his breath, he stared at her, unable to believe he hadn't burned her but reluctant to check.

She grinned, and his heart clenched so hard he had to suck in to get it pumping again. "I said I want you again," she confirmed. Her eyes lasered him, still glowing with desire. "Here. On the bed. In the shower. On the rug downstairs. Wherever you want. What do you say?"

Oh, God, yes. "Are you sure?"

Still holding his face, she pressed her lips to his. "I'm sure for once in my life. You make me feel incredible."

He kissed her back, then took her hand to pull her with him until they were both on their feet. His head swam in circles, too fast to be blamed on punching his power. "That's 'cause you are," he panted, "and I'm gonna spend all night proving it to you."

****

Gypsy opened her eyes to her tin-tiled ceiling. The sight remained the same, but she felt different. Sore. Oh, goddess, she was sore all over, inside and out. Deliciously so. Smiling, she stretched, enjoying each little twinge as proof of a long, erotic, unforgettable night.

The bed was empty beside her. A page of torn-out notebook paper lay on the other pillow. She picked it up. *Gone fishing—Ethan* was all it said.

Her smile stretched wider. He wanted to be normal, whatever that meant these days. What could be more normal than a country-bred man spending a Saturday morning fishing?

She showered and dressed in her favorite skirt and sweater. She entered the kitchen, and had just poured herself some coffee when Ethan came thumping in with a stringer of three glossy, speckled fish. "Breakfast."

She eyed the stringer. "Fish for breakfast?"

"Used to have it all the time back at Hope Creek. You got cornmeal?"

"Sure," she said, heading for the pantry cupboard.

"Sit. I can do it."

Inordinately pleased, she lowered herself into a chair with her coffee. Was this normal? Was this how a real relationship with a man went—this give-and-take? She hated to trust her own judgment even now, but she ventured a playful tone. "Careful. You're starting to sound domesticated."

He raised an eyebrow. The gleam in his eye made her even giddier and started her wondering how short she could cut her workday. "If you're not busy after breakfast," he said, "I can show you how undomesticated I am."

While breakfast cooked, she thought, not for the first time, about his siblings. He'd told her all about them, finally. They seemed to have come to terms with their abilities, according to Ethan. His eldest brother ran Hope Creek with his wife. Morgan owned a B&B with her husband, and his youngest sibling, Elsa, divided her time between storm chasing in the Midwest and an estate in California owned by her fiancé. None of Ethan's siblings had opted to rid themselves of their powers. Why Ethan? What made him hate it so?

Right now, he almost seemed happy.

Shut up and take the gift for what it's worth while you can, she told herself. The snarky self-reproach took a shot at her good mood, but she hung stubbornly onto it.

"I'm gonna seal up that porch today," he said. "Do you have a ladder?"

"Sure. Why?"

"No reason."

She eyed him over the rim of her coffee cup. Ethan was a lot of things, but a terrible failure at looking innocent. She grinned. Let him have his secret, then. She'd find out later. For once, she was with a man whose secrets resulted in delight, not dread.

What a nice feeling. "I'm actually going to go into town for a bit this morning. There's a woman who wanted a past-life reading."

"Okay." The fact that he didn't even raise an eyebrow at her unusual side job spoke volumes about how accustomed he'd become to it. Did he even realize?

Pure contentment carried her all the way into town, her bicycle basket loaded with candles specially selected for her appointment. The woman wanting the reading had just arrived in town, and the little rented apartment had given her strange déjà vus as soon as she moved in. She'd come to Gypsy's shop seeking advice, and today, Gypsy hoped to connect the woman with whatever wanted her to remember it.

If she could keep her mind on her job. Daydreaming, she almost ran into a hay bale stacked in a sidewalk display outside the dentist's shop.

"Look out, Speedy!" called a familiar voice.

Gypsy stopped the bicycle and looked around. Rich ambled toward her down the sidewalk, a backpack hoisted over his shoulder. He stopped before her. "Heading into work?"

"Just for a little while. You?"

"Heading home. Quiet night, for a change." He studied her. "You look different today. New clothes?"

Blushing, she shook her head.

He snapped his fingers as if remembering something. "Haircut. Once a month like clockwork, right?"

Smiling, she shook her head again. "New attitude."

Rich grinned back. "Bet this new attitude drives a motorcycle."

"He would, if he could get it out of the shop."

With his grin fading, Rich put a hand over the front bar of her bicycle. "Gypsy, just don't get too wrapped up in this guy, okay? I don't want to see you get hurt again."

"I won't."

Looking pained, Rich added, "I know you think

that, hon. You always think that, and the people who love you wind up picking up the pieces afterward."

"I thought you liked him."

"He *seems* nice," Rich said firmly. With an earnest look, he added, "Call me if you need me. Day or night, understand?"

"I will."

"Okay." He released the bike. "Going to meet a couple of the guys for breakfast so we can razz Colin about his pretty fire house date."

She laughed. "He's a good kid. Don't you go riding him too hard."

"Ah, he can take it. He's a good sport."

Smiling, she waved goodbye then made her way to The Holistic Mystic.

She opened the shop then gave the air its weekly smudging with a mild blend of incense. The spicy scent lifted her spirits even more. In some small corner of her thoughts, she worried that this wonderful, unfamiliar feeling of total serenity might come crashing down the same way it always had in the past. After her initial happiness in a relationship, her bad judgment in men showed itself, and things inevitably went sour.

But this time, it felt different. This time, she wasn't searching for a relationship to fill some void in her life. She accepted her life as it was, and knew that if she didn't, she could change it. Hadn't she proven that by kicking her last bad judgment off her property? Very simply, she liked Ethan, even if she couldn't call what they had anything as permanent as a relationship.

What did that mean for her heart when his bike was fixed and he decided to go?

The shop door's bell jangled. Her client walked in,

a twenty-something blond woman in a jeans and a peace sign T-shirt. "Hi, Gypsy."

"Hi. I have a table set up in the back. Tea or coffee?"

"I'd love some coffee."

Gypsy went to get it, relieved that the woman's arrival had given her an excuse to stop worrying. The universe could do a lot, but sometimes, even karma needed a little help.

Chapter Fourteen

The truck with the roofing supplies arrived later than Ethan had hoped. They'd called his cell to confirm delivery, but on the way the truck had gotten a flat. He'd used the time to finish sealing the porch. The truck came and unloaded its specially ordered cargo of fish-scale tiles. He was just beginning on the newly arrived roofing when a patrol car rolled up outside the gate.

Seeing Hollis and his deputy emerge from the vehicle, Ethan groaned. With a fatalistic grimace, he descended the ladder to meet the officers as they came through the gate into the yard.

Burt gave a few proprietary barks to let them know whose yard they'd entered. He came up beside Ethan.

"Morning, Mister Sutter," Hollis began in a conversational tone. "Or is it afternoon yet?"

"Might be. Haven't checked the clock."

"What are you doing up there?"

Sigh. "Roofing." Ethan indicated the pile of tile and nails beside the ladder.

"Mind if we ask you a few questions?"

Ethan wiped his hands on a rag. "Thought we did that already."

"Are you familiar with a Mister and Missus Watson?"

"Can't say I am."

Hollis's pale eyes narrowed. "How about a five-year-old girl by the name of Sophie?" He chuckled a purely companionable way that Ethan didn't buy for a minute. "She swears an angel saved her from an apartment building fire. Her family's beside themselves to thank the man who did it."

"That's nice."

Hollis took another step toward him. "The man drove a black motorcycle with saddlebags and a Montana plate, Mister Sutter."

Ethan went rigid. The deputy went rigid. Beside him, Ethan sensed Burt going rigid. Even the wind and birdsong seemed to die down. After an eternity of seconds, Ethan made himself relax. "Are you here to charge me with something, Officer Montgomery, or is this just a friendly social call?"

"I've got you, Sutter. Don't think for a minute I don't. As soon as you strolled into town, I started getting fire calls, and I've got eyewitnesses putting you at each one. You so much as light a match in my town, and I'll put you away."

Ethan said nothing. The page in the little spell book swam in his vision.

"You listening to me, Mister Sutter?"

He snapped his gaze back to Hollis. "Heard every word."

"Good." Hollis touched the brim of his hat.

When they left, Ethan strode back to the ladder and resumed his work. The cheerful anticipation of the happiness on Gypsy's face when she saw his work had been all but smashed to pieces. He worked with grim resolution, wanting to finish as much of the task as possible before the cops dragged him off to prison for something he could neither prove nor disprove.

Maybe his life was just like that. Maybe he didn't deserve to be happy.

Gypsy got home just as he was taking an early-afternoon break. She leaned her bicycle beside the repaired gate and walked through with her mouth open. "What did you *do*?" she asked, her eyes alight.

In an instant, the morning's work, worry, and dread were worth it. Ethan smiled. "Repairs. You know, that roof wears like iron. It was in great shape, even with some tiles missing. The people who roofed it originally must have laid down a layer of—"

Gypsy sprang at him and flung her arms around his neck, knocking him back a step. "You're wonderful," she said, then kissed his cheek.

Warmth filled his chest, but he squashed it, not trusting it, not trusting the way it made him feel. He turned the focus back onto her. "How was your consultation thing?"

She smiled back. "Past-life reading. But you don't want to hear about that stuff."

"Sure I do."

She eyed him. "Really?"

Anything to save him from liking that warmth in his chest too much. "Tell me. What's a past-life reading, and how did it help her?"

Still looking suspicious—which only made her more irresistible—she pulled up a lidded five-gallon bucket and sat, heedless of any paint that might get on her clothes. "Okay. Turns out, this woman's great-great grandmother lived in Pickering when she was a little girl, in the very same apartment building. So, it wasn't a case of past-life, so much as a good spirit welcoming her home to Pickering."

"That's pretty coincidental."

"Oh, there's no coincidence to karma."

He clenched his jaw. That probably went for bad karma, too.

She studied him. "What's wrong?"

"I got a visit from Hollis this morning, reminding me whose town this is."

"Oh." She eyed him through those long, dark lashes. "What did he have to say?"

"He can't be sure yet, but I have no doubt he's trying to peg me as the person who set the last two fires in town." Ethan shrugged. "I'm screwed, no matter what I do."

"What you are," she said, rising to her feet, "is amazing—with or without your ability." She kissed his cheek. "You haven't let this power beat you, Ethan. You've allowed it to make you even better."

He snapped his head around to stare at her. She meant it; the earnest look in her eyes dove right down into the bottom of his soul and fed a hunger he hadn't known he possessed.

He had never once felt in control of his power. It had always controlled him, jerking him around with a compulsion to use it because that's what he should do for people in trouble. Faced with a burning building, he'd always gone inside.

But he could have walked away. Without his ability, would he still have chosen to enter those buildings and search for people? He took a long, shuddering breath, and gave the darkest parts of himself their most thorough search in twenty years.

And the answer surprised him.

A weight spilled off his shoulders. He angled a look at Gypsy. "You know what? To hell with Hollis."

Her inky brows shot upward. "Am I talking to the same Ethan who drove up to my shop last week?"

"As a matter of fact," he said, lifting a stack of tiles to his shoulder, "you are." He grinned.

****

Who was this man? As Gypsy helped Ethan repair missing roof tiles—from the ground, since there was only one ladder tall enough—she wondered what she'd done to earn this tenuous gift from fate. She tried to offer him compensation for the money he'd shelled out for the specialty roof tiles, but he refused. Room and board were payment enough. He claimed the labor was voluntary—his own way of working through the noise in his head, not an invitation for payback on her part.

How could he not see his own selflessness?

Or maybe he was beginning to see. When they broke for dinner, she went inside to prepare a hefty harvest chicken salad. He joined her several minutes later, bearing a few clipped asters from her front border in a water glass. When she beamed at the gesture, he returned it with such a boyish grin that her heart gave a wild thump. She checked the clock and wondered how fast they could get through dinner.

Burt loped in from the great outdoors with burdocks in his coat. He took over dinner prep while she brushed out the dog's thick fur, chastising him as she worked through the snags.

"He's just being a dog," Ethan said from his place at the cutting board. "Aren't you, buddy?"

Burt wagged at Ethan, and the ache in Gypsy's chest was almost too much to bear. Too good to be true.

She pushed aside her worries with impatience. "I think I should ask Colin to help you with the rest of the roof. I'm not much use to you without a second ladder."

"Already called him. He's coming tomorrow afternoon and bringing one of Rich's ladders for you. Rich will be here to help out tomorrow, too." Ethan smiled again. "Said he'd commandeer a ladder truck if we needed it. He might have been joking."

She narrowed her eyes at him. "You've been planning this."

He sobered. "I travel a lot, so I don't need much, and I hardly touch my money. My brother and sisters don't need it. This is as good a use as any." He turned away to dice the cooked chicken. "Maybe better."

"What happens when you run out of your money spending it on everyone else?"

"I haven't, really. Just you."

That plain-spoken revelation startled her into silence, and for a while she just sat there, marveling at him.

Gypsy had spent many a night in her big house alone except for Burt. The only chatter that filled her living room on those nights was that of the television, tuned to whatever movie happened to be on. Tonight, she did the same old thing, with one exception: Ethan sat beside her on the old couch with a big bowl of popcorn between them. They squabbled cheerfully over buttery handfuls of the stuff, and mostly ignored the classic movie playing out onscreen. Burt lay on the rug, patiently awaiting a kernel or two. Gypsy couldn't remember having such a good night in years.

Years.

She had spent five years helping the people of

Pickering…and ignoring herself. Ignoring how much she needed this. Not needing a man. She could get along without one; that much, her bad experiences had taught her. But companionship with another human being? She'd never realized how much she'd craved it.

At the end of the film, Ethan guided her upstairs and made love to her, so gently and skillfully she imagined she must have dreamed him up. The real Gypsy Ronan must still be blissfully asleep, fantasizing this entire happy accident. How could it be anything else? How could her luck have changed so dramatically? If that were so, she prayed to Gaia that she might never wake.

The following morning, she was rolling her bicycle to the gate for a day at The Holistic Mystic when Colin and Rich pulled into the driveway in Rich's battered pickup truck. The truck bed was loaded with construction supplies—ladders, tools, lumber, and buckets of what looked like paint. Gypsy blinked. "He wasn't kidding."

Rich and Colin emerged from the vehicle. "You needed help," Colin said, "and I'm on holiday break, so I have all day."

"I'm just here for the beer and company," Rich said. He aimed a grin at her. "Kidding. Ethan bribed me. Said he'd start volunteering around the fire house if I could help him get this done in a day. Plus"—he gave her a heart-warming shrug—"it's you asking, so…"

"Oh, Rich, you're just perfect." She hugged him hard.

Rich seemed mildly startled by her affection. He gave her a grin when she released him.

"All right, all right," came Ethan's voice. He

sauntered to the gate. "Drive the truck around to the carriage house. I have a dolly set up for moving the equipment."

Gypsy hadn't realized she owned a dolly. Probably one of the carriage house's many unearthed treasures. She eyed Ethan. He never failed to surprise her.

Catching her watching him, he pecked her on the lips. "Go do your thing. When you get back, we'll have turned this place right around."

Rich and Colin watched the exchange, Colin with that boyish, shame-shame grin at their public display of affection, and Rich with a raised eyebrow.

"Go on," Ethan urged again. "Daylight's a-wastin'."

She stole a look at the pile of tiles beside her house, then at the equipment loading down Rich's truck. Stunned into silence, she mounted her bicycle. She couldn't begin to add up the numbers on a job this big if she had to pay for it.

Rich seemed to see the progression of her thoughts. "Don't get all obligated, now. This is spare whitewash left over from old lady Hosley's house. It'll do for touching up your siding and fence, and it isn't costing anyone anything but some time…which I'd be spending at home drinking beer today."

Gypsy switched her look of admonishment to Colin. "Don't you touch that beer."

The boy grinned. "I brought energy drinks instead."

"Off to work with you," Rich said. "Make sure you remember your address, because you might not recognize the house when you get back, and you'll pass it right by."

She didn't doubt it. She glanced back to the carriage house, where Ethan had disappeared to gather roofing materials, then gave Rich and Colin a smile that went all the way to her heart. "You're the best."

Rich smiled. "That's what they tell me. See you later."

When she got to her store, Kayla was waiting. "I'm so glad you're here," Kayla said, taking Gypsy's hands. "I wanted to ask if you'd do the favors for my wedding."

Gypsy beamed. "Of course I will! It'll be my gift to you."

"Oh, it's going to be expensive," Kay protested. "I can't let you—"

"Hush. Yes, you can. I'll enjoy it," Gypsy assured her. She shushed the rest of Kayla's protests then went to her compounding table to prepare some new pumpkin-and-ginger scented drawer sachets. Humming, she pulled open drawers of the apothecary bench to gather materials. It seemed everyone was full of good karma this morning. It almost made it seem like Ethan would never really leave.

Her humming faltered, but she pushed on as if nothing were wrong. Kayla didn't appear to catch the hitch.

Good, Gypsy thought. She'd have hated to spoil anyone's good humor. Putting on a brave face, she puttered around the shop. Customers trickled in to look at her fall display in the front corner. Kayla rang up the purchases on the vintage-style register. The machine's bell chimed with each transaction, a merry counterpoint to the glum mood trying hard to sneak in under Gypsy's mask of cheer.

The sun shone brightly through the front window, illuminating the colored apothecary jar and stained-glass colors of the geode slices hanging there. The familiar scents of her shop swirled around her. Soft music floated through the air under the murmur customers doing their early holiday gift shopping. Why shouldn't she be cheerful on a day like this?

Oh, Hollis, why can't you just leave him alone and let me be happy?

The day rolled on, time as oblivious as ever to humankind's woes or well-being. She busied herself counting her blessings, as she usually did when struck by a funk.

The shop emptied out around dinner time. The music now playing on the shop's sound system filtered through the air under the muted hush of Kayla restocking jewelry. The young woman's footsteps thumped back and forth across the wide plank floors. After several minutes, Gypsy sensed Kayla standing across the counter from her. "I'm here if you need to talk," she said finally.

Gypsy looked up from a supply catalog. Kayla watched her with shrewd blue eyes. "I've been quiet all day, haven't I?" she asked with an apologetic shrug.

"Yes, but your silence is like a jackhammer." Kay's smile softened the teasing jab. She rounded the counter then sat on a stool beside Gypsy. "It's the man staying with you, isn't it? Ethan?"

"He isn't hurting me."

"I know he isn't. I knew he wouldn't the minute I met him, or I would've had it out with him right there. But something's wrong." Kayla angled her head. "It's been bothering you all day."

Gypsy eyed her shop assistant. "You're too smart for your own good. Or maybe mine."

Kayla grinned. "Just perceptive. I had a good coach." She crossed her legs. "So? Talk to me."

Gypsy pursed her lips. She couldn't tell Kayla about Ethan's ability without betraying a trust…but she could talk about her own worries.

Especially her worry for her heart when he left.

She sighed. "You'd better put on some tea and get those scones out of the back room."

****

Ethan finished putting Gypsy's tool box in the carriage house, then he closed the door. He rubbed a sore shoulder. A long day…but well worth it. With the extra pairs of hands, he'd finished the roof patching and even painted the newly shored-up bookcases in the living room. Rich and Colin had gone about half an hour ago, one protesting impending hell from the fire chief, who was expecting him for an evening hose drill, and the other pleading impending computer games.

Burt spotted him as he emerged from the carriage house and trotted over to join him. Dusk had just hit.

A eerie wail came from close by. Ethan, who'd never been a stranger to the sounds of wildlife, never even flinched. He scanned the tree behind the carriage house. Sure enough, a series of squeaky *Whoo-ooo-oot*s came from one of the higher branches. He spotted a plump little bird sitting far out on a limb strung with the last of its autumn leaves. Ethan drew a stick of jerky from his pocket. He bit off half then gave the other to Burt. They listened to the owl while the breeze died down for the night.

Standing in the graveled drive, Ethan studied the

old farmhouse. Not much he could see in what illumination Gypsy's carriage house floodlight threw on an evening of gathering cloud cover, but he remembered each patch had looked pretty good when they finished it. The kid had whitewashed all the thin spots on each side of the house. Good as new, as far as the bones of the building were concerned. Now, the old house could stand whatever a harsh Vermont winter might throw at it.

So he shouldn't have any qualms about leaving.

He glanced down at Burt, who stared expectantly at him after finishing his treat. "Don't look at me like that. They say you're supposed to leave a place better than you found it, don't they?"

Would it be better when he left?

His cell rang, saving him from the dog's keen-eyed recriminations. He pulled it from his pocket.

"Mister Sutter?"

"Yes?"

"Roy at Clemens Automotive. Your parts came in this morning, and your bike's finished. Can you be here before closing to pick it up?"

Wait. What? Ethan checked the caller ID to be sure no one was pranking him. Nearly closing time, according to Pickering's social clock. They'd said his parts would take days. Was he really about to be handed his ticket out of here before everything blew up in his face?

Or pushed out of here.

He glanced down at Burt. What about Gypsy?

"Mister Sutter? You there?"

"Yeah, yeah. Thanks for getting them in quicker. Be there in ten minutes."

Roy thanked him and hung up. Ethan jammed his cell into his back pocket and stood there in the drive, looking at the touched-up house and feeling worse than he'd felt since leaving Hope Creek. Like a coward, who cut and run at the first sign of difficulty.

"Well," he said to the dog, "maybe she'll do better when I get myself and my problems out of her life."

Burt didn't look any more convinced than Ethan felt in saying it.

He gathered up his keys, sunglasses, wallet, jacket, and the dog leash. A few steps toward Gypsy's gate, he stopped to wonder if he had everything. The answer was depressingly simple. Everything he owned worth having, besides his bike, was already on him. What he didn't have, he didn't need.

He opened the gate and led Burt through, refusing to look back at the house.

Halfway to town, the scream of sirens set his skin crawling. What new catastrophe would Hollis blame on him now? He walked faster.

Burt whined and tugged forward on the leash. When Ethan didn't respond, the dog barked and jerked the loop right out of his hand, then bolted down the sidewalk.

"Hey!" Ethan chased after him and was quickly passed by two fire trucks. He glanced skyward, searching, and found a column of smoke rising against the dark sky. The smell of a structure fire assaulted his nose a second later. *Must be one hell of a...*

Burt skidded to a stop at the door of Gypsy's shop. So did the fire trucks. Barking fit to be tied, Burt threw himself against the door. Through the windows, Ethan glimpsed the flicker of fire.

Fear shot down his spine as if the flames had engulfed his clothing. He lunged at the door. "Gypsy!"

The fire trucks behind him didn't even register. Ethan called on his power and grabbed for the door handle.

"What are you doing, Sutter?" cried a voice. "Get back! It's a full-on Roman candle in there!" Rich Pettit grabbed Ethan's coat sleeve and tried to haul him back.

"Gypsy's in there!" Ethan roared, tearing his sleeve from Rich's grasp to slam against the door again. "She's gotta be! Look at Burt!" The shepherd rammed himself against the door, whining, barking, and when he didn't succeed, circling their feet with desperate looks.

Rich grabbed an axe from a nearby firefighter. "You sure?"

"She isn't home." Ethan tried to peer through the windows, but one of the firefighters herded him back. "Christ, come on, man! I'll go in there myself!"

Rich moved forward. "All right, you need to back off, Sutter. Let us do our job." He pushed the face shield of his helmet down then waved to the men hooking up the fire hose to the nearest hydrant. "I want two more axes over here. Get that hose charged up. Let's make it rain!"

Ethan watched them rush about in an orchestrated frenzy. The flames' reflection glinted off the face shield on Pettit's helmet. Every second could be costing Gypsy her life.

The hell he would back off. Ethan gripped Burt's leash and hurried down the alley at the side of the building. Busy with their work, the firefighters didn't see him.

Behind the building, he unleashed his power, not caring if anyone saw. The steel door at the back was hot enough to peel its dark-green paint. Ethan ordered Burt back, then jerked at the door. Nothing. He hadn't really expected to get in.

That way.

He took a deep breath and dropped Burt's leash. "Stay," he ordered the dog. Then he punched his power as high as it would go.

His hands flashed white. The air rippled around him as the bubble of his power settled into place. He gripped the door handle again, then pulled with all his muscle. Superheated, the lock shattered. Ethan ripped the door open.

Smoke and flame poured into the alley.

Barking once, Burt charged into the building.

"Burt!" Ethan shouted. Then he heard a thin cry for help. Without a second thought, Ethan rushed inside.

"Help!" cried a voice, barely noticeable under the roar of fire. He might not even have registered it but for Burt, who galloped across the floor to a bookshelf leaning akilter against a charred wall. "Help!"

For a heart-stopping instant, Ethan feared it was Gypsy, crushed under that oaken monstrosity, but the woman trapped in the gap between bookshelf and wall, crumpled on the floor and covering her face with a cloth, was blond.

Kayla.

The woman's blue eyes widened as he approached. He didn't doubt he was glowing like a damned street light. One look at his hands confirmed the shimmer of his power still pulsing, rippling, fading, then resurging again. He used to feel comfortable blaming the fires for such an illusion when the people he rescued questioned it. Crystal-clear in the flash of firelight and his power, he saw the glint of her engagement ring.

Her fiancé was Andrew. An artist. God, he had to get her out of here. To hell with his power.

She pulled the cloth free only long enough to say, "My foot! I'm stuck!"

Ethan shouldered up against the bookshelf and hauled it back. He looked down to find Burt seizing the woman's belled sleeve and pulling. The dog's back arched with effort, but once Ethan budged the shelf, Burt finally succeeded in wrenching the woman free from a fallen timber. As soon as she was free, crawling, coughing, Ethan let the shelf fall back against the wall. "Where's Gypsy?"

"I don't know! Front of the shop. The door! The door was—" Kayla choked up with another barrage of coughing, then clapped the cloth back over her mouth and nose.

Ethan thrust a hand toward the open back door. "Get out! Get out of here. Go, Burt!"

The dog—good God, that amazing dog—circled before Kayla's feet. Whining, he guided her toward the door where Ethan had ordered him. Woman and dog disappeared into the smoke escaping from the open door. *Truckload of jerky with your name on it, moose. If I get out of here.*

Gypsy.

He bolted toward the front of the shop with his power on full-blast. The bubble of air around him, regulated to ward off the lung-damaging heat, could only do so much to keep out likewise-hot debris. He ducked a falling statuette. "Gypsy!" He squinted through the smoke and gloom, murmuring a prayer he barely recalled from his childhood with the Rathbones. Half a step. Half a step. *Oh, please, God, don't let her die.*

Fires on television and in movies had it all wrong. They presented a well-lit space with a clear enough floor to allow an actor to move about safely and look good doing it. The director could get it all on film in beautiful full color. Audiences would gasp and ooh and shriek, and be satisfied that their celluloid heroes would emerge triumphant.

The reality horrified Ethan no less after charging into dozens of them: a murky, colorless minefield of debris as hazardous as deep-sea scuba diving in uncharted waters. Without a sense of direction, a person could get hopelessly lost and run out of breathable air. In seconds, a fire could do a lifetime of damage to body and lungs.

He didn't worry for himself. Anything that happened to him was only cosmic penance.

But Gypsy... All those people she was determined to help, whose lives she wanted to change for the better...

And then he saw her, crumpled in a tangle-haired heap at the base of the front door.

Terrified for her, he almost lost his grip on his power. The bubble flickered. Shouting her name, he bolted forward. She was limp, unresponsive. Her skirt smoked at the edges. Ethan swore and pressed his hand to the bare skin of her leg. Hot. Christ, she was hot as a new sunburn. He punched his power again. The buzz in his hands intensified, pushing the bubble outward around them, driving off the heat and quenching the smolder of her clothing. Her skin cooled to just above normal temperature.

Only a little time left. His bubble was similar to a scuba tank, too. Only a little viable air remained inside it. Once he breathed that up, he risked suffocation as much as any victim of a blaze.

He reached for the door handle. It didn't budge. He tried the lock.

Not locked—but they couldn't get out.

Why the hell was the door jammed? He saw no debris blocking it, and had seen none outside, either.

Reluctant to leave her, Ethan scanned the tiny pocket of visible space around them for anything he could use to break the glass.

His desperate gaze landed on a trio of geodes littering the floor. The sharp spears of the largest one pointed at him as if accusing him for every wrong he'd ever committed.

Or like a sign.

He snatched it up and drove it, two-handed, into the pane of glass forming the top half of the door.

The glass shattered. Smoke poured forward through the gap. Flames lunged at the fresh air seeping in. Swearing, Ethan forced the fire back and pulled Gypsy into his arms. "Hey! Help! Over here! We can't get out!"

No one answered. The fire truck parked outside had deployed its men and its gear. The snaking hose disappeared around the side of the building.

Were they trying to come in the way he'd done? What the hell were they thinking?

Ethan turned to run to the back door—

—just in time to see an ax swinging at him.

He dropped, the only thing he could do to avoid the gleaming blade that sped past over his head. The masked firefighter wielding the weapon disappeared back into the smoke like a wraith.

Crouched with Gypsy in his arms, unwilling to lower her to the scorching-hot floor he could feel through his boot soles, Ethan scanned the area. His heart pounded, and the flames held at bay by his power pulsed in answer to the question repeating in his head like the voice of Gypsy's owl: *Who? Who? Who?*

He gathered Gypsy up and made for the back door. No telling when his power would give out. He'd never pushed it to its breaking point. He glanced down at Gypsy.

He'd never had a reason.

Another shape came out of the smoke. Ethan tensed, then saw that it was the same firefighter who'd been carrying an ax. He must have dropped it, and for an instant Ethan was relieved—but then the firefighter upended a table into Ethan's escape route.

"What are you doing?" Ethan screamed, but it was no use. The firefighter grabbed another table then hurled it against the first one. The back door—their only way out—would be all but buried. On purpose.

The shock of the situation cleared, and realization set in with horrifying clarity.

He didn't matter. He'd never been a decent human being in his life, and whatever happened to him in a fire was just reparation for that. But Gypsy? A woman whose heart was so good, she cared for him in spite of himself? And this person wanted her to *die* here?

Adrenaline punched through his veins. Grimly, Ethan barreled through the rubble with Gypsy's face protected against his chest.

The firefighter slung books and geodes at him. Unable to stop the debris from falling through the shield of his power, Ethan turned and took the hits on his arms and shoulders. There was no time to defend himself. Not and get her out before his power failed.

The firefighter gave a muffled roar and lunged at him. Ethan loosened his grip on Gypsy in reflex. She slipped, and he caught her, one-handed, against his torso with a curse. Fury flooded after the adrenaline. He swept out a hand, not giving a damn if it glowed like Christmas anymore. Flame rushed along the floor, following his order, and built a seething wall between himself and the firefighter. Ethan grabbed Gypsy tight and bolted through the wreckage toward the back door.

Right into the grasp of another firefighter.

Not trusting anyone, Ethan wrestled against his grip. The fireman shouted something unintelligible over the roar of the blaze. Ethan held onto Gypsy with everything he had. The fireman tried pulling her away. With a feral snarl, Ethan warded him off.

Something over Ethan's shoulder caught the fireman's eye. With a startled-sounding shout muffled by his face shield, the man raised a staying hand toward something behind Ethan.

Their madman was back.

The fireman tried to stop him, but the madman flung burning debris at them, oblivious to the charring of his fire gear. The missiles sailed at the other firefighter, who'd been trying to pull Ethan and Gypsy out of the building. Tripping over broken table legs and tumbled shelving, their would-be rescuer crashed backward against more of the rubble and disappeared into the smoke.

So, not everyone was against him. What the hell was happening here?

Before Ethan could process that, his adversary lined up with him and raised his hands. He'd found his ax. The blade began to arc toward Ethan.

He didn't even think twice. He punched his power with everything he had.

White light blinded him, burst across the floor, sped up the walls, surrounded them all. The stinging glare forced him to shut his eyes. He flung his arms around Gypsy and ducked his head against her shoulder, holding her tight, shielding her with his body from whatever came next. His last thought rushed through his entire being on the heels of his power blast.

Please let her live. I'll do anything.

Chapter Fifteen

Gypsy woke to the same filtered sunlight and the same tin-tiled ceiling she'd seen for the past five years. The same patchwork bedspread. The same walnut dresser and cheval mirror.

Except today, something was different. Her lungs burned. Her body ached. And then she remembered.

A letter, stuffed in with her shop's mail, hand-delivered.

You had your chance. You had lots of chances. You never noticed me, even after I did everything for you.

Rich Pettit's handwriting, even though he hadn't signed it. She hardly had time to process all the times she'd been with him, in what she'd thought was friendship, but he'd clearly viewed it as something else. He must have thought the note would burn up in the...

Fire. A locked door. Desperation. The terrifying realization that Rich's friendship had been an obsession. The despair of knowing that once again, she'd made a terrible mistake and trusted someone so very wrong, and this time, she'd pay for it with her life.

All those oils, those candles. A perfect accelerant to a fire that would burn fast and burn hard, swallowing her without a trace.

An then, an angel had come for her. A spirit of flame, glowing, taking her in his arms. Shielding her, guarding her, carrying her to safety.

Ethan. Using a power he despised to rescue her.

Oh, goddess, where was he? Had he gone, disappeared from her life as he had from the lives of countless others whom he'd saved? Would he run again?

Leave her? The one man who'd ever truly deserved her love?

Love.

Gypsy sat bolt upright. Her head whirled, but she forced herself to leap out of bed. Stumbling, she lurched against the wall. An umbrella hanging from a Shaker pegboard clattered to the floor.

Rrrruff! Burt burst through her door, and only then did she realize it had been ajar. The shepherd herded her back toward the bed with overjoyed barking and desperate attempts to lick every inch of her within his reach. Protesting, laughing, she tottered back then sat hard on her mattress. Even that small resistance left her gasping for breath while the dog leaped up beside her to slobber her face.

"Sorry," came a familiar voice. "Couldn't keep him out."

Ethan strode into the bedroom. Still heaving for breath, Gypsy caught the scent of food. She inhaled, not even caring what it was, just glad to be alive to enjoy it.

"Steak and eggs," Ethan said, as if reading her thoughts. "More steak than eggs. You gotta get your iron and get that oxygen back up."

No wonder she felt faint. Gypsy put a shaking hand against Burt's ruff, pushing against his attempts to reach her face.

Ethan swiped a hand toward the floor. "Down, moose."

Burt hopped off the bed.

Cocking his head, Ethan studied her. "How do you feel?"

"Close to passing out." She struggled with hazy memories of the moments just before the fire. "Kayla!"

He set her breakfast on the nightstand. "She's going to be all right. She's still at the hospital, getting treatment. Burt got her out."

"Burt?"

The shepherd wagged, but stayed obediently in his spot on her rag rug.

Tears welled up. Mortified, Gypsy put her face in her hands. She'd trusted Rich. Betrayed again, and this time, by someone she'd thought a friend. Her judgment was terrible.

Except for Ethan. And now that he'd revealed his power, the power he loathed, he'd flee as soon as his motorcycle was fixed.

And her shop was in ruins. She'd have to go home to Lubbock with her tail between her legs.

"Hey. Gypsy, it's okay. They caught him. Rich is going to jail after he gets out of the hospital. He can't hurt you."

Her heart squeezed, and what little oxygen remained in her lungs whooshed out. She panted for air and avoided Ethan's gaze, hiding behind her hands. It wasn't the thought of Rich that hurt.

A large hand covered her knee, warming the skin through her pajama pants. "What are you worried about?"

She shook her head.

"Gypsy." Gently, Ethan pried her hands away from her face. His fingers curled around hers as he crouched before her. "You're okay."

She stared at him, memorizing his face, each lash framing his hazel-gold eyes and each contour of his sculpted jaw and kiss-inviting lips.

Not for her, anymore.

She gathered her pride and lifted her chin, sniffing back her tears. Her heart clenched, but she steadied her breath and worked through it, clinging to the last of her courage. She needed to be able to let him go. Love didn't force itself on someone.

"You're going to leave, aren't you? They saw you. That's why you never stay anywhere." She managed, with effort, to keep her voice steady.

Ethan ducked his head, and her heart dropped into a bottomless well of misery. There it was. The very last time she'd go through a broken heart. Her life stretched out ahead of her, long and lonely. She'd be that kooky old woman in a conservative town, the one all the neighborhood kids feared, whose house they dared one another to approach.

"I've had a lot of time to think this past week," he said. "See, working on projects might occupy your hands, but it does nothing for your head. I guess what I've been trying to fix all this time is me. But I'm not broken." He raised his head to look her in the eye.

Searching his face for some clue to his thoughts, she came up empty. Those gorgeous hazel eyes roved over her, just as searching. She couldn't force words from her still-raw throat.

"I always hated my power," he went on. "I hated myself. Hated going through life as some kind of freak who couldn't be who I am in front of anyone. It still bothers me, carrying around this power, even now."

So, he still had it, she realized. Fixing himself hadn't meant ridding himself of his ability. Her attempt to help him had gone up with the rest of her livelihood. What, then?

He rubbed her knee. Gypsy relished the touch as if it would be the last they'd ever share, even though her heart was breaking. She closed her eyes on the pretense of residual illness, when really she couldn't bear to look at him and know he'd soon be far away.

"But," he said, interrupting the ringing hollowness in her soul, "it bothers me a lot less if it helps me protect you."

She snapped her eyes open to stare at him, wondering if she'd only imagined his words. The Chariot card flashed in her mind, and it all made sense. *Oh, goddess, say it,* she begged him silently.

He cocked his head. A half-smile curved his lips. "I've been on the road for two years, leaving behind place after place without a second thought about it. I made up all kinds of reasons to go…but what I was looking for was a reason to stay." He reached up to stroke her face. "You're it, honey. If you want me."

Her fragile hold on self-control shattered. Tears poured forth, and she gasped back a sob. Could he possibly mean it?

"Oh, God, don't cry. Shit, Gypsy, I'm sorry. You're still not well—" With another curse, he stood, then snatched a few tissues from the box on her bedside table.

The Tower card began to make sense, too. His sacrifice. He meant to keep his power. For her.

She struggled to her feet as he turned back. Putting her hands over his, she nodded. "Yes. Please. Yes." She had to pant for breath between those few words.

Still looking pained, he wiped at her tears with the wad of tissues. "Sorry," he said again. "Not very good at taking care of someone."

"You're wrong," she insisted, stroking his face. She paused to catch her breath. "You're wonderful at it in so many ways." She stared back at him, adoring the warm look in his golden eyes.

The faint chime of the doorbell interrupted them, and even then, she thrilled at his clear reluctance to leave her. She clasped his hand and moved toward the bedroom door.

Burt darted out the door. They descended the stairs together behind him.

Hollis stood on the porch with a bouquet of flowers. "I'm glad you're better," he ventured, shuffling his foot awkwardly where he stood on the board Ethan had laid over the drying porch.

Still holding Ethan's hand, Gypsy offered Hollis a rueful smile. "Hollis…"

The officer's gaze switched from her to Ethan and back again. "I get it, I get it. I just came to check in on you and see how you're getting on. These are…just friendly." He smiled. "Had you pegged wrong, Sutter. I admit it when I'm wrong."

"It's all good," Ethan said with a cordiality that surprised her.

Gypsy opened the door wider to accept the flowers, admiring the mix of orange, gold, and purple. "Thank you," she murmured.

Hollis nodded, then turned his attention to Ethan. "Chief McIntyre and the boys at the fire house have been asking about you. They're a man short, now, and they want to know when you plan to start your training."

Gypsy raised her brows at Ethan.

He grinned back. "Yeah, you've been under the weather a while. Mac says I have a knack for fire rescue." He rubbed Burt's broad head. "Isn't that something?"

She beamed. "*You're* something." Bursting with happiness, she reached up on tiptoe to kiss him.

"Want some breakfast?" Ethan offered Hollis.

"Nah. Got to get back to the station. You two have a good day."

"We will," Ethan responded. He closed the door and turned to Gypsy. "Don't worry about a thing today. Colin's coming over, and we're going to work on clearing out that carriage house. After that, we'll catch some fish for dinner. Sound like a good plan?"

He was staying. In her house. In her life. Anything sounded like a good plan. Giddy—and not just because she was still recovering and light-headed—she threaded her fingers through his. "I foresee an absolutely amazing day." Rising up on her tiptoes, she kissed him again, then followed him to the kitchen.

Epilogue

Ethan pulled into the long gravel drive of Hope Creek in the gleaming maroon convertible. He approached the long, low log house at a crawl.

"You made it all the way across the country in this car, Ethan," came Gypsy's amused voice from the passenger seat. "Are you going to baby it up the driveway, too?"

"I don't want the stones to scratch the paint," he complained. He steered the newly restored car around a particularly suspicious rut filled with water from a recent rain.

She giggled. The sound had him wondering whether they'd be missed if he detoured to a hotel to extract more interesting sounds from her. He shot her a simmering look.

She stopped in mid-giggle. After almost a year together, they didn't need much conversation to get on the same page. She was thinking hotel, too. He grinned. "We can't. They know we're coming today."

She gave a grumble, but her hand slithered along his thigh with promising eagerness.

"You ever been in a hayloft?" he asked airily.

"No. You going to give me the tour?"

"Oh, I'll give you a tour, all right," he added as they stopped in front of the house. He gave her a peck on the lips. "I'll get the bags."

He'd barely shut off the engine before the front door burst open. "Uncle Ethan!" shrieked a redheaded little girl. "Mama! Daddy! Uncle Ethan's here!"

Allyson and Kincade Murphy emerged from the house. "Come on in!" Allyson invited. "Everyone else is here. Good thing we finished off that old barn for a guest house."

Ethan glanced across the drive at what had once been the ruins of a burned-down barn. In the old barn's place stood a beautiful, rustic cabin with more than enough room for half of Montana. "You've been busy."

Kincade approached. With a nod over his shoulder, he indicated Gypsy's softly rounded belly. He grinned. "So have you. How's married life?"

"Weird," he admitted. "Good weird. I like Vermont."

Cade sobered as the women shepherded the Murphys' chattering daughter into the house. "I guess 'Welcome Home' isn't quite the right phrase to use, then."

"No, it's good," Ethan said. He looked his foster brother in the eye. "It's good to see you."

Cade nodded. "You, too," he responded warmly…and for once, Ethan really felt it. Maybe Cade had always been that way toward him, and Ethan just needed an attitude adjustment to see it. He glanced toward the main house door, where Gypsy had disappeared in a swirl of gauzy skirts and lace.

Cade passed him a grin, which Ethan returned. Just like that, everything that had always been so wrong, so contentious between them, spilled away. No matter where he went, where he settled, he'd have a home and family here. One that accepted him, whatever he was, however he'd come to be that way. The warmth that spread through Ethan's chest stunned him. He stood there with his brother on the porch, looking out to the horse paddocks dotted with mares and foals, happy to absorb that feeling in silence.

"Ethan!" echoed two female voices.

His foster sisters Elsa and Morgan jogged toward them from the guest house. Behind them trailed two men Ethan had only seen in pictures, but he recognized them as his sisters' husbands. Meeting them was a long time coming.

"Kind of strange to have this old place overrun with family again," Cade said.

"Yep," Ethan said, "but it's good."

Cade gave him another smile, then clapped him on the shoulder. "Let's get in there and catch up." He raised his voice. "I thought you'd be next in line for having kids, Harry!"

Elsa's dark-haired husband, Harry, grinned at Morgan, who carried a tow-headed baby boy in her arms. "He thinks it's a competition," Harry rumbled.

Trent, Morgan's husband, nudged Harry. "You better get started, then."

Ethan shook hands with his brothers-in-law, then they filed inside in a flood of cheerful, noisy greetings. A beagle wove around everyone's feet, barking happily, then chased after Cade and Ally's little redhead. With a smile, Ethan remembered Bailey as a pup who'd chewed everything in sight.

Still on the porch, Ethan took a final glance around the old ranch. Hope Creek. He'd always thought it a misnomer. What hope had there been for a miscreant like him?

Apparently, plenty.

Turning into the house, he caught sight of Gypsy's long, dark, curling hair amid the crush of his family.

Family. With his very own on the way, and a chance to do it right. That warmth stayed in his chest, then flourished when Gypsy saw him looking and smiled.

And suddenly, he knew. If it was a girl, they'd name her Hope.

A word about the author...

Nicki Greenwood graduated SUNY-Morrisville with a degree in Natural Resources, which of course has nothing to do with writing novels. She has also worked in a bakery, an insurance agency, a flower shop, and a doctor's office, which have nothing to do with writing, either. She did spend an awesome two years as an assistant editor for a publisher, and now does freelance editing on the side. Nicki still holds down a day job, which manages to get her out of the house once in a while. Since 2010, she has written eight novels, including the award-winning Gifted Series.

Nicki lives in upstate New York with her husband, son, and assorted pets. If you can't find her at her computer, you can always try the local Renaissance Faire. Visit her at http://www.nickigreenwood.com.